THE GODHEAD COMPLEX

ALSO BY JAMES DASHNER

The Maze Runner Books

The Maze Runner

The Scorch Trials

The Death Cure

The Kill Order

The Fever Code

Crank Palace

The Maze Cutter Books

The Maze Cutter

The 13th Reality Books

The Journal of Curious Letters

The Hunt for Dark Infinity

The Blade of Shattered Hope

The Void of Mist and Thunder

The Mortality Doctrine Books

The Eye of Minds

The Rule of Thoughts

The Game of Lives

Adult Books

The House of Tongues

#1 *NEW YORK TIMES* BESTSELLING AUTHOR
JAMES DASHNER

THE GODHEAD COMPLEX

AKASHIC
MEDIA ENTERPRISES

All rights reserved. Published in the United States by Akashic Media Enterprises, also doing business as AME Projects. Visit us on the web at AkashicMediaEnterprises.com. Printed in China by We Think Ink. Interior formatting by Hannah Linder Designs.

Publisher's Cataloging-In-Publication Data
(Prepared by The Donohue Group, Inc.)

Names: Dashner, James, 1972- author. | Dashner, James, 1972- Maze runner series. Maze cutter trilogy. Title: The Godhead complex / James Dashner.
Description:
Identifiers: Subjects:
[Red Bank, New Jersey] : Akashic Media Enterprises, [2023] | Interest age level: 012-018. | Summary: In the second book of The Maze Cutter Trilogy ... Sadina and the islanders are up against both man and nature as they navigate their way to Alaska. There, they hope to meet the mysterious Godhead, unsure of what separates myth from truth. But the Godhead, now led by Alexandra, is fractured. Within the cracks of their sacred trinity, secrets are revealed that blur the lines of good and evil forever. One person's God is another person's Devil.--Publisher.
ISBN: 979-8-9859552-2-4 (hardback) | 979-8-9859552-3-1 (ebook)
LCSH: Good and evil--Juvenile fiction. | Quests (Expeditions)--Juvenile fiction. | Survival-- Juvenile fiction. | Belief and doubt--Juvenile fiction. | Sacred space--Juvenile fiction. | Alaska-- Juvenile fiction. | CYAC: Good and evil--Fiction. | Quests (Expeditions)--Fiction. | Survival-- Fiction. | Belief and doubt--Fiction. | Sacred space--Fiction. | Alaska--Fiction. | LCGFT: Dystopian fiction. | Action and adventure fiction. | BISAC: YOUNG ADULT FICTION / Dystopian. | YOUNG ADULT FICTION / Science Fiction / Apocalyptic & Post-Apocalyptic. | YOUNG ADULT FICTION / Action & Adventure / Survival Stories.
Classification: LCC: PZ7.D2587 Go 2023 | DDC: [Fic]--dc23

ISBN 979-8-9859552-2-4 (hardback)

First Edition

To Tessa Shaffer, who has poured as much of her heart, soul, blood, sweat, and tears into this series as I have. I'm forever grateful for her work and her friendship.

PROLOGUE

Night of the Evolution

31 Years Ago

Nicholas wasn't one to avoid danger but he didn't exactly go chasing after it either—except tonight. Testing the latest variant of the Cure required Nicholas to walk directly into the devil's den, or as the locals in Denver, Colorado called it: **Crank Palace**. He pulled his black hooded cloak tighter around his face so that no man, woman, or Crank could see his features. In his right pocket he clicked two syringes together like Chinese medicine balls as he walked, each hypodermic needle circling the other in a relaxed rhythm as he entered the hallowed gates. *CLICK CLACK, CLICK CLACK . . .*

Screams and wails surrounded the inner walls of the dismal place. Fires ignited from Flare pits. Smoke hung in the air and bodies hung in the shadows. No matter how many times he'd visited these hellholes, and he had proudly visited them all, nothing prepared Nicholas for the fresh curdling cries of desperation he felt vibrating through his whole body when he walked through the gates. Screams of death that Nicholas imagined as souls being cooked from the inside out.

He continued to circle the syringes around each other in his pocket,

CLICK CLACK, a dance of opportunity for someone tonight within the sacred walls of the original Crank Palace. *What better way to rescue the past from itself but to come to Colorado?* Nicholas felt someone approaching and looked to the footsteps behind him. A Crank stumbled past. He needed to be more careful with how his test went this time around. The last test subject nearly drew unwanted attention. In testing the Cure, he needed those possessed with only the purest of minds. And even then, his most recent experiment proved that anyone's intentions, anyone's mind, could change in an instant. A person became a different version of themselves when they were dying, and not just the part of them that slowly turned into a Crank. Even when using his telepathic gift, Nicholas found that a person could say almost anything when they themselves were closer and closer to the end, but when given the chance to live . . .

That's when their own beliefs, fears, and desires came back into awareness quicker than what could be controlled. Quicker than what was safe.

Nicholas needed to be more selective this time.

And he wanted someone past The Gone.

If this **worked** as well as it worked last time, he needed to be sure the Cured Crank—reverted back to healthy DNA—could stay under his study for years to come without waver. Nicholas didn't know how long the Cure held true. *A year? Two years? A lifetime?* He wasn't sure of that, but he knew the variant within the syringes in his pocket worked more quickly than imaginable but might someday wear off just as quickly. Many more studies were needed.

A Crank more human than not walked past Nicholas and let out a deep-bellied groan. A sound that could have been from hunger or the vocalized grief of having his deepest memories resurface. A groan of one's sanity slipping away. Nicholas walked on. He wouldn't choose a walking Crank, no. He needed to choose a Crank more dead than alive. One on the ground who writhed in pain perhaps, but one close enough to death that the promise he or she made to Nicholas would forever be kept.

He had tested variants of the Cure on so many Cranks that he had lost count.

Of course, somewhere hidden in the journals of his library were the observational notes, the number of experiments and trials that attempted to prove his hypothesis right time and time again: that DNA changes from the Flare could be reversed, and that the same Cure that erased the Flare could unlock a multitude of dormant DNA in the human body. Dead-end genomes that scientists had called "junk DNA" for centuries in their scholarly journals. Nicholas tried to hold back his smile, thinking of the discovery, but how could something so monumental as evolution not make him feel like a God?

But it was a fleeting feeling, to be sure. *CLICK CLACK . . .* he circled the two syringes together as he watched the Cranks before him. A failed experiment was a failed experiment. Successes were only temporary. He reported back to the Villa what they needed to change in the next batch. Side effects, advanced symptoms, deaths. Most deaths happened naturally—not everyone's DNA was reprogrammable and not everyone's body could take the Cure. Death was a natural part of scientific advancements, even those **deliberately** caused by the advancer. As when Nicholas' last Crank subject shouted about the Cure within the walls of Crank Palace and put Nicholas' life in danger. *"I'm turning back. My hands, look! He's cured me! This man is a God!"* The Cure itself was at risk as soon as one muttered of its existence. The Crank had promised to stay silent and obedient but as soon as his life became his own again, he betrayed his own thoughts and Nicholas had to end the life he brought back that night. *Easy come, easy go,* you might say. Nicholas wanted to test on someone past The Gone, someone easier to influence. Manipulate. Control.

Nicholas wandered toward an alley behind the westside buildings as it started to rain, and he squinted at the sight of a Crank on the ground with limbs as limp as a butchered deer. But huddled over the Crank sat another, and Nicholas couldn't test on two subjects at once. He tightened the hood of his robe again, but the falling rain enhanced his telepathy and he couldn't help but overhear the woman's thoughts.

I'd take this pain from you if I could. I wish I was infected with this, not you. Nicholas stopped walking and looked on from the shadows of the alley.

Why the hell was someone healthy inside Crank Palace?

Nicholas wasn't infected, but his presence would be swift and purposeful. This figure in front of him seemed to be mourning her long-lost love. *Had she no fear of the Flare?* The only reason Nicholas proved fearless was because he had been a test subject of his own unique study, something the Villa knew nothing about. Using one of the variants as a preventative, Nicholas knew it couldn't harm him with the Flare but might just protect him from it. What he didn't expect were the powerful side effects—weird and frightening things like telepathy.

Human DNA was a funny thing. For a Crank, it was about healing. For the non-infected, the Cure resequenced DNA structures that had been left abandoned in humankind, opening new pathways and abilities whose potential had been lost or never discovered. Like clicking in the last pieces of a puzzle.

But Nicholas' gift of telepathy was also his curse.

He could trust no one.

"Can you help us?" asked the voice huddled over the Crank writhing in pain. Nicholas read her mind again. *Please. Please say you can help us.* He suddenly felt naked, as though she could see right through his cloak to his hand that held the Cure. "Help us." She spoke with an unwarranted confidence.

Nicholas was drawn to her. Her assuredness. Her fearlessness. He walked from the shadows, closer. "What makes you think I can help you?"

"Because you're not infected." *I can tell you're different.*

Nicholas danced with her thoughts again as the rain came down harder.

"And why do you think that?" he responded.

"Your eyes." *Please help us. I'll do anything to save him.*

Nicholas leaned in and asked an impossible question. "Would you sacrifice your life for his?"

Without hesitation she answered, "Yes."

He changed his mind. He'd do something unplanned that night. Something he had never done before.

Once he saved the wretched Crank on the pavement of the alley, he'd also inject the fearless companion with the Cure and study them both, bring them into his inner circle and create the future one day at a time.

One infected, one not.

"I'd do anything to save him. *Please.*" She whispered without tears, "Just tell me what you want me to do."

Nicholas palmed the two syringes in his pocket. "I'll ask for your silence. Not just now, but as we leave the walls and for every single day beyond that. Whatever happens."

"You have my word." Her thoughts and intentions aligned. "Can you save him?"

"I can try. But I'll have to inject you, too, just in case you have an asymptomatic infection." Nicholas wouldn't tell her of the DNA **resequencing** she'd undergo, needing to know how her gifts evolved naturally, if they evolved at all.

"Anything. Please. You're a Godsend. Thank you."

"God is nothing but a complex, we are all Gods. You'll soon find out." Nicholas gently tapped the inside of her arm to find the vein. He wondered how the sequencing might align her unique strands of DNA. "You'll come with me after this to New Petersburg so that I can keep you under observation."

"Alaska? That's a little far from Colorado?"

"Yes, Alaska." Nicholas engaged the syringe slowly so as not to flood her body too quickly with the Cure. "Not bad in a Berg." He smiled and watched her face relax. "You mustn't make a sound when I inject him next. Not a cry, not a scream, not a shout for the world to hear. If you mutter anything louder than a sigh of relief, I will have to-"

"Of course." She watched on and Nicholas pivoted to the Crank with skin so thick the needle needed extra force to penetrate. "What's your name?" she asked.

"Nicholas."

"Thank you, Nicholas. We'll forever be in your debt. My name is—"

"Doesn't matter." Nicholas stood up from the damp ground and put the emptied needles back in his pocket. *CLICK CLACK* . . . "From now on you'll be known as Alexandra, and he'll be known as Mikhail."

PART ONE

Natural Selection

I don't know what awaits us after the Gone. I guess I might 'meet my maker' as someone in the Glade once said. Or I might just meet myself again . . . my whole self, memories, real name, all that. Maybe at the end, the broken pieces of life all come together.

Maybe they'll make sense. Or maybe they won't.

Maybe it's a little of both.

—*The Book of Newt*

CHAPTER ONE

Forging Ahead

I

ISAAC

The flames danced higher from their nightly fire, and Isaac watched as his friends carried on in a circle around the camp as if they were all back on the island after a feast. As if everything were the same as it ever was. But, no. Everything had changed. He could see that change most in Jackie's face, how the loss of Lacey and Carson took the spark out of her eyes. Or maybe killing a bald-headed half-Crank with her bare hands changed her. Either way, with every mile they traveled closer to the coast and farther away from the broken Grief Walker, away from Lacey and Carson, Jackie seemed further and further away too.

She didn't talk about what happened all those weeks ago, and Isaac understood that perfectly. He never wanted to talk about losing his mom, dad, and sister either. Talking about it made it real. And it didn't need to feel any more real than the empty space that remained in their place. Isaac half-smiled and half-frowned at Jackie, the only way he knew how to send a sympathetic but supportive look, letting her see that he knew the grief and torment of what she was going through. It wasn't just the loss of her friends that Isaac understood all too well, but the feeling of what Old Man Frypan once called 'survivor's guilt'—the feeling of still being alive when those you loved weren't. Jackie half-smiled and half-frowned right back at him.

"Hey, who wants to hear a spider bark?" Dominic stood up to stretch, and before Miyoko could push him out of the circle, he did it again. He let one rip. Since escaping the Bergs, Dominic's gas had become the biggest weapon of destruction the group had to avoid. Trish glared at Dominic. She had a steadfast rule of not farting near the campfire.

"You're going to catch us all on fire one day, you know." Trish rolled her eyes and then inched closer to Sadina, intertwining Sadina's fingers with her own. After Sadina and Isaac were kidnapped, Isaac couldn't help but notice Trish tethered herself more than ever to Sadina, in whatever ways she could. Isaac understood that too. He was thankful for the group, but he himself felt untethered, as if a bad wind could come along and just blow everything away. Maybe because they slept outside as if they were on the run. He missed the safety of the yurt he'd built back home. He looked around at the trees and available resources; it'd take some time, but he could build a shelter here for everyone.

"Thanks for dinner, ol' Man," Isaac said as he collected the carved wood they used for bowls and helped clean up. Isaac had never seen Old Man Frypan happier than when they settled in between the mountains, eating rabbits and plants and cooking for everyone when he had the energy.

Minho leaned back to stretch. "You even managed to make Roxy's stew taste better, which I swore wasn't possible."

"Some kind of spiky herb he added from the forest," Roxy added as she helped Isaac clean up.

"It's called Rosemary. I don't know how I remember that, but I do." Old Man Frypan inched closer to the fire.

Roxy took all the bowls from Isaac and stacked them together. "I'll forage first thing in the morning, go out a little farther east and see what I can find up there."

"I'll go with you and maybe find some squirrels to hunt." Orange tugged at the annoying burs that had gotten stuck in her hair from hunting earlier. "Ow! These things really hurt for how small they are." The weeds, vines, and brush had weapons of their own in this part of the world. The harshest things back on the island were rocks, water, jellyfish, and the weather, but out here there were too many dangers to count. Every day it seemed like Isaac learned something new to watch out for. Besides Cranks and giant killing machines.

"How's your insect bite?" Isaac asked Dominic.

"I don't think it bit me. I think it was a stinger." Dominic looked at his bicep. "Kinda looked like a bee but that sucker was way bigger. Do you think Grievers can shrink down and fly?" Everyone but Old Man Frypan laughed.

"Grievers are nothing to snark at," the grizzled veteran said, and the group hushed out of respect.

"Maybe the bees bite out here?" Miyoko asked.

"I don't see any teeth marks." Dominic examined his arm even closer.

Roxy went over to check on the poor guy. "Hmmm. . . . It's not ants or you'd have more of them with the same marks. Sounds like it could have been a murder hornet. That's not good."

"A murder hornet? Is my arm going to fall off?" Dominic looked at Roxy, concerned, and Isaac couldn't tell if he actually believed it. "Am I going to die?"

"I bet that sucked the gas right out of you!" Trish laughed until Sadina elbowed her.

Roxy held in her own laugh. "I'm just messing with you. It'll probably be sore for a few days, but you'll be fine." She looked closely at Dominic's arm, then patted it lovingly. "Lucky he didn't get you more than once."

Miyoko and Trish combed their fingers through Orange's ginger locks and removed the spiky balls of nature that had attached themselves, tossing her hair into a bird's nest. Despite Minho and Orange being more intimidating than Ms. Cowan at times, Isaac was glad to have their leadership within the group. Without Orange they'd all be dead.

He sat back down by the fire, taking everything in. The wind kicked up and the sparks of the fire reminded him of the sparks in the forge. He'd give anything to go back to being a blacksmith apprentice at home, but he had a feeling that even life on the island wasn't exactly *"life on the island"* anymore. The fire made Isaac feel safe, and the smoke had a way of cleansing the group enough that they all didn't smell like the hammers of hell in between stream baths. The wind pushed again, longer and harder. "Anyone else notice it's getting colder at night?" Isaac had only felt it in the last few days, but right before dusk the temperature dropped further and each *whoosh* of the wind lasted longer than the day before.

"Yeah, it sure is," Dominic answered.

Ms. Cowan inched closer to the fire. "Never had this kind of chill back home."

The flames flickered and highlighted the shadows of stress on Cowan's face. Along with the drop in temperature, she had been uncomfortably quiet the last few nights. Isaac imagined that the weight of her decision to leave the island and to go against the government must have continued to weigh on her, especially after losing Wilhelm and Alvarez. But there was no way she could've known the trip would result in so many deaths.

"You think everyone back home is doing okay?" Isaac asked her, but Cowan didn't blink. Slowly, one by one, heads looked up in her direction.

". . . Ms. Cowan?" Isaac asked again.

Even Orange, Minho, and Roxy, who had never been to the island, waited on Cowan's response but she just stared at the fire.

"Mom?" Sadina shouted over the fire.

Ms. Cowan finally blinked, "What's that, dear?"

"Do you think everyone back home is doing okay?" Isaac asked again.

Cowan looked at him as if it were a trick question. "Yes, of course.

They're all fine, I'm sure." But the way her voice lowered slightly at *'they're all fine'* gave Isaac a pang in his gut. A pang that said it was them, the eleven **souls** sitting around the fire just then, who *weren't* fine.

"How many Bergs are on your island?" Minho asked while adding wood to the fire, and everyone from back home looked at each other.

Trish replied. "None of us knew what that . . . thing you call a Berg was until we flew on it."

"No, we didn't have Bergs on the island. The islanders weren't meant to leave . . ." Cowan's last words seemed coated with regret. Isaac felt the mood shift along with the cold air but Cowan finally snapped out of her trance. "Look, if we hadn't left the island, Lacey, Carson, Wilhelm, and Alverez would still be alive. I know that." She took a slow deliberate breath. "But we owed it to humanity to work for a Cure, and if we'd succeeded . . . we could have saved hundreds of thousands of lives. Maybe millions. Who knows."

". . . if there's that many people left," Roxy responded in the grimmest voice possible.

"We can still do that," Miyoko said while she finished the braid in Orange's hair. "The Villa Kletter talked about wasn't far from where we were when we arrived on land. Maybe a few miles?" She paused before adding, "I think she said it was a two-day hike before she . . ." and Isaac knew why she stopped talking when she did: because there's no polite way to say *before Kletter got her throat slit open.*

Sadina chimed in at that. "Yeah, we were supposedly really close to the Villa. And that's why Letti kidnapped us and kept saying the same thing: not to trust the people there or Kletter."

"You trust a word that came out of Letti's or Timon's mouth?" Isaac didn't think he had to remind his best friend that the two crazy people who forcibly took them probably weren't the best ones to take advice from. Sure, there were moments when Isaac thought that maybe Letti and Timon were helping to protect them from something, the way they allowed them to leave clues for the rest of the group to stay on their trail, but they'd never fully explained what the so-called Evolution was or how people could die.

"I vote we go home," Dominic said, and a silence fell over the entire group, even from Minho and Orange, whose home sounded awful.

The fire crackled. "We could all go with Minho to Alaska," Roxy added optimistically, but the mention of Alaska made Old Man Frypan stand up and leave the circle. He had understandably seen enough of that place to last several lifetimes.

"I didn't live this long just to go back to the the Maze. I'd rather die right here than step one foot in that Godforsaken country." After his airing of grievances he sat back down. "Some wounds aren't meant to be re-opened."

What might happen if they *did* go back home, Isaac wondered. The way they left on the *Maze Cutter*, mysteriously leaving after the whole island got knock-out drunk from poisoned wine, might have seemed like the best solution at the time but what would Cowan say if they went back? Lie and blame it all on Kletter? *"She poisoned everyone on the island and kidnapped us."* Or be honest and say, *"Hey, we tried to save the world but it turns out there's a lot more to it. A bunch of scientists wanted us dead, the Cranks have evolved, and some of us escaped thanks to two orphans from the Remnant Nation. No big deal. We're back!"*

And even so, what if by returning to the island they only caused more people like Kletter to come after Sadina and the islanders again? The Gladers of old wanted to protect the immunes and their descendants from ever being found. It seemed selfish to put everyone back home at risk again. But what did that mean? Spending the rest of their lives on the run?

"Alright then. Should we put it to a vote?" Cowan asked. And just like that the nightly campfire improbably turned into some kind of government meeting. Isaac had never wanted part in any kind of decision making. He'd just wanted to learn how to forge and be a blacksmith. But his throat felt itchy with the pressure of needing to speak up.

"I motion we move to vote," Dominic said as he stood up, sounding like a stranger. Isaac wasn't sure what he wanted to do when they reached the coast. . . . Stay in the wilderness and build a yurt? Go home to apologize for ever leaving? Go to Alaska and finish some mission they didn't understand? See the Maze of old? Go to the Villa to find the scientists? It was too much, as usual, for him to process.

Sadina also stood up. "Mom, can't we just—"

"No. We had a democracy at home and we'll have one here." Cowan acted as if this entire trip hadn't revolved around Sadina and the possibility that her blood might change the world. Also, poisoning your people because they might not agree with you wasn't exactly what Isaac would call a democracy. "We'll vote by show of hands. Only vote once."

Issac looked at Sadina and mouthed the words, "I'm sorry."

2

SADINA

At times she had been glad to have her mom on the trip with her, but this was not one of those times. Why couldn't they discuss the decision for a few days and present options, and listen to everyone's opinions? Why did her mom always have to do everything in such a public forum? *Like the poisoning at the amphitheater.* Sadina never would've brought the entire town together just to poison them all and then sneak away and pretend to be taken forcibly.

If the truth wasn't an option, why couldn't they have disappeared in the middle of the night on the ship and left a note about their true intentions? If a cure was such a good and noble thing, then why hide what they did? It shouldn't have mattered that some of the island Congress disagreed—that's always the case. Sadina just wanted logical sense sometimes. Like now. Why couldn't they sleep on it and have an open discussion in the morning?

But her idea of what was fair didn't matter. It never did with her mom.

Sadina couldn't control what happened next any more than she could control having special blood. She could only hope her friends chose the best option—whatever that might be. Letti and Timon thought Kletter was evil enough that they killed her the minute they had the chance. They could have killed Isaac and everyone else in the group except Sadina if they wanted to make it easier on themselves to manipulate her, but instead they let everyone live. *And weren't they working with the Remnant Nation somehow?* They never killed anyone else, despite having the chance to do so. It was the one thing Sadina kept coming back to because she couldn't shake how fast they'd killed Kletter. Because *the Villa was bad.*

"Vote with me," Sadina whispered to Trish.

"Wherever you go, I'll go." Trish clasped her fingers around Sadina's and held her hand fiercely, so tight that Sadina's knuckles hurt.

"Wherever you are, I'll be," she whispered back.

Sadina's mom cleared her throat. "Let's handle this like a proper vote. Meaning, no outbursts, no arguing. Whatever has the votes will be what we do, period. Understood?"

Everyone in the group nodded their heads but said nothing.

Sadina couldn't tell if her mom was being more of a mom at this moment or more of a senator. Both titles sometimes put off a "because-I-said-so" tone to them, something Sadina could have done without. *What if the majority vote isn't the best way to spend their time?*

"All those in favor of staying here, raise your hands," Sadina's mom asked. Old Man Frypan's hand shot up as if it were connected to a shooting star in the sky. Jackie's hand joined his arm in the air. But theirs were the only votes for staying, and once *the senator* pointed at them each as if to say "Your vote has been seen," Old Man Frypan and Jackie's hands lowered.

"Why do you want to stay here?" Dominic whispered to Jackie, but Sadina's mom hushed them all.

"All those in favor of going back home, raise your hands," Sadina's mom announced next, but Dominic's hand was the only one to go up. He looked at Jackie with a frown as if her vote and his combined could have tipped the scales of the majority and they'd have all just gone home. Sadina looked over at Isaac. She thought for sure Isaac would've voted to go back home. All he had talked about in the last few days was setting up his own forge, fishing at the Point again, and checking in on the gray-haired firstborn of the island, Ms. Ariana.

Sadina nodded to Isaac; he must have been waiting to vote with her and for that she was thankful. *Why was she so nervous about this?* She took a breath so big that all the little bones in her neck cracked. She couldn't believe Old Man Frypan actually voted to stay put, night after night forever, because even her body ached from sleeping on the stony ground. The tiniest rock or clump of clay woke her up in discomfort every night. Trish made Sadina a woven grass pad to sleep on but it didn't help much. There weren't enough grass pads in the whole mainland to keep her there. Heck, even the wooden boards and half-broken cots on the *Maze Cutter* were more comfortable.

"Next vote." Sadina's mom cleared her throat again as if that made whatever she had to say next more official. "All those in favor of going to Alaska, raise your hands."

Sadina watched as one by one, Minho, Orange, and Roxy raised their arms with confidence. If Sadina had to be anywhere when trouble came, she'd want Minho and Orange to be around. She couldn't shake the feeling, like a tickle in her spine, that Alaska was where she was supposed to be. Letti and Timon might not have known everything but the one thing they knew for sure was that the Villa wasn't going to help in the way Kletter thought it was. Or the way Kletter *lied* that it *could*. Sadina squeezed Trish's hand and locked eyes with her. One set of clasped hands rose because Trish wasn't letting go of Sadina—not even to vote. Because Trish had Sadina's back no matter what. Even if Sadina was wrong.

But Sadina looked at Isaac in confusion. *Did he forget to vote?* She waited for his hand to go up, but it didn't.

"All those in favor of going to the Villa, raise your hands." Cowan asked the final question, the only option left, and Sadina watched as Isaac and her mom both raised their hands, along with Miyoko. How could one of her best friends and her mom both think that they knew better than her when it came to what she did with her own DNA? Sure, Kletter scared them into coming off the island but were they all forgetting how she killed the crew of eight people before she got there? What if Kletter was just a master manipulator? What if those eight people she killed were all scientists too? There was just too much yet to learn and it sounded like going to Alaska to meet the Godhead was the only way they'd have answers. *Real answers.*

Sadina shook off Trish's hand. "The Villa? Really? You do remember scientists were to blame for all of this in the first place?" She couldn't hold it in. "The Flare Virus. The Flare Coalition, WICKED, the Maze, the Trials—and here you are voting to just trust those in the same position?" Sadina couldn't believe she was the only one to question things. Isaac and her mom lowered their hands, but they didn't say anything.

How could they not *speak?* Sadina had so many questions running through her head that kept her awake at night. Like what if . . . what if the scientists wanted to infect Sadina and the islanders to send them back so that everyone on the island, all the way up to poor Ms. Ariana of the firstborns, got infected with something new? What if it wasn't about curing anyone at all? What if all they wanted were fresh new test subjects? What if the trials never ended? Who could Sadina actually trust? All questions that floated through her mind and kept her up at night.

"Well, I guess it's decided then. Alaska has the votes," Sadina's mom said with failed enthusiasm.

"What if we took the top two and we all voted again to see if—" Dominic suggested but Sadina's mom cut him off.

"This isn't a swimmers' champion bracket like Midsummer Day on the island. These are the majority rules. We are going to Alaska."

Even though her vote for Alaska won the majority, Sadina hated how they'd reached their solution. Why did Isaac's vote, Jackie's vote, and Miyoko's vote feel like betrayal?

Sadina watched as Old Man Frypan pulled out his Book of Newt and Jackie stared deep into the fire. Isaac finished cleaning up dinner with Roxy and everyone but Minho looked heavy from the responsibility of choosing what path lay next.

"Alaska it is." Minho tossed a handful of brush onto the fire and it seemed to sizzle and clap with approval.

"You okay?" Trish asked Sadina.

"Yeah," she replied without thinking.

"Are you lying to me?" Trish shot back.

Sadina stopped to think. Trish was right, she knew her better than anyone. "Why do I feel like this is the last time we'll all be together? That not everyone will go to Alaska?" She waited for Trish to make the face she always did when Sadina was being extra dramatic, but it didn't come.

"I know what you mean," she replied instead. "I kind of had the same feeling."

3
ALEXANDRA

She stood alone on her balcony and watched in wonder as the full pallet of colors from the Aurora Borealis filled the sky like never before. The milky-green of the northern lights had never left, coating the town in a fog-like feel. But tonight, the sky lit up to reflect all the colors of the rainbow. Bright blues, oranges, and purples appeared as ribbons after so many years without them. Pinks hung low, pulling at the purples, and if Alexandra looked closely enough, she could even see a swirl of red racing above as if to announce something more. Could it be? *Yes. It was time.*

Alaska was ready for the Evolution.

Alexandra was ready.

And this moment she embraced before her was all too perfect. The lights danced in the sky, named lifetimes ago after Aurora, the Roman Goddess of Dawn and the God, Boreas, of the north winds. It was nearly midnight, but to Alexandra it was the dawn of a new day. The Evolution. She took in a deep breath full of cold Alaskan air and imagined the ancients-of-old and how they must have been shocked upon seeing the lights for the first time. Alexandra had the luxury of time and knowledge that they had lacked. Unlike them, she didn't need to create any fairy tales to tell the people of Alaska about Gods and chariots, she'd simply tell them the truth. The sky was no place for Gods. The only Gods needed on Earth were stationed on the Earth. Scientists. Academics. And those who were blessed with the infinite knowledge of the world—*like her.*

Even without ever viewing this many colors of the Aurora Borealis before, it took Alexandra only one look at the sky's brilliance for her mind to flood with information. Instant facts about the event—and it was truly an *event.* The solar winds were more active than ever. Coronal Mass Ejections operated independently from solar flares and blasted particles millions of miles toward space and into the magnetic field of anything in its way. They were blessed with particles that danced with oxygen from the lower atmosphere and produced green flowing curtains of light. Bright blues struck the massive display in places where magnetic winds mixed with nitrogen, and the rare purple lights woven from hydrogen molecules in the atmosphere.

To see such magnificence and not understand it would be a . . . sin. Yes, a sin.

She took note of the emerald swaths that spread farther and stronger than the other colors, just like she would soon be the strongest voice of the Godhead. A green no longer murky but one that held bright life within it. How she wished Nicholas and Mikhail could see her triumph over Alaska like the lights that floated in front of her.

In a way, Nicholas *was* there to see it. She turned and opened her balcony curtains just enough so that Nicholas' severed head, in its sealed glass box, could take in the view. With the eyelids removed, Nicholas' eyes bulged out to remind her of his outrageous expressions when he presumed to have read minds. The color of his face and the frayed skin of his neck made her stomach twist, thinking how much pressure Mannus must have used to release each muscle, tendon, and bone from its place.

She found humor in the fact that part of the Godhead was literally just a head now. Nicholas, always the scholar, would've appreciated the play on words. "As soon as they find the rest of you, you're out of here."

She set the glass box on the table. She didn't think discovering Nicholas' body should have taken so long, but with all the traveling he did and all of his secret trips, no one had even noticed the weeks without him. No one missed him. She certainly didn't miss him hovering over her thoughts. The freedom that Nicholas' death afforded her went beyond the ability to finally execute her plans, it freed her mind from his intrusiveness. Even now, she looked forward to the day she'd be fully and finally freed from him once and for all and not have to stare at his **decaying** face. But she needed to keep what remained, just long enough for Mikhail to know that *she* was in control now.

She was the One above all. The Goddess of the new Dawn.

Bright, colorful streaks swirled prominently above, brighter than ever before, and below Alexandra's balcony the Pilgrims came out in flocks to look up at the night sky. People pointed upward, arms skinny from a weak harvest season and their mustard yellow cloaks dirty from everyday life. But this moment allowed them hope. And she, Goddess Romanov, would be the one to deliver on that hope.

A knock at the door made her ears buzz. She shook the noise from her head and quickly shuffled to place a cloth cover over the glass box holding Nicholas' head. "What is it?"

Flint swung the door open as if the rapture was upon them, out of breath like a flight of stairs could kill him. He'd never have survived in the times of the Maze. Sometimes Alexandra thought of sending Flint down there just for a week or three to prove it.

"Well, what is it? You're fluffing and puffing like the world's on fire."

"The lights. The skylights!" Flint pointed to the balcony as if Alexandra didn't have her own eyeballs.

"Yes. Of course the lights are back." Alexandra moved the covered head of Nicholas closer to the balcony so he could watch her change the world. She smirked. How many times had Nicholas begged her to be patient. Begged her not to be brash. "The lights are a sign of the Evolution. Everything is evolving, Flint. This is just the beginning."

"People are crying in the streets. Talking of sacrifices."

"Don't be an idiot." Alexandra dismissed his fear.

"I'm scared there will be more Hollowings tonight." Flint stood at the doorway, neither in nor out—exactly how he acted within life—teetering on the edge of faith or fear. Alexandra had no time for teetering. The Evolution was finally, after years of pause, upon them. "Nicholas should calm the people and—"

She cut Flint off, "*I* will calm the people. Tell the Pilgrims their Goddess will address them tomorrow and that if any Hollowings take place tonight, I'll see that the sacrificers are the next to be sacrificed. Can you handle that?"

He nodded. He bowed. He left.

Alexandra ripped the cover from Nicholas' box.

"Enjoy the view."

CHAPTER TWO

Kindling & Kin

I

SADINA

A chill in the air shivered her awake. She tried fixing the grass mat Trish had made her but she couldn't get comfortable. Her family's lineage from Sonya had never felt like a burden before; at times on the island she had felt admired and special, even protected—but none of those feelings seemed to follow her on their journey to the mainland.

Ever since the group arrived, Sadina had felt unsafe, vulnerable, like her own life was at risk of being extinguished before discovering why her family's DNA could help. And maybe if more of her ancestral bloodline had been alive, the pressure could have been spread out among others—brothers, sisters, cousins—but Sadina was the only child, just like her parents. Sadina slowly and quietly stood up from her makeshift sleeping spot next to Trish and moved closer to the fire. She walked past her mom, Old Man Frypan, and Minho, all still snoozing. Minho slept with his boots on. Orphan soldiers did weird things.

Sadina sat cross-legged on the ground closest to the fire and rubbed her temples as she looked into the dying flames. A rustle in the trees to the left startled her. She looked back to the sleeping bodies and counted shadows, then felt beside her for something, anything, to use as a weapon. Her right hand found a rock; she held her breath and listened as the rustling grew. *What was that?* An animal, maybe? But how big? Minho had told stories of the animals they hunted where he came from. Animals bigger than anything they had on their island, and Isaac had told stories of the strength it took to kill the half-Cranks. Sadina wasn't sure she could kill anything bigger than a spider; she never had a reason to before. What if she was forced to crunch the life out of something under her own weight? The disturbance grew louder and closer. Sadina looked at Minho's boots and thought the best thing to do with the rock she'd grabbed might be to throw it at Minho and wake him up. He had guns, knives, and if things got really bad he had some kind of ancient artillery that blew up when you pulled a pin from it. Sadina tensed when a dark tall shadow, hunched over in shape emerged from the tree line. Sadina's eyes widened to take in as many details as they could, but the dying fire made it hard to see more than the outline of a person holding something long and thin. A weapon. She was sure of it. Her heart filled with all of its special blood and beat faster and faster until she realized that her fear had gotten the best of her.

"Don't mind me." The whispered words floated in the air and the shadow stepped closer to her. "Just taking my hourly piss and feeding the fire." Old Man Frypan's image came into focus before her tired brain could identify his voice.

"Oh Shuck, you scared me." Sadina exhaled and dropped the rock beside her.

"Nice. And I'm sorry. Didn't mean to scare you. What are you doing up?"

"Couldn't sleep. Too anxious about Alaska."

"Imagine my excitement." Frypan broke a stick in two and leaned both halves on top of the dying fire. It didn't take long for the flames to catch on, flickering to bright life.

"Sorry." Sadina didn't know what else to say. "I've heard all the Glader stories of old, but to be honest, they always felt more like history lessons and not real life until I saw that first Crank."

"The Cranks . . ." he scoffed, "They ain't nuthin' to hardly worry about. Time did what they could with the Cranks, the people though. . . . They're the ones you have to watch out for."

Sadina pulled her knees to her chest. "What do you mean by that?"

"I mean . . . how do I say this . . ." Frypan pulled up a log to sit next to her and shifted his weight in thought. "The island has been a safe place, a safe haven, for many, many years. Those born there in that safety, they don't know the evil that existed, that still exists, in the outside world. Which is good, it's the whole point of the safe haven— but what I mean is . . ."

"You're talking about the people at the Villa?"

"I don't know if the people in the Villa are good people or bad people. I just know that they don't know us as well as we know each other. And we don't know what motivations they might have." Frypan's voice was somehow stronger in a whisper. "Or the motivations of The Godhead."

"If they really want to cure the Flare, that can only be good, right?"

"Ava Paige wanted to cure the Flare, too." He said it with the utmost spite.

"Just like anything, I guess. Someone's motivations can be good but their actions could be bad. Or their motivations could change . . ." Sadina looked up to the stars and tried to find the biggest one. There was no way she could fall back asleep thinking about all this now. *What if the Godhead had good motivations but bad plans to execute?* Just like her mom had the best of intentions by holding the vote but the act of "democracy" ruined the vibe in their group.

"Everyone from here to the great beyond has motivations, and when you meet someone—try to meet their motivations as well. See if you can figure them out." Old Man Frypan tossed another twig into the fire. "See, Cranks don't scare me anymore because they can't think past their primal urges. People, though . . . people are manipulative, motivated by power, greed, and things you and I aren't capable of."

Sadina wished things could be black or white—the cure or no cure —she hated all this gray area where people like Ava Paige lived. "Do you think I was an idiot to vote for Alaska?"

"No." The old man answered her almost too quickly for her to believe it.

"Am I being naive to trust the two people who kidnapped me?" She asked, hoping for a more honest answer, even as she realized how ridiculous the question was in the first place.

"I can't tell you who to trust." He said it gently and slowly like her grandmother Sonya spoke. The elders had a way of speaking that made the words themselves hold more weight. All their life experiences stood behind those words and made them feel heavy.

Sadina wished for an ounce of wisdom from her grandmother about all this, but Grandma Sonya died years ago. "So . . ." Sadina looked at the fire as she thought out loud. "How did you know who to trust?"

Old Man Frypan put another piece of wood on the fire as if the answer required patience. He sat back down and softly said, "You trust yourself more than anyone else."

"So, I shouldn't trust anyone else?"

"You're jumping to it too quickly." He slowed down his words, "You trust yourself first, and after that you trust those *who trust you*." He stoked the fire, its flames reflected in his glistening, wizened eyes. "The only mistake you could ever make is trusting the trustless."

2

MINHO

Orphans had no parents.

Orphans had no siblings.

Orphans had no friends. . . . Only enemies.

Minho sat up and reached for his knife; when he pulled the sharp blade from its sheath, he realized he'd only been awakened by the sounds of the group making breakfast. Old Man Frypan snapping twigs. Roxy cutting root vegetables. Dominic humming a song. He slowly put his knife back in its holder and avoided eye contact. Mornings, when he floated in that dreamlike battleground between sleep and awake, he often didn't know where he was and grabbed his weapons on instinct. In those early moments of the day, he reverted back to his Orphan days. Ready to shoot. Ready to stab. Ready to survive. Maybe the group knew his reflexes were on overdrive and that's why no one slept too close to him. Sometimes he had a good solid sleep, so restful that even in his dreams he wasn't anywhere close to the Remnant Nation, but the further he went from his training ground the harder reality seemed to snap back when he woke up. He moved his knife to his hip and reminded himself that he had friends and he had a mom, now. And, most importantly, he had a name. His name was Minho.

"Orange . . . ," Roxy said in a way he imagined a mother's tone might sound when something isn't wrong but not exactly right.

"Yeah?" Orange took a glimpse at Roxy's bowl.

"Here." She motioned for Orange to hold out her hand. "I think this potato you found me is a rock." She plucked the rock out of the bowl and into Orange's open palm.

"Oh." Orange laughed at the potato-looking chunk of rock. Minho had never heard her make such a sound, a cluster of small laughs like Trish and Sadina made.

"Orange is trying to break our teeth on break-fast!" Miyoko yelled with her own chortle.

Minho watched as Orange bounced the rock in her hand, a thing she could use to kill three people without so much as a thought. Anything an Orphan held in their hand became a weapon.

He wondered if she felt the same disorientation in the mornings, if she, too, had to slow her heartbeat in order to keep the practices of the Remnant Nation at bay. The Orphans were in training from the age of four. Trained to fight. To kill. To survive. Until then, were they cared for by nannies until they were able to stand and balance their own weight? He didn't know. His earliest memory was Griever Glane forcing him to kill a mother wolf in front of her cubs. He turned the wolves into orphans only to later die the same death as their mother. Was that what the Remnant Nation did to him?

"Your eyes are open but nobody's home." Roxy looked right at Minho as if what she just said were a question. She had funny ways of saying 'good morning,' unlike Sadina's mom who spoke gently and said things like, "rise and shine, kiddos."

"Getting there." Minho didn't have the heart to tell Roxy any of these dark thoughts. Both past and present. He watched Orange closely with every bounce of the rock in her hand. Every time it met her palm he waited for her to peg Miyoko in the temple for laughing at her. Pelt Dominic in the ass for being such an ass. But she didn't. She just tossed the rock up in the air and watched it fall.

If having friends was changing Orange, maybe there was hope. Maybe leaving the Remnant Nation meant they could also leave the Nation's imposed beliefs behind.

Orange vaulted the potato-looking rock farther up this time. As it dropped to eye level her elbow swung in a way that made Minho's own muscles flinch from years of training. Orange flicked her wrist with hand-to-hand combat skills and gave a hard backhand that sent the rock flying into a nearby tree. The islanders gawked at her precision. Minho smiled.

"Whoa," Dominic said. "I wanna learn that."

"Do it again!" Miyoko grabbed a stone from around the campfire. "Is this one too big?" Orange repeated the trick, big heave into the air, quick swing of the elbow, backhand that sent the rock flying. This time a little closer to Dominic, whizzing past his ears.

Minho sighed, even as the others cheered. Orange was a good fighter, but she deserved to be more than that.

Humanity deserved the right to evolve. Didn't they? Be better than this?

Born fighters could evolve into born leaders if given the chance.

Maybe even nameless Orphans who killed dozens of trespassers on sight could turn out to be something more. Something much more.

Just maybe.

Or not.

CHAPTER THREE

Secret Mission

I

ISAAC

Isaac didn't plan on bringing up the Timon and Letti thing again, especially not while they cleaned up camp, but Sadina just couldn't let it go.

"The reason I trust them—that I think maybe Kletter lied . . . I mean, she killed her whole crew. Eight people. That's enough right there not to trust her. But besides all that, the reason I think I trust Letti and Timon, is that they *trusted us.*" Sadina paced while Isaac folded up her grass mat. She kicked up dirt behind her with every step. "They said it themselves, they could have killed the rest of the group, just like Kletter, but they let them follow our clues. They trusted us."

Isaac handed her the mat. "That wasn't them trusting us, they only manipulated us into thinking everything we did was something they wanted us to do. They were frantic half the time, and . . ." Isaac stopped himself before saying *and they didn't even trust each other.* Did Sadina not remember what Letti pulled on Timon when they came across

Roxy and Minho for the first time? The whole gunfire in the air, mentions of betrayal. Something about how not even Timon knew the plan.

"I just think we need to go to Alaska. *I need to go.*"

It wasn't worth arguing over something that had already been decided. "Good thing we're going then." Isaac put his arm around her and pulled her into a hug. Even if Sadina had chosen to go back home, he'd have supported her. She was the closest thing to family he had, and family didn't always have to agree.

"And how the hell are we supposed to get there?" Dominic asked, still sour from being the only islander to vote to go back home. It wasn't that Isaac didn't want that, of course he did, but he didn't want to go do it as a failure. He wanted to make the rest of the island proud, to at least say they tried. If they went back now, they'd be returning with more questions than answers.

"Yeah, how are we supposed to get all the way to Alaska?" Miyoko asked as she packed up what smaller pieces of firewood were already cut.

"Well, we can backtrack along the coast and pick up the *Maze Cutter.*" Cowan cleared her throat. "New Petersburg is along the Gulf of Alaska, traveling by ship will save us all time and energy."

Ms. Cowan was probably up all night worrying about how to be the most diplomatic in these decisions. Isaac thought with the vote over and done with that Sadina's mom might be more relaxed, or less stressed, but the circles under her eyes looked darker than ever and she moved slower than Old Man Frypan.

"Minho, can you steer a ship?" Isaac asked.

"I can get us there." Minho didn't flat out say he'd never steered a boat before, but as far as Isaac was concerned if he could steer a Berg and a Grief Walker then he could handle the *Maze Cutter* just fine. Plus, enough of them had picked up details on the journey to the mainland to help him out.

"We could stay close to the coast, and come in to hunt as needed," Orange said while packing up.

Ms. Cowan cleared her throat again, but this time said nothing.

2

Minho and Orange led the way from camp, but the vote had slowly divided them into three distinct groups: Minho, Orange, Roxy, Sadina, and Trish in the lead, those who voted for Alaska. In the middle was Isaac, Ms. Cowan, and Miyoko, the three who thought the Villa was a better choice. And trailing behind were Jackie, Dominic, and Old Man Frypan, all of whom didn't want to go anywhere and were moving at a speed to prove it.

Isaac never paid much attention to the politics on the island because he never had a reason to. The sets of laws back home were kept and there was rarely an issue that divided anyone. The last real division in politics on the island had been when they added laws about being near the water during a storm after Isaac's family's accident. It was clear some people were upset that there weren't laws made earlier and others were upset that there needed to be laws added and abided by. Isaac didn't care either way, because no law in the universe could bring his family back. But he hated the feeling of everyone's vote and differences in opinions now seemingly splitting the whole group apart. He hated it!

He could barely see Sadina's group ahead on the trail and he lost sight of Old Man Frypan's group behind him ten minutes ago. He only knew they were somewhat close by hearing Dominic making up a ridiculous song about every single thing they walked past.

"Hey, let's rest a minute and let them catch up!" Isaac called ahead to Sadina's group.

Ms. Cowan cleared her throat with a nod.

Miyoko whistled and waved Sadina and her Godhead-driven crew to fall back. It was almost as if once Sadina had decided to go to Alaska that she was going with or without the rest of them.

Ms. Cowan sat on a log and pulled out her canteen. Isaac waited to see which group came back into view first, but something wasn't right about the way Ms. Cowan drank the water, taking small sips, pausing after each one. The way she lacked the enthusiasm for conversation she once had. Maybe she was just homesick like the rest of them, maybe the guilt of those they'd lost still weighed heavy on her, but Isaac couldn't help but wonder. "You okay, Ms. Cowan?" he asked.

"Of course, why?" She looked up at Isaac from the log, but even the way she tilted her head seemed off.

"You just seem out of breath. Or like it's hard to swallow maybe?"

And that's when he noticed the mark on the woman's neck.

The trees stopped shaking their leaves. The wind off the coast stopped blowing. The birds stopped chirping. The only thing that didn't turn silent in that moment was the rash on Cowan's neck that seemed to scream obscenities. What was that from?

She cleared her throat yet again, locking eyes with Isaac.

Panic rushed through his mind. The Flare. The variants. Infection. He couldn't unsee the image of the half-Cranks. Of Jackie killing one with her bare hands. Isaac couldn't help but clear his own throat. The thought of a virus hit him like a hammer to metal on the forge, igniting sparks of fear in his gut; the heat of the unknown rushed through his body.

The Flare. The variants. Infection.

3

Isaac followed Ms. Cowan into the brush. Maybe it was just poison. Maybe the rash was just a rash. They'd been surrounded by plant life for days, plants they had never seen before, some with spiked weapons that attached to clothing and skin and some that Roxy claimed could kill you with so much as a touch. Maybe that's all it was.

He tried to catch up to her. "Ms. Cowan . . ." He waited for a response but heard only the sounds of vomiting. A sound he'd heard often enough from Jackie during the *Maze Cutter* voyage, but never a sound he heard from Cowan before. He followed the gut-wrenching noise. Bent over and heaving, Ms. Cowan's body purged the evil from inside as she leaned her shoulder against a tree.

"Shit," Isaac let out before apologizing. "Sorry."

"It's okay. I'm okay. Just allergies." She quickly composed herself and fixed the handkerchief around her neck.

"Ms. Cowan . . . you sure?" He pointed to the spot where the material covered her scabbed skin. Cowan touched the rash as if covering it with her hand might make Isaac less **suspicious**. "We've got to tell everyone and—"

"No." Cowan stood up taller. "Everyone will overreact. I'm fine."

"You can't hide vomiting from the rest of the group. You remember how bad it was on the boat. Especially with Dominic." He was trying to break the ice, reminding her of the Dominic-Vomit-Domino-Effect that ensued every time Jackie got seasick. Jackie barfed, and then if Dominic were close enough to hear it or see it, he'd throw up. And he barfed with such gusto that it usually made someone else in the vicinity throw up too.

Cowan gave a pathetic smile. "Good times, for sure. It'll be okay. I'll figure this out, alright?" She cleared her throat, like a crack of thunder, and the sound of it made Isaac shudder. The smell of her vomit made him shiver. "And please, don't say anything to anyone. Please."

Isaac could only nod.

CHAPTER FOUR

Safety & Divinity in Numbers

I

MINHO

"You really think we'll run into Cranks out here?" Orange asked as they walked through the spotty forest. She eyed Minho's hold on his weapon as she dangled her own gun by her side. The trunks of the trees creaked as they swayed in the wind; the branches and leaves sang a haunting, whooshing tune.

"Maybe," Minho answered. Whether Cranks or something else, he'd be ready. Especially when the rest of the group took bathroom breaks in and out of the woods. Even wild dogs protected each other when one of them had to do their business. Orange seemed to be letting the islanders rub off on her, but Minho couldn't let his guard down so easily. "You don't?"

"I think the worst of what we could possibly run into . . . is back in Nebraska." Orange grimaced, and Minho silently agreed. Even before meeting people like Roxy and Ms. Cowan, he knew that the way of the Grief Bearers, not to mention their priests and priestesses, wasn't right.

The constant guards. The rigid schedules. Training and watch duty for hours, being forced to kill anyone that approached the fortress walls. "And call me crazy, but I think the Remnant Nation must've collected all the Cranks in the world for their sick Crank Army and that's why we haven't seen much of any out here." She waved her weapon in front of the coastline as if to prove her point.

Minho looked at Orange to see if she was kidding. "I thought only the lowest level of soldiers believed in that rumor."

Orange frowned and raised her eyebrows. "I thought only the dumbest of soldiers didn't."

"Cranks can't be trained. And they can't be taught how to shoot." He tried to reason with her. "The rumor about an Army of Cranks is just something the older officers threatened to send off the younger soldiers to in order to scare them straight. To make them think that if they ever disobeyed they'd be turned into brainless slugs fighting the same war whether they wanted to or not."

"Sometimes rumors turn out to be true." Orange said.

"Name one."

"I don't know, maybe the rumor about Grief Bearers throwing Orphans off cliffs when they turn eighteen." She gave him a knowing look. Meh. She was only half right; sometimes they threw Orphans over the cliff before they turned eighteen—like Minho.

"Everything's always exaggerated." He understood the ritual and why the Grief Bearers sent away their strongest soldiers for a forty-day pilgrimage. It was obvious—to weed them out and find the ones strong enough to become Grief Bearers, help train the next generation.

"They still threw you off a cliff."

The sound of swift rustling in the brush returned Minho to the present moment. Roxy, Trish, and Miyoko stepped out from the thicker woods and back on the trail with Old Man Frypan.

"Did I hear that right? They threw you off a cliff?" Frypan asked and everyone's eyes swerved to Minho.

Roxy looked the saddest. "They what . . . ?"

"It wasn't that high of a cliff." Minho didn't know why he felt the need to defend the Grief Bearers. It was more about him not being viewed as vulnerable to the others. "Everyone goes through it. It's a rite of passage."

"Sounds like they weren't very nice," Frypan said with a massive roll of the eyes. "Much less trustworthy."

Minho shrugged. He was still learning what real trust meant, and hearing that Orange believed in such a thing as the Crank Army rumor made him realize he couldn't ever tell her his real reason for going to Alaska was to join the Godhead. Because if Orange believed in childhood rumors then she surely still held on tight to her training. She'd been taught to kill the Godhead, and Minho wanted to *join* the Godhead. He didn't know how he'd separate from the group when they arrived in Alaska, but there was something in his blood that screamed at him: *You are one with the Godhead.*

And he believed it.

The Orphan named Minho was one with the Godhead.

He'd prove it in time to everyone else but for now it'd be his guarded secret. He was still learning about life outside the walls of the Remnant Nation, but he knew one thing for sure: Gods could not trust men.

2

ALEXANDRA

One's tolerance of the cold depended on genetics, and Alexandra always knew she had good, adaptable DNA because of her ability to withstand frigid temperatures. Or maybe it was mind over matter that she'd developed from strengthening her principles with the precepts and the Flaring discipline. Whatever the cause, others around her had bundled up in their mustard-yellow cloaks while she was comfortable with only a thin veil of cloth wrapped around her shoulders. It made her strength visible, which helped her to stand out even further from the crowd. It told the Pilgrims that she was their fearless leader.

She was their God among men.

As she moved closer to the eager crowd before her, the sheer cloak gently moved and folded with each step, like the Aurora Borealis in the sky. She pointed to the heavens above and spoke, throwing all the eloquence she could at the words.

"The sun shines on us now with a new energy. The Alaskan lights have returned to the night sky with all the colors and all the glory of the Universe." Only two Pilgrims clapped at this; the rest gawked at her in confusion. She couldn't blame them. "Were you not blessed to behold the colors of the sky last night?" Alexandra worked daily on strengthening her mind and controlling her thoughts and emotions, but times like this when it felt as though she were speaking to children, only the digits helped.

"The lights are a sign of the end times," a man murmured, and although Alexandra was prepared for their doubt to show up in many ways, she couldn't help but be annoyed. The Pilgrims of countless religions had been wishing the end times upon them for longer than recorded history. Why was every generation bound to the hopelessness of the generation before it? Why couldn't something so grand as the Borealis be a sign of good things to come?

"The northern lights are a promise of hope. They are telling of the times ahead, the evolution of the world to come and—"

An ungrateful and uneducated Pilgrim interrupted her. "Red appeared in the sky before the Sun Flares!"

Alexandra stood tall and recited the digits in her head. She was far too tired from a sleepless night to coach the citizens into their future. Always, she was forced to comfort their feeble minds. But today, shifting their perspective took more time than what she had patience for. Always more time. She hated progress halted by such lack of foresight.

"The sun will never flare or scorch the Earth again," she said calmly. *I hope.* "Nicholas foretold times just like these. Your Godhead has prepared you, have we not?" She enunciated every word as if to cut their doubt and fears in half.

"The Godhead is good!" a woman in the crowd shouted as she held her baby up in the air. Those around her murmured in support and raised their voices together to repeat, "The Godhead is good!"

Alexandra smiled. All it ever took was one voice to guide the others back to faith. She made eye contact with the woman holding the baby and nodded in gratitude. She remembered the faces of those who supported her just as much as the faces of those who spoke against her. Glaring back at the others who'd expressed fear, she said the words herself along with the crowd while peering deep into their eyes, "The Godhead is good. The Godhead is good."

The people breathed and chanted as one, a single organism moving and swaying together with each word. Something caught Alexandra's eye. Movement in the distance. A hooded man walked in the opposite direction of the town's square, his back to the crowd. But she didn't need to see his face to know whose shoulders lay beneath that cloak. It could be only one person: Mikhail. And Alexandra knew exactly where he was going.

"The Godhead is good," she chanted again. "The Godhead is good." And she watched Mikhail disappear around a corner, turning left toward the former home of Nicholas. Their former God.

CHAPTER FIVE

Dear Nicholas

I

MIKHAIL

He knocked on Nicholas' wooden door again. Two knocks, pause, two knocks, pause, and then a burst of knocks in succession. Then even harder, until the blood pooled within his skin and formed a fresh bruise along his pinky. *Patience, dear Mikhail.* That's what Nicholas would say, but the panicked feeling had followed Mikhail around all morning, and now it intensified. *He had the same dream again.* The dream that only visited him when things were off course. Mikhail knocked one last time, ever louder. He tried the door. Locked.

Nicholas' intuition was so strong that all Mikhail had to do was think about stopping by for something, anything, and Nicholas usually met him at the door. He was *always* at the door. Well, unless he'd left on one of his trips. *Was he gone?* Mikhail searched his memory, but his memory was shit. Complete mush ever since Crank Palace. At least when he was a Crank he had all his memories. But now, even the things his brain remembered, things he knew for sure, he couldn't pronounciate. Wait, that last word didn't sound quite right in his head. That happened, a lot. Pronounciate?

He reached for his keys to open Nicholas' door, not wasting time to remember which key out of the six in his collection would work, trying them all.

One by one, the keys failed, until the fourth, a red dot painted on the metal, did the trick. "Nicholas?" Mikhail whispered in case he forgot something he should have remembered again, but as soon as the name left his mouth, the overpowering smell of rot filled his every sense, gagging his throat. Mikhail coughed to clear his airway, he couldn't find oxygen. Only decay, and he knew the smell of death all too well from Crank Palace.

Ever since Mikhail's senses came back to what Alexandra called "healthy again," Mikhail believed that there were no good smells left on earth. His sensory nodes performed ten times what they did before and amplified all the worst stench of all the worst cities. Flare pits that smelled like charred skin and bones. Soggy, foggy days that reeked of moldy earth. The odor of sewer water that hung heavy in the air after a storm.

But this . . . Mikhail choked on it.

"Sir?"

He walked through the great room slowly, immediately spotting Nicholas' robe, lifeless on the ground, draped over a cushion. Nicholas would never have done such a thing, discarding his holy robe on the floor, even in his own apartment. Mikhail coughed again, using his own robe to cover his mouth. Finally, when his eyes adjusted to the dim lighting of Nicholas' apartment, he realized it wasn't a cushion that Nicholas' robe covered, but a bloated body. It took him a handful of seconds to realize what he was looking at—not because his brain was confused, but because he had never before this moment seen a body without a head.

2

ALEXANDRA

3, 5, 8, 13, 21 . . .

Sitting at the table, she recited the numbers out loud as she pulled closer the hard-cased, red-leather briefcase with Newt's blood inside. Despite having it in her possession, she still felt anxious. Alexandra tapped the glass case holding Nicholas' head three times, then five times, then eight times while she waited for Mikhail. She understood the power of the digits better than Mikhail and Nicholas ever did. For one thing, Mikhail was too erratic to remember the numbers in their organized sequence. But Alexandra knew the infinite loop of numbers and could recite them at any length. It was as if the digits were born inside of her and she birthed them into existence with every reciting. Each number equaled the sum of the two before it, creating within the string of digits their own frequency sequence. The Evolution was always inside of her, and the time had come to bring it to others now. She'd guide them as their one true God, no longer a divinity of three.

Even though she risked dropping the vial of sealed blood every time she held it, she couldn't help herself as she whispered the digits and pulled out one of the vials.

34, 55, 89, 144 . . .

The small sealed tube grew warm in her hand, a warmth of possibility that fueled her through the coldest nights for the last thirty years. She'd waited for this moment when she'd finally no longer have to answer to Nicholas. When she could choose who was blessed and who would be changed like she once was. Never mind the irony that he'd been the one to choose her, after all.

She often wondered why he did so, chose her of all people all those years ago, but her intentions, even now, were always pure. As pure as met her needs and wants, anyway.

It was Nicholas' intentions that had changed over the years.

What started as a relationship based solely on survival allowed Nicholas to manipulate her until his end. For years she let him think that he was greater than her, but now it was her turn. She'd once read a funny word in an old book: switcheroo. That described it delightfully. Just like the Aurora lights returning to the skies of Alaska, she'd step forward to brighten the world with Subject A4.

But despite her love and appreciation for numbers, she didn't know what in the Mazes of Hell "A4" meant. An arbitrary letter and number that once perhaps held great meaning was just a symbol now. But even numbers had vibrations to them. Did A4 vibrate with the frequency of Newt? She wasn't sure. Four wasn't a holy number. It wasn't in her digits. But the lab tape on the vial, with Newt's name on it, was undeniable; this had to be the sample of what was left after Nicholas injected her and Mikhail each with variated sequences of Newt's DNA. But even three decades later, Alexandra never thought the word "Cure" fit. What it did for Mikhail was much more than that. It was a miracle. A cursed miracle. Parts of Mikhail had returned to human while other parts remained animalistic—like the urges of insanity. Madness. Traits of the Cranks. Things that terrified her even while she subdued them.

What the slightly variated sequence of DNA had done to her was even more astounding. She'd received clear knowledge. Clear as the glass box in which Nicholas' head nestled. Intuition that not only predicted future events but also received elements of the past, as if her very own cells, once upgraded, carried the knowledge of previous civilizations within them. As if the wireless internets of old were alive again and only she had access to them directly from her brain. Preposterous? Yes. True? Also yes.

The re-wiring of her DNA had been subtle but powerful, unlike the hellfire Mikhail had to go through. His body had to physically reproduce cells that were being eaten by disease. His cells undoubtedly held no knowledge. It took him months to be able to speak like himself again, and even after that he was never truly the same. Nightmares haunted him at every sleep. Nicholas expected Alexandra to grovel at his feet day in and day out with gratitude for saving her dear Mikhail, but Alexandra had watched him change twice, and the transition back from The Gone was somehow harder. Because he didn't come all the way back.

To her, he was still gone.

His mind was more fragile than ever, still completely mad. Being asleep in the dreamworld for only ten minutes could sometimes send him spiraling into paranoia. But his visions never made clear sense. And because of her gift she was able to see clearly how the Evolution was meant to unfold. How it was exactly what the world needed to continue. She tried to tell Nicholas and Mikhail the things she knew, but they wouldn't listen. To be fair, they might not have understood, anyway. The world needed more brilliant minds like hers to keep advancing. Visionaries. True Gods and True Goddesses. Damn, she had an ego.

The Evolution wasn't for everyone, to be sure. No. It couldn't just be handed out like loaves of bread on Sunday. There needed to be tough decisions in who advanced and who stayed within the confines of their own minds. And she certainly couldn't let it be wasted on the population already infected with the Flare. It was a sacred thing, the Evolution.

She carefully set the vial back into the leather briefcase.

Years ago she'd have died for the mere chance that Mikhail might live. But now . . . now Alexandra would give him only one chance to join the Evolution or she'd erase him. Erase him without so much as a blink of regret.

Sadness, perhaps. But not regret.

3
MIKHAIL

Mikhail controlled his breathing, outside in the crisp Alaskan air, just as Nicholas had once taught him: inhale for three seconds, hold his breath for three seconds, exhale for three seconds. He repeated this without thought. The trinity. The power of three. The breathing was an attempt to control his anger but the efforts were wasted. There was no inhaling and exhaling and no mindful meditation that could calm him now.

His brain clicked with anger. The smell of Nicholas' apartment hung within his nose as if a rat had crawled inside his skull and perished days ago. Thoughts became sounds within his head and those sounds were the symphonies of war. Guns firing. Knives stabbing. Swords swordifying. Mikhail's feet took double the length of steps as he walked to Alexandra's building.

Could a crazed Pilgrim have decapitated Nicholas? Possibly, but there was no doubt in Mikhail's mind that Alexandra was the voice behind the command. When he couldn't find the Coffin, the sealed red-leather case that held Newt's blood, in Nicholas' apartment, he knew who'd taken possession. Her love for power had finally outweighed her love for mankind. Or her love for a kind man. Nicholas was mad, but he was kind. And without his guidance, Alexandra wouldn't be held to any standards . . . and Mikhail wouldn't either. He didn't have the capacity.

He searched his memory for Nicholas' voice. Memories fragmented in Mikhail's mind, blips of conversations, faded glimpses of events, but he knew for sure, surer than sure, that their former master had planned to release the Cure. He'd even warned Mikhail of all the ways Alexandra might try to get in the way. Mikhail ran through his mind like a maze runner to remember what Nicholas told him to do next, but he really only needed to remember one thing.

The Golden Room.

Nicholas insisted that when it came to Alexandra, *"She doesn't know what she doesn't know."* But how could he not have seen this coming? Or did he know of his own end at Alexandra's hand but wanted to save Mikhail from the unavoidable fear that comes with such knowledge? The walk, the building, stairs, the hallway. He was there.

Heat rushed to Mikhail's hand as his fist formed tight to knock on Alexandra's door, but she opened it before his flesh hit the wood. He immediately smelled vinegar and seaweed. Alexandra drank green tea so potent that the herbs smelled like fish, and she only used vinegar when she was deep cleaning. Cleanliness was next to Godliness, he knew this, but coating things in vinegar didn't make someone a God.

"You're late," Alexandra said as she opened the door further to reveal a table, set with the red-leather Coffin case on top. *The Cure.* Mikhail inhaled for three full seconds, smelling the putrid vinegar, and held his breath for three seconds. "You're thinking that will help you? Breathing exercises?" She squinted at Mikhail as she tilted her head. He exhaled for three seconds.

"I'm thinking it will help *you.*" He needed to keep his calm and wits about him, couldn't let his anger cause him to mis-speak, couldn't reveal more information than he meant her to know. He too had secrets. *And she didn't know what she didn't know.*

"You shouldn't worry about me, *dear Mikhail.*" She openly mimicked Nicholas' term of endearment for them both.

"What did you do? Who killed our Great Master?" Mikhail pushed past her and walked closer to the table that held the Cure. Alexandra touched the edge of a black cloth draped over another object, the same way Nicholas' robe had been draped over his dead body. Mikhail shuddered. Behind the smell of vinegar was another smell. Death. Twice in the same hour, that stench.

"He was never our Master. Maybe he controlled you like a puppet, but fate is my Master." With one long sweep, Alexandra pulled the black cloth to reveal a clear glass case. And there it was, inside. The head.

Mikhail coughed. The breath left his lungs so quickly that he couldn't stop. Nicholas' head. The former Godhead's eyes looked right past Mikhail with a terrifying, horrifiable, blank stare.

"You have his head? For what? For this moment?" Mikhail turned away from Alexandra and from the part of Nicholas in the room. He inhaled. Held his breath. Exhaled. Three seconds each.

Alexandra walked over to Mikhail and placed her hand lovingly on his shoulder, but there was no love. Not anymore. "Don't go erratic on me. The principles have done this to Nicholas." Mikhail pulled away from her touch, from all the vinegar in the air. Her apartment would never be clean again—and she would never be a true God. Not like

Nicholas. Not like him.

"The principles . . ." He knew them well, woven tightest into his brain, despite his difficulties. But he couldn't understand how Alexandra justified murder as fitting into those principles. Nicholas had created the Godhead with the essence of three truths:

Patience in all things.

Integrity in all acts.

Faith in fate.

Mikhail spun around to face Alexandra, close enough for her to smell the rotting flesh of their Master trapped into the fibers of his robe. "You haven't even planticipated what Nicholas—"

"Planticipated?" Alexandra cut him off with laughter. She never tired of correcting him. So what if he combined two words that meant the same thing. It was just one of many ways she reminded him that he wasn't as gifted as her. Who gave a Crank's ass if he never spoke in front of the people of Alaska like her?

Mikhail had bigger plans. Wars were fought with actions, not words.

He held Alexandra by the shoulders, sure now that she could smell the death still trapped on his clothing. He needed her to be as disgusted by her own crime as he was. "What you did is irre—" Mikhail waited for his brain to catch up with his thoughts, his visions. "Irreversible. Irrevocable." He waited for her to correct him but she didn't.

Alexandra wiggled out of his arms. "Yes. Evolution *is* unstoppable. You're right."

But that's not what Mikhail meant and she knew it. His eyes followed her as she walked to the red-leather case, disengaged the locks, and swung it open. He knew all her power moves. He knew she couldn't help but dangle that vial of Newt's blood in front of him and drone on and on about the Evolution. He inhaled. Held his breath. Exhaled. Three seconds each.

She traced the vial with her fingers as if to taunt Mikhail. "You can do this with me, you know. We can do this together."

"I'll never be like you." He walked closer to her, close enough to smash the vial in a moment's rage if he so chose. *Would he choose?* Would he let the crazed part of his brain win? The part that urged him to show the outside world all the chaos he felt within? "You don't understand the process and all of the . . ." He paused, waiting for the train of his thoughts to pick up the passengers of his words. "The . . ."

Alexandra never showed patience. "Faith in fate will always come to be." She taunted the principle as if she'd made it up, as if her manipulations could be called fate.

"And what'll you do with those who don't qualify for your advancements? What about those who qualify but change for the worse?" He'd tried for years to prove to Alexandra that *her* shift after receiving the DNA upgrade had changed her in a bad way. The sequencing or whatever it was of Newt's blood gave her an arrogance that entered any room before she did. She might refer to them as her gifts, but to Mikhail they were a curse. A lust for power not unlike those scientists of old.

She didn't appear fazed. "Everyone's gifts are different. Just because your gift is—"

He yelled at her. "*Life* is a gift! *I got my life back.* What you're doing . . . is selfish. You'll leave half the population behind, and . . ."

He paused as Alexandra lifted the vial out of the case. She dangled it between her fingers like a child with a toy. Except . . .

Except there was *something else* about that vial. Something he didn't quite understand but understood perfectly at the same time. His thoughts lifted then emptied out of his brain as if an awakening had taken place. He pivoted to the door and avoided her eyes. "I'm sorry. I'm losing it. Grieving for Nicholas. I'll . . . I'll go on a pilgrimage to process it all and we'll talk when I get back."

"Pilgrimage. Is that what you call it when you disappear for weeks at a time?" She placed the small container back in the Coffin, perhaps even with a smirk. But for once, her smug look didn't bother him. Mikhail had just found out how little *she knew* without her even knowing.

"Nicholas was a good man who saved my life and I'll honor him in my own way." He lifted the hood of his robe. "You'll address the people?"

"Don't I always?" Alexandra quickly snapped back.

The people of New Petersburg loved this woman. Trusted her. Worshipped her. But they were fools, all of them. She wasn't as in control as she thought. He looked back, just briefly, to the red-leather case that held the vial with Newt's name sprawled across it, but the number . . . the number belonged to another. A4.

A4 was *dear Chuck,* as Nicholas called him.

A4 wasn't The Cure.

Alexandra didn't know what she didn't know.

CHAPTER SIX

The Fire Goes Out

I

SADINA

The closer they got to the coast, retracing the steps of the *Maze Cutter*, the more anxiety she felt and the less she slept, grass mat or not. She rolled over and the full moon illuminated Old Man Frypan placing sticks on the dying fire. Usually a half inch of wood could burn up to one hour, but the skinny stuff they found closer to the coast was all brush and fizzled out much quicker. She was thankful to see Frypan awake, not just for the warmth of additional fuel to the flames, but the questions running through her mind were the kind that only he could answer.

She stood up as quietly as she could and walked over to join him. "You don't sleep much, do you?" she whispered.

"When you get to be my age, sleep doesn't matter much. I'm closer to the Great Sleep and I suppose I'll get some rest then." When he turned away from the fire to grab more brush, she could see part of the tattoo from WICKED on his neck.

"My grandma had the same mark. Well, not the same number . . . but you know what I mean." At least Sonya had long hair that covered her neck, but Old Man Frypan just had his subject number out in the open, like a twisted version of a smile. A constant reminder to anyone and everyone of where he'd been. Sadina took a deep breath. "I never understood all you went through. I still don't, but I have a better idea." The lame attempt at gratitude didn't do her thoughts justice. Until now, all that history she'd been taught had seemed so stale and banal, in a weird way almost made up. But the Cranks and the death were all too real. And although she wasn't being poked and prodded, she already felt like a test subject.

"You think they'll put me through any . . ." She couldn't find the right word for what she was afraid of. *Trials* and *tests* didn't seem to cover her concerns.

"Nah, they'll just take your blood. They'll get all the vials they need and that'll be done."

"They took your blood way back then?"

"They took a lot of things." His frown hid a thousand thoughts and feelings, she was sure.

Sadina let the heaviness of it all sink into her bones and there fell a silence between them. The shadow of a figure appeared from the left.

"You two having fun without me?" Trish sleepily walked over to join them.

"The moon's too bright, kept waking me up," Sadina lied. It seemed like she couldn't take a deep breath without Trish asking her what was wrong. She reached for Trish's hand and squeezed. She loved Trish, she really did. So much. But she wished things could be as easy as life on the island, when the worst thing that happened was getting chastised by the elders for swimming too far out. Out here, death seemed to lurk at every corner and ever since getting kidnapped, it felt like Trish was just waiting for the next bad thing to happen. Almost as if she wanted to get it over with.

"Sorry if we woke you," Old Man Frypan said to Trish.

"I felt Sadina gone and I freaked a little, till I saw shadows by the fire." Trish tried to downplay her reaction, but even in the dark, with only fire and moon lighting her face, Sadina could see Trish's heart racing. Her tenseness stressed Sadina out.

"Everything's fine. I just couldn't sleep is all," Sadina reassured her.

Frypan pulled out his pocket-sized copy of *The Book of Newt.* "Reading always helps me sleep."

"You must've read that a million times," Trish said. "I'm surprised you don't have it memorized."

"I do. Mostly."

Sadina said, "I feel kinda guilty admitting this, but despite Newt being my great uncle, I only read it in primary school with the assignments they gave us."

Frypan shrugged, tapping his copy. "You know, it's not like Newt was a god, that's not what the book's about. Newt was human. But he was also brave and the kind of soul that a person could count on. He had a responsibility to his group, just like you two have a responsibility to this group. You and your great uncle are more alike than different."

Sadina's life was so drastically different from her great uncle's that the words seemed outrageous.

Frypan continued. "I read this to calm the parts of my mind that are stuck somewhere I don't want them to be. I hear Newt's voice when I read it, and it's a hell of a comfort."

Sadina had always thought of Newt as somewhat of a myth or legend. She was thankful for these talks with Old Man Frypan to help her see that he was just a kid like her once. "You really think I'm like him, or you're just saying that to make me feel better?"

He shook his head. "You've got his kindness and you've got his instincts. Everything will be alright. Don't look at this blood in you as a burden, look at it as your opportunity to rise in your own way. Let the way you live your life be your legacy, just like those before you."

"Thank you," Sadina said as Trish leaned into her and kissed her cheek. "Although I bet you weren't that cheesy back then."

"I'm gonna go back," Trish said. "I can't take these all-day hikes and then stay up all night partying like you two." She kissed Sadina again and whispered, "I just wanted to check on you."

Sadina nodded. "I'm right behind you. Dominic'll be singing his good morning song like a rooster at first light." She walked over to the fire and stacked a few twigs like the roof of a yurt. "You gonna get some sleep tonight?" she asked Frypan.

"I may or I may not." He sat up tall and looked her deep in the eyes. "Hang in there, kid. You're gonna be okay."

And on hearing that Sadina couldn't help but wrap her arms around Old Man Frypan in a hug because all she needed in the world was to hear someone tell her that she was going to be okay. Here he was, a Glader of old who had seen more unsurvivable things in his life than most, telling her that *she would be okay* with an amount of sincerity that only the purest of souls could muster up. She squeezed the wonderful man. "You too. We're all here for you, and we'll get through Alaska together." His hug back felt like it held all the support of those from the Glade long ago. Her great uncle Newt, Thomas, Minho, Teresa. . . . As if they were standing right behind them.

"Alaska . . ." Frypan laughed as he pulled away. "Don't go telling on me, but I ain't goin' to Alaska."

Sadina pulled back to make sure she heard him right. "You're not going . . . ?"

"Not in this lifetime." His eyes widened as he shook his head.

"But . . ." She couldn't think of the words to protest, wanting to wake every single person in camp just then and do what Old Man Frypan asked her not to—tell them he wasn't going to Alaska. She knew that going just might kill him inside, but going without him felt like it might just kill her. "Please. You . . . I can't go without you."

"I'm sorry, child. I'm sorry." He turned his attention back to the fire and the conversation was over.

2
ALEXANDRA

She stared at the glass case that held Nicholas' head and traced the corners of the box with her fingertips. She wanted the hideous, severed thing that housed Nicholas' bulging eyes gone from her living space for good. She could summon Mannus to come take the head back, give it an ocean funeral. He did murder Nicholas after all, and part of the pact of any murder had to include disposing of the body. Right? Or she could pawn the head off on Flint and demand he feed it to the wild pigs at the outskirts of town, but she knew the man couldn't keep a secret and the sight of even the slightest death might weaken his knees enough to crumble. No, she could think of only one proper burial place for Nicholas' head—the ruins of the Maze, underground.

She'd go in the middle of the night under the light of the Aurora Borealis. She didn't plan on burying it so much as setting the head there as a warning, a rotting-flesh-reminder to Mikhail whenever he had the itch to go visit. Whenever Mikhail went missing for days at a time, Alexandra pictured him in the Maze wandering around like an imbecile lost to his own devices. She wasn't positive that's where he went, but it's where she always pictured him, lost in the Maze. Or maybe he was just lost in the Maze of his mind. Despite her clear-knowing, there were times when that man's madness created black patches within her. Gaping holes of no awareness.

"Goddess!" Flint burst through the door without knocking. She quickly covered the glass case with cloth. Flint was easily sparked and it didn't take much to send him into flames. But as annoying as his traits of overreacting were, she could manipulate him to start the fires that *she* wanted stirred about and spread.

"For Flare's sake, what is it now?" She gazed at him with stern eyes. "You entered without knocking again." She reprimanded him the way a mother might a child.

"It's Nicholas!" His face flushed with obvious fear.

Alexandra froze. Ice filled her nerves. "He . . ." She expected him to point at the glass box but he just paced wildly within the same four corners of her rug.

"He was found dead in his study. His body, well, part of it, was found." Flint's face now drained of color, as if he were the one to find their former God.

Alexandra quickly recovered. "Yes, I knew he was missing." She showed the requisite amount of shock and horror one might when their closest associate turned up dead and headless. "The news frightens me. Who could have possible murdered one of the Godhead?" She demanded Flint share any rumors he may have heard.

"There are no leads, Goddess Romanov." He stood still with a waiting, submissive look. Was he waiting for her to console him, or was he finding it hard to console her? "What would you like me to do?" he finally asked quietly.

"I need time to process. Leave, now. I'll prepare a statement to address the **Pilgrims** of the Maze on Sunday. Arrange it."

"What about Mikhail?" Flint asked with glaring concern, and for just a moment, Alexandra considered the possibility of framing this whole thing on Mikhail. He'd left on his latest pilgrimage, and she didn't know where. But she could easily cause an uprising, throw the people against him and raise her Goddess above all, without dispute.

Of course, doing so might cause a war within the city limits, and war was the last thing she wanted. War was low vibration, and the Evolution was about *raising* the vibration. She needed to use her proclamation on Sunday for good, not to point fingers of blame and cause more violence that didn't suit her needs.

No. She'd use Nicholas' death to propel her plan forward and to plant faith in the hearts of those who seemed to have lost all trust after seeing the new colors in the sky. Her ears buzzed with the possibility and the skin of her face pulsed with heat. She touched the top of her head and her fingertips grew cold. She touched her ears and they buzzed louder. She closed her eyes and saw flashes of red. Bright red, as if the sun shone inside the room. In her mind she heard the Pilgrim who spoke of the red sky before the solar flares.

Red. *Could it be that her own evolution was still unfolding?* No. Madness. But she feared madness. Oh, how she feared it.

"Goddess?" Flint's voice sounded far away. "What about Mikhail?"

Alexandra recited the digits and tapped her fingers along to the count so that every thought, action, and vibration of her mind, body, and spirit embodied the sacred numbers. *What about Mikhail?* The question posed in Flint's voice echoed through her mind but the red shapes in her vision spread to black. A tingling warmth came over her body, then a searing heat, and she felt herself falling.

"Goddess!" It was a single word, shouted as if from a dream.

3
MINHO

Old Man Frypan woke up early every morning, but an early-riser didn't make him a quick-mover. Minho guarded the trail for another one of Frypan's bathroom breaks and he thought of asking the old geezer which was worse: the Maze and the Trials of the past, or the invisible Maze and trials that stayed intact within his mind. The Orphan named Minho knew all too well how growing up in the Remnant Nation felt like a prison, but it seemed only he could see the walls at times. They didn't have Grievers in the Remnant Nation, but they sure as hell didn't have friends either, and that was one thing he envied about Frypan. Friendship: how to be a friend and how to have a friend, were still things Minho had to learn.

Isaac walked up to Minho while the rest of the group waited on Frypan. "Can I talk to you for a minute?"

"Sure." Minho didn't adjust his stance. But something about the look on Isaac's face made him grip his gun even tighter.

Everyone else seemed occupied enough. Miyoko and Orange were picking weeds that looked like flowers; Jackie was poking Dominic's arm where the murder hornet had stung him; Trish and Sadina were lost in some kind of dreamy conversation.

"Over here . . ." Isaac lowered his voice and pointed away from the group. They stepped to the side, shielded by a couple of trees.

"What's wrong?" Minho asked, still not letting his guard down. Never letting his guard down.

"I need . . . um, I don't know what I need," Isaac stuttered, and his nervous energy was contagious.

"Something's wrong." Minho raised his eyebrows as if to tell Isaac to just spit it out already.

"What are the symptoms of The Flare?" Isaac blurted out, but the Orphan didn't really know. His medical knowledge consisted of how to kill someone without making a sound and tending to battle wounds in the field.

"The Flare? Don't worry about the Flare, you're all immune, right?" Minho watched Isaac's face closely but the nervousness didn't fade. What did these people ever have to worry about on the island with their young and nearly perfect lives? He pictured them playing games on beaches, kayaking through streams, dancing every day.

Isaac pinched the skin between his thumb and forefinger. Something definitely wasn't right. "I mean, if we were to run into someone, out here, who might have signs of something. How do we know if they're infected or if they just have . . . say, allergies?"

Minho pivoted to turn his gun on Isaac. "You have symptoms?"

Isaac put his hands up. "Whoa, whoa, I'm not infected. I'm just curious!"

The fear in his face made it evident he didn't know the slightest thing about guns. Minho didn't have his finger anywhere near the trigger and he didn't have the butt of the gun against his shoulder to prepare for kickback. Orange would've known from Minho's stance that he wasn't a threat. But the islanders thought having a gun within 100 feet was dangerous, so Minho used the misunderstanding to his advantage. "Tell me the real reason you're asking. Now."

"Okay, fine. It's Ms. Cowan. She has a rash, but it's just a rash." Isaac paused. "So far."

"The coughing. She said it was the dust in the air. Damn." Minho held the gun tighter in frustration but then let it tilt toward the ground.

Isaac let all the oxygen out of his lungs. "And the cough, yeah, I forgot about the cough."

Minho hated this. The rest of the group had started to call for them —they were ready to move back down along the coast. Minho looked hard at Isaac. He thought about the countless times he'd been forced to kill healthier people than Cowan—at just the possibility that they *might* have been somewhere where someone was infected. And now Cowan had three symptoms: Rash, the cough, and Minho had noticed her being lethargic lately.

"You can't say anything," Isaac said. "No one else knows."

Minho thought about the possibilities. "I thought she had magic blood or something? Come on, let's go back."

"You're not going to kill her . . . right?" Isaac tried to keep up with Minho's steps as he walked back to the group.

"Of course not," Minho replied. He really didn't want to kill anyone ever again, but he would if it came down to it. But there were complicated dynamics that came with these new friendships of his. In the Remnant Nation he'd be punished if he *didn't* kill someone in this same circumstance, but out here he'd be punished if he *did*. He could only imagine the response of the others, especially Sadina. Actually, Roxy might even go crazier on him. There were too many new rules that Minho had to keep track of, and he tried to think of all the possibilities quickly.

"What are we going to do?" Isaac asked.

"I'm not going to kill her, but she can't get on the boat. No arguments."

Even if the *Maze Cutter* were the biggest ship known to man, having an infected—with anything, much less the Flare—on a floating vessel wasn't a good idea. Cowan was lucky they weren't in the Remnant Nation—it'd be the Flare pits for her.

"We can't leave her out here alone . . . ," Isaac offered.

"She won't be alone." Minho locked eyes with Isaac until the other boy's eyes reflected the unwanted understanding. Isaac shook his head, but Minho nodded. "You've got to stay with her. Take her to the Villa to get help. No arguments."

"I'm sensing a pattern. Not a good one."

"Look," Minho said, "if Cowan has something it could be a virus or it could be a genetic reaction." He paused, wondering if he should admit what he really thought out loud. Old Man Frypan certainly always did. "I'd shoot her dead right here behind this bush if it were up to me and it'd be done. She'd be safe and we'd be safe. But you all have this little experiment going on and if Cowan's sick, that means Sadina's blood—at least *half* of it—might not be as precious as everyone thinks." Minho finally let his gun fall to the side. Sometimes it just all seemed pointless.

"I didn't think about that." Isaac slowed; his shoulders slumped. Minho had really ruined the kid's day.

They walked back into view of the group. Trish and Sadina were doing some goofy dance-thing as everyone clapped but Minho couldn't keep his eyes off of Cowan. He looked her up and down. His training and every last one of his instincts screamed at him to shoot her, but he couldn't, he just couldn't—not if he wanted to have friends. Minho looked at Orange, Roxy, Old Man Frypan. Were these friendships worth ignoring his instincts?

"By the way," Isaac said from behind. "Don't say anything. I'm not supposed to tell anyone."

For some reason, that statement annoyed Minho more than anything else he'd heard.

Weak, he thought. *All of these people are weak.*

PART TWO

Believing the Belief

Nothing feels good and nothing feels bad, anymore. Nothing feels right or wrong. Hot or cold. Happy or sad. Exciting or dull. I heard an old saying once: Ignorance is bliss. They even named that damn Crank drug after such a notion. The Bliss. All these things relate to each other, and I neither care nor don't care.

I might be losing my mind, or I might finally understand the whole of it.

—*The Book of Newt*

CHAPTER SEVEN

Control Subjects

I

ISAAC

He waited for a chance to talk to Ms. Cowan alone, but day turned into night. He had to wake her up while everyone else slept. "Psst . . ." He gently shook her shoulder while avoiding the rash near her neck. "Ms. Cowan. We—"

"What? I'm fine." She slowly opened her eyes and tried to smile but the corners of her mouth drooped. So did the corners of her eyes. She was more than just tired. This lady was sick.

"You're not fine, and I talked to—"

"I'm not coughing anymore. And my throat felt tight before, but it's not now." She sat up, groggily rubbing her eyes. "It must have been those plants where we. . . . Somewhere, or the bugs when we slept. . . . Somewhere. An ant bite, maybe." She lifted her hands in the air as if it were all a bad dream. "I was allergic and now—"

"Your neck," Isaac whispered. He didn't want to mention the

change in her speech patterns. She used to talk in such a refined manner and now her thoughts were all over the place.

"My neck's fine. It's not itchy anymore."

"Itchy? You said it wasn't!" He took a deep breath and looked around to make sure he hadn't awakened anyone else. Being responsible for Cowan weighed heavily on him. He had to get her to the Villa. What if something happened to her before they got there? What if she infected him? He focused on whispering as quietly as he could while still making his words clear. "We're going to the Villa. You and me." He made it sound like a fun vacation.

Ms. Cowan didn't respond but her eyes and her open mouth made it look like she wanted to protest.

"It's not an option, it's an order. From Minho." Isaac paused and waited for the backlash, for her to be disappointed in Isaac for blabbing, telling Minho, the guy with a gun of all people. But she just took the news. Did she even understand what he just said?

"Okay. Thank you," Cowan replied.

"You understand what's going to happen? We're going to have to split from the others"

"We've got to get to the Villa." Cowan said it like a government decree, as if she had already been thinking it before he brought it up. And suddenly the heaviness in Ms. Cowan's eyes made sense to Isaac; she wasn't afraid of being sick—the sadness and weight in her eyes were all about knowing she had to split up from Sadina. Isaac felt the same heaviness wash over him in that exact moment. The likelihood that once they did separate, they may never see each other again. The world was hard enough to navigate together, and there were too many things that could pull them apart, but he'd voted for the Villa and he needed to keep his promise. If Isaac could have saved his own parents he would have in an instant. He owed it to Sadina to try whatever it took to get Cowan the help she needed.

"Ms. Cowan . . . we might never see them again."

"That isn't an option. We will see them again." She said it firmly, but it didn't erase the doubt in Isaac's mind. Going to the Villa felt like it would take him further from anything that reminded him of home again. Like Sadina. "I appreciate your help. If I can admit it. I'm a little . . ." Her eyes traveled slowly from the stars above back to Isaac.

"Scared." He answered for her.

"I'd say you don't have to come with me, that I could find the Villa myself, but I don't know if that's true." A tear dripped out of her left eye.

Isaac felt the silly urge to wipe it from her face. Thank the gods, he relented. "You and I voted the same: to go to the Villa. I gave Minho my word that I'm going with you. We'll figure out what this is."

Ms. Cowan took a deep breath and reached for Isaac's hand; it held all the comfort of a mother's love. He decided he'd look after this lady, not just for Sadina, but also to make his own mom proud. "Kletter wasn't entirely truthful about everything with you kids."

Isaac pulled back a bit from her touch. "What do you mean?"

"Sadina's blood is important, yes. But . . ." She paused.

"But—what?"

"Well, didn't you wonder why I let eight other teenagers trot along on this adventure if it was just about Sadina's bloodline? We all come from immune blood. Every single person born on the island comes from a bloodline of immunes." Isaac hadn't thought about it before, but she was right. "It was never about just one of us. It was *all* of us." Cowan coughed. "Well, except for you." Her words stung Isaac like he imagined a Griever might sting. Hard and fast. "You'll remember you weren't originally on the roster to come . . ."

Isaac did remember, all too well. Sadina had to beg her mom to let him on board. "You wanted to spare me. Because of everything I'd been through." The grief and the trauma from losing his family. Everyone always meant it without actually saying the words. He wasn't sure which was worse, them not saying the words or if they had said them: *You can't come because your family is dead.* It coated almost everything in Isaac's life with a stain, ever since the accident. If someone was nice to him, he had to wonder if the interaction was sincere or if it was under the blanket of *because your family is dead.* Even Sadina went out of her way to include him at times, like inviting him onto the *Maze Cutter* at the last minute.

Not that he minded—he really didn't. It helped. But what was Cowan getting at?

"You're right," she said. "I wanted to spare you because you'd been through so much awfulness. But also, without a single living family member left back on the island—you don't have any control subjects to your bloodline." Cowan let the smallest laugh escape before she covered her mouth. "I'm sorry. I just find it so ironic. That you weren't supposed to be here with us, but it's you who I need the most—I trust the most—to help me now."

"Control subjects?" Chills went up Isaac's spine. "You . . . you lied to everyone." The chills inverted and then went down his whole body. *What was Cowan saying? That everyone who boarded the Maze Cutter was a test subject? Dominic, Miyoko, Jackie, Trish, and poor dead Lacey and Carson too? A test for what?*

"Scientists use controls in an experiment. The control group stays unchanged, and in this case it's the family members who stayed back on the island. The Villa can compare those who receive treatment with the control group to find out if—"

Isaac held a hand up. "What treatment? I thought this was about taking Sadina's blood. Creating a cure from Sonya and Newt's bloodline?" He no longer whispered and he didn't care who heard him within camp. It was time everyone else woke up to Kletter's lies, too.

Ms. Cowan motioned with her hands for Isaac to lower his voice. "Part of what Kletter wanted to see was how immunes might react in the evolved environment of the world today." Somehow, she managed a smile. "The environment isn't so great for me."

Isaac didn't understand how she could be so damn happy sometimes. "You lied to everyone here."

"Half of the truth isn't a lie. Everything we came out here for is still true."

"What about Alaska? We need to tell the others everything now and they can come with us to the Villa and—"

"No. The Godhead will explain everything. There's too much that I don't know, but the Godhead will answer. Kletter was trustworthy but she was no God." Isaac was sure about only one of those things: *Kletter was definitely no God.* "Sadina needs to go to Alaska and work toward the Cure. They'll come to the Villa in due time. Plus," Cowan coughed again, "if it comes from us, from me, they'll be as angry as you are. They'll refuse. Sadina will never forgive me if she found this out now but if it comes from the Godhead, it will all make sense." She fixed the fabric around her neck to further cover the rash.

Isaac thought about what had been said. She was right about predicting Sadina's reaction, and that's exactly why Isaac couldn't go along with all the lies. He could only cover up so much for Ms. Cowan and the rash wasn't one of those things. He had to put his foot down.

"We *have* to tell them the truth about this, about your symptoms," Isaac said, pointing at Ms. Cowan. "There's no way around it and there's no half truth to it. We're telling Sadina . . . so if anything happens . . ."

His heart contracted in pain and he walked away. He knew the horror of losing a parent all too well and he didn't want that to happen to his best friend without warning. Sadina deserved to know. She deserved to know that when she said goodbye to her mom, it might be the last time they ever hugged.

CHAPTER EIGHT

A New Journey

I

MINHO

Two more hours until they reached the *Maze Cutter* and everyone could rest. Minho didn't know for sure that they'd find the ship in the next couple of hours, but the feeling grew in his gut. Orphans didn't have much, but they had instincts. Like flying the Berg. Like meeting Roxy and not killing her despite everything he'd been taught.

"Careful," he said to Orange. The ground they walked changed from small stones to sharp-edged rocks that stuck up at all angles. It seemed like the trail could turn into a big cliff looking over the ocean at any moment. He could smell it, hear it. "We're almost there. Two hours or so."

"I'll believe it when I see it." Orange walked just ahead of Minho. He knew her competitiveness wouldn't allow him to spot the ship before her. "Sorry. I like to be first. Blame the Grief Bearers."

"I get it." He slowed down and looked behind him, waited for the islanders and Roxy to catch up. Orange was the only one he trusted to go ahead of the group and not get herself killed or lost. He'd once seen her kill three rabid wolves that came at her from the woods without warning. Everyone thought she was a goner.

"Hey." Orange dropped back. "Before they catch up . . ."

Minho didn't hear Dominic's obnoxious singing, so they had at least a few minutes. "Yeah?"

"You're lying, right?" She placed the tip of her boot on the edge of a jagged rock as if to trace the blade of a knife.

Minho shook his head. "No. What're you talking about?"

"About helping the Godhead? You're going to Alaska to end them, right?" Orange's eyes might as well have been question marks.

Minho's teeth clenched with the pressure of betrayal. He forgot about *that* lie, and he couldn't tell his fellow Orphan the truth. He had to let her believe that he lied to the islanders and not her.

"I promised I'd get them to Alaska," he replied vaguely. Never mind that his goal was to *join* the Godhead, not destroy them as they'd been conditioned from birth. Orange would probably kill him quicker than she'd dispatched those wolves if she found out. "After that, we can figure out a plan."

"Hmm. I figured you'd have a plan. Just checking." She sounded suspicious, but oh well, he thought. She looked up to the trees and pointed at a sparrow landing on its nest with food in its beak. Back in the Remnant Nation she would've used that momma bird and baby for target practice. Was she trying to send a message? Returning her attention to Minho, she asked, "You ever wonder about your mom? Who birthed us?"

"Not really." It was the second lie he'd spoken in the last ten minutes. Not only did he think about his past family sometimes, he thought about them all the time. In the periphery of his mind. The Grief Bearers had drilled into them that they were orphans. *You have no family. You have no friends. You have no name. Only Enemies.* And by constantly telling him that he had no family, Minho knew he'd had one. He imagined them all the time.

"Animals were meant to raise their own. We weren't created in a lab, manufactured to grow up and protect their walls, right? Someone birthed us." She glanced back over her shoulder as if she didn't really think he was listening.

Minho thought about the birds again. If they were bigger, like pigeons or doves, he would've shot them for dinner but they were barely worth a bite of meat. "Birthed us, yeah, then they were thrown into the Flare pits. Great thing to talk about." That's what they'd been told, anyway. But of course, rumors always tiptoed their way around the Orphan barracks.

"But did you ever wonder, what if your parents aren't dead?" A quirky smile spread across Orange's face as if she knew something he didn't.

"No. I never wondered that." He placed the thought up there right along with Orange believing in some kind of massively organized Crank Army. It was silly, naive. Unfounded. Thankfully, the roar of the ocean had grown louder and the salt in the air had intensified, meaning this conversation could be over soon.

"Hear me out," she continued. "What if the Grief Bearer who raised you was your dad? What if they wore those hooded cloaks to hide how much we look like them?"

Minho had the slightest notion that someone on the planet might be related to him. Especially Griever Glane. Orange was full of wild ideas. "Well, if he was . . . he's dead now."

Roxy came into view with Miyoko, soon followed by the rest of the group. Minho started walking again, alongside Orange, and their movement caused the bird to fly away. "What made you think up this, anyway?" he asked.

"Because if they lied to us about one thing, who's to say they didn't lie about more?" She was right, nothing outside of Remnant Nation had turned out quite like he'd expected. Minho looked around at the vast openness of nature, the trees, the animals, the sky, the clouds. Peaceful. Their whole lives they'd been warned about the the outside, but the only real threat since leaving the Remnant Nation was *from* the Remnant Nation. They'd seen few Cranks in the wild, and the most dangerous thing about the islanders were Dominic's various unsavory habits.

"You think you have parents that are still alive?" Minho asked.

"Me? No. Ever seen anyone with hair like this? Me neither." She walked over rocks that grew bigger and bigger. "But Skinny and I used to joke that maybe we were related because we both had the same birthmark."

"Really? Let me see."

She showed him the thin smear of ropy, white skin on the outside of her elbow. "His was exactly the same, but maybe it's just a scar from some lovely childhood torture. Like the ropes."

Minho remembered. The Grief Bearers hung them by the arms until they were all pins and needles, almost numb. Then they'd lower them, hand over a gun, order them to shoot at targets, which faced each other in a zigzag pattern, only feet apart. Missing a target meant hitting another Orphan.

Minho examined the birthmark again. "Doesn't really look like a scar. Maybe you were born with it."

"Well, whatever. I like to think it matched because we were family somehow."

He saw a familiar look in her eyes. That feeling of trying to replace the complete abandonment that came with being an Orphan. "Maybe you were." The problem was, the abandonment had no name, had no face, only had a feeling. And that feeling was present in everything. Minho instinctively checked his own elbow, but no birthmark or scar.

Time to move on, he thought.

Luckily Orange did just that. "So after we find the boat we'll hunt for supplies. A week's worth for ten people is—"

"Seven." Minho rubbed at his elbow. "There's only going to be seven."

"What's that supposed to mean?" As soon as she asked, Minho realized that he *did* trust Orange or he wouldn't have said anything. *Maybe he could trust her with his secret after all.*

He looked behind them to make sure no one could hear. "Cowan and Isaac need to stay behind." He whispered even though the rest of the pack was a good bit behind them.

Orange didn't seem to care all that much. "What about the third person, you said seven?"

He shrugged. "I just have a feeling someone else will choose them over Alaska when they find out."

"Find out *what?*" Her curiosity finally appeared ignited. "You have to tell me."

"Swear on Skinny's life you won't spill it."

"I swear on his soul."

Minho took wider steps as the path changed again. The rocks along the trail were smoothing out. They had to be close and were just turning a corner of jutting land loaded with palm trees. "Cowan's sick. Isaac's going to take her to the Villa."

And then there it was, all at once. The ocean. Vast and blue and sparkling. Endless. Forever. The most stunning thing he'd ever witnessed. Without thinking he'd stopped walking and could only stare.

"Holy ship." Orange said.

She pointed ahead at an inlet on the coast below them. A ship, alright. As big as a Berg, floating on the water as if it had always and only known peace. Remnants of missing letters along the side made it clear:

The Maze Cutter.

He felt as if he was looking upon the Maze itself.

A ship as solid as any Grief Walker. Ugly, but solid. Ready for use.

Maybe even a vehicle fit for a God.

2

ISAAC

The mood of the group shifted once they found the boat. Miyoko couldn't stop smiling, Dominic sang louder than usual, and Roxy and crew were downright celebrating.

But not Isaac. He didn't have anything to celebrate. Finding the

Maze Cutter felt so final. Once everyone boarded the ship, he might never see them again. An anxiety churned deep inside his stomach that wouldn't settle. Seeing the *Maze Cutter* again, he couldn't shake the memory of Kletter arriving on the island with eight dead bodies rotting on the deck of the ship. Was Minho different? He had an arsenal of weapons, after all. The people who went to the island with Kletter were once on her side, too. Of course, they only had her word for it. And now Minho's.

While the others hunted and gathered for the long journey ahead, Isaac set up a secret forge deep off the coast of the beach with scraps of wood, concrete, and metal he found. He needed to prepare for the worst and have something that resembled a knife if he needed it. More than that, it was the break he needed. The therapy.

He pounded metal on metal, *CLANK, CLANK, CLANK*, hoping the noise didn't echo all the way to the beach. He hammered the hot steel three strikes at a time to mimic a birdsong.

"Oh look, it's the future Captain Sparks," Sadina said as she pulled tree branches away to clear a path. "What are you doing?"

Busted.

"Making a knife." He didn't look up. He couldn't.

"Minho and Orange have plenty of weapons, and grew up using them. I think if anything happens we'll be—"

"It's just in case." He banged the metal harder. He didn't want to tell her. Not here. Not now. Not ever. That her mom was sicker by the day and that it was up to him alone to save her or it'd be up to him to kill her.

"I guess it's good to get some smithing practice before you get back to the island. The real Captain Sparks might finally promote you." She smiled with innocence, with the ease of someone whose life had never been turned upside down. Thinking of going back to the island was like imagining his parents and sister alive again. It was a stretch to even create the images in his mind, they were too far away. And soon, Sadina and the memory of her would be just as far away.

"You think we'll ever be home again?" He tried not to sound hopeless, but who knew if Minho and the group wouldn't settle into a new home once they got to Alaska.

"Yeah, I do. It's our *home*." She said it without question, but Isaac wasn't convinced. If a family could be taken away, then a home just as easily could cease to exist. "I know things are different. I know when we go back, nothing will be like it used to be." She moved closer and finally reflected the amount of heaviness that Isaac felt. "Trish has been a little *extra* since we got kidnapped." She let out a fake laugh that she only did when things were the furthest from funny.

He couldn't return it. "Well, from what Jackie said, Trish almost didn't make it through that. Cried every day and every night, it was all they could do to keep her from dying of dehydration after all that crying." He looked over at Sadina but she wasn't changed by this information, so he added, "You know people can die of a broken heart." Sadina rolled her eyes. "She loves you."

Now, a sigh. "I know. She just loves me in a very heavy way right now. I can't even get up at night without her coming to check on me. Plus, since we got back with everyone I haven't had much time to talk to *you*." She nudged him.

She was right, they hadn't talked much since he saw the rash on Ms. Cowan's neck because Isaac couldn't lie to his best friend. He did his best to create natural distance between them, and Trish's overprotectiveness lately helped the effort.

Isaac forced a smile. "It's alright. We're always going to be close even if we're not right next to each other." Sadina nodded but that wasn't enough for him. "Promise?" he asked.

She recited the motto they'd had since childhood. "From the sea to the sky, I promise."

He hadn't thought about the saying in years. "From the sea to the sky."

Isaac went back to pounding on the metal to flatten the knife he'd made, and with Sadina looking on, it was almost like they were back home and she might start begging him to cut out of work early for the day to go for a swim.

"Can I tell you a secret?" Sadina asked and Isaac's stomach

dropped. How could she trust him with a secret and he not return the favor?

"Of course." He wished he hadn't promised Ms. Cowan to keep quiet until the day they boarded the ship. *Should he tell Sadina?* It wasn't his whole secret to tell, but Isaac felt so much guilt about keeping this from his best friend.

"I'm a little scared about what happens when we get to Alaska. What if they want to separate me from you guys? Trish can't take that." She fumbled with a rock in her hand, and Isaac had to wipe his face to hide the springing emotions. Her question wasn't a "what if" to Isaac —it was guaranteed to happen. She was about to get separated from her mom and her longtime friend before they even left for Alaska.

"You're strong enough to get through anything. And Trish might surprise you, too. Just hang in there." He hammered back away at the knife.

"When you're done with that, can you help me make something too?" Sadina held up a piece of metal wire in her hands. "Found it on the beach."

"Sure thing. What do you want to make?" He leaned over the makeshift forge. He only wanted to make her happy and hoped she didn't hate him forever when it came time to leave.

"Something for Trish." She also had a small piece of wood. It only made him wish *he'd* created something for her to remember him by.

"Sadina . . ." He *needed* to tell her. He had nothing to give but the truth. That her mom was sick. That he wouldn't be getting on the ship to Alaska.

"What? You're looking at me like you have some deep dark confession to make." She laughed nervously but then got quiet. "Look, if you're going to tell me you've always been in love with me or some weird sappy shit—"

"No. Nothing like that. I don't think I'm your type, anyway." He rolled his eyes but Sadina started to laugh again, and he realized he couldn't be the one to tell her. Not now. "I just want you to know that I really would go from the sea to the sky for you."

"I know." She gave him a questioning smile.

He wanted her to understand. "If we ever get separated, I'll find a way back to you and everyone else."

"Isaac! Stop being so weird, we're not going to get separated." She snatched the hammer out of his hand, almost burning hers in the process.

"You're right," he lied.

3
ALEXANDRA

With the ranks of the Evolutionary Guard to protect her, Alexandra confidently walked in front of the crowd that had gathered for Sunday Maze Mass. The air was icy on her arms and face, despite the sunny skies above. She folded the mustard-yellow wool cloak around her arms, holding tight to the disguise she'd once worn to fool Mannus into doing her bidding to kill Nicholas.

It was time for a good old-fashioned uprising.

It was time for the Evolution.

"You're sure you feel up to this?" Flint questioned her strength as she walked to the stage. She'd thought by getting rid of Nicholas that she was done having people question her.

"Flint, I told you, the fainting was just a spell of grief that came over me. I'm fine." But it hadn't been from grief. She had no idea what caused her to black out. She handed Flint her cloak with a look that said *don't ever question me again*.

"Hello, Faithful Pilgrims!" Alexandra faced the simmering crowd and waited until all had eyes on her. The group before her included those who were silently devout, praying in basements, all the way to the extremists who performed rituals and Hollowings. She looked for Mannus' horns which typically stood out in the crowd, but there was no sign of him. She needed to speak with him, make sure he'd kept his word and that the arrangement between them was still private. She didn't trust any of the Pilgrims, much less one who'd killed a member of the Godhead. "Faithful Pilgrims, I bring sad news today, but first I bring you news of hope." She placed both her hands over her heart as if to brace the people of Alaska for Nicholas' loss.

A crazed Pilgrim, almost naked, with jittery eyes as wide as two soap dishes, screamed at her. "The lights are solar flares! We're doomed!" Those around him faltered in their faith, murmured agreement. She hated how easily the fear of simple things could affect their simple minds. She had almost no patience for this, for the uneducated. She counted the digits in her head while the crowd calmed again.

"No, the lights are our hope." She waved her hands before her, slowly, like the movement of the Aurora Borealis. She turned on the melodrama. "The colors in the sky represent the colors within us. Our light within is coming back, and just like the skies above have evolved, it's time for us, too to Evolve." Murmurs again rumbled through the Pilgrims, and Alexa wondered if they even knew what the term "evolved" meant. Society had been stuck in survival mode for so long that she doubted many of them had an ounce of hope left for the future, any hope that life could ever be anything more than what it was right then. But it needed to be.

"My Pilgrims, we are at a crossroads in civilization and it is our job to choose faith. It is our choice to change history. And it is our responsibility to stand strong." She again allowed space within her speech for the crowd to react and they did. She spotted a set of horns moving through the crowd, and as she made eye contact with Mannus, he tapped the side of one of his horns. She had all but forgotten her promise to remove those damnable things from his head.

"What is the news?!" The crowd chanted for her to go on.

"The news is of hope and our ending peril. The hope that we will soon become greater and more than we ever imagined possible in the past. We will become not only resistant to the Flare but Evolve with gifts that will allow each and every one of you to become a God within your own right."

She held up her hands to the sky as she took a breath but the crowd didn't cheer, they only rumbled in confusion at this. Impossibly, she'd overestimated them once again. Surely they'd understand what she said next. "But the sad news I bring to you today hurts my heart to announce." She cleared her throat and lowered her head for dramatic effect. "Our God Nicholas was brutally murdered by those who opposed his plans regarding the Evolution." It wasn't a complete lie.

"Murdered!?" Gasps arose from the crowd.

Pilgrims moaned in mourning and turned to each other for support.

"Yes. It is true. Our dear Nicholas died defending his vision for this land. For each of you to have the privilege of living a Godly life." She paused and rubbed her temples. The loud buzzing in her ears started again as if she couldn't speak of Nicholas' death without her body having a visceral response.

"Who murdered him?" a loud scratchy voice asked and Alexandra looked up to see Mannus, the murderer, asking her. She squinted at him and shook her head before addressing the crowd.

"We're looking into who could have committed such a hideous, blasphemous, violent crime."

"The Hollowings must be increased!" a tattooed Pilgrim shouted. "Two a day!"

Alexandra turned to Flint for crowd control but he was useless. "No! The Hollowings must stop at once. Nicholas asked this of us and it is the one thing we can do to honor his memory, to be more Godlike in his absence." She reached for the mustard-yellow cloak from Flint. The Pilgrims clamored too many phrases for her to hear all at once, and calming them was much harder than she'd anticipated. The disbelief draped over the crowd's faces, and this was the outburst of emotion that she needed in order to manipulate their reactions for her plans. She let them erupt and share each other's pain a little longer. The more she let the outrage and fear simmer, the easier it would be to steer them into her intentions.

The fear that annoyed her so much could be used to her advantage, now. "Dearest Pilgrims, you must understand the full truth." Her eyes met Mannus' in the crowd and she quickly looked away; she would not be sharing *that truth*. "You must realize that this horrible news comes about because Nicholas had discovered a Cure, an immunity to the

Flare." The crowd became quiet just as she had hoped. It was as if her eardrums had ceased to function all at once. Perhaps they weren't too far out of her control after all.

"A Cure? Finally? Could it be true?" a woman in the front row asked gently as she reached out to the Goddess. Alexandra took her hand and squeezed it as she answered with a giving smile.

"Yes." She needed to cement their shock. "What he discovered is a preventative that keeps you healthy from the world's deadliest virus, but also will boost your DNA to be smarter, stronger, and more gifted in all areas of your life."

Nicholas had indeed discovered a way to be immune to the Flare but she'd never tell them the rest of it, that the same variant which kept them resistant could also cure the half-Cranks to be whole again. She didn't want Alaska to turn into a refuge for Cranks. They'd likely be more dead inside than Mikhail and cause more Hollowings. Alexandra knew the majority of people might agree with her, that they'd be hesitant to let half-Cranks back into society. Those abominations of the world, no matter the internal ratio, belonged on the outskirts of every town and in the Flare pits of Crank Palace.

"When can we get this Cure?" the same woman in the front row asked.

"In due time. Patience is necessary, dear Pilgrims. But soon we will eradicate every strain of the Flare and each of you will Evolve to the infinite potential of the human race. Capabilities that until this moment, only members of the Godhead have possessed." The time was right. She made a show of unfolding the cloak and she swung it wide around her shoulders before securing it at the neck.

"You all will become Gods and Goddesses, if you accept the Cure. Some will oppose this advancement in medicine, but let me be the first to tell you that those who oppose the Evolution are as evil as the Flare itself." The crowd cheered at her fanfare just as she knew they would. "Those who oppose the Evolution are themselves responsible for the death of the God Nicholas." The crowd booed along with her. "The Cure is on the horizon. It is the dawning of a new day, and Alaska will be both home of the Maze and now home of the Cure."

The crowd's faces lit up with hope, and joy, and something so intense that she hadn't seen from the Pilgrims in a long time. A fight in their eyes. A willingness to do more than just survive. Hysteria. Fanaticism. Exactly what she wanted. "New Petersburg will be the most powerful of all cities, the highest of all populations. No longer a place to be feared, or to be looked down upon. New Petersburg, the sight of the Maze—will rise again."

The people cheered louder and louder. She breathed it all in like fresh air.

She was their only remaining God.

Their one true Goddess.

4

Alexandra felt dizzy. Was this how Nicholas felt with all the power he'd once held? Her ears buzzed louder with each step she took into town. Now that she was the singular God, she wondered if her head could take the pressure. Her hands shook without reason, which she tried to hide from the Evolutionary Guard.

"Goddess Romanov!" shouted someone from the crowd chasing behind them, but the guards knew to keep anyone from getting close to her. She wouldn't be touching them on their foreheads, their noses, and then their mouths like dear Nicholas did. She'd never touch them at all. "Goddess Romanov, I've done your bidding now you do mine." The voice of the follower rang clear.

"Stand back." The Evolutionary Guard pushed the man with horns. "She'll speak again next Sunday."

But Alexandra held up her hand to stop them. "I'll speak to this one now." She motioned the Guard to give her space, "Please. Allow us privacy." She knew such a request might cause suspicion and that heads might roll if she invited this monster of a man up to her quarters for a private talk. The middle of the street, south of the square would have to do. The Guard hesitated to leave her side, as if they knew

Mannus was a Godhead killer. She motioned with a little more threat for just a few feet of privacy.

"You've got a kindness owed to me, Goddess." Mannus tapped his right horn.

"Yes, I do. Thank you. It will be done." She smiled so that the Evolutionary Guard allowed her to comfort a spiritually lost Pilgrim.

"When?" Mannus forcibly demanded the when and the how of it, but the more he pushed the more she'd delay. She didn't come out from under Nicholas' reign to be bossed around by anyone ever again. She couldn't let Mannus forget who the true God was.

She held her hands in front of her, palms up to show dominance and leadership as she spoke to Mannus. "Dear Pilgrim, do you have faith?" It was something simple she'd learned about body language and casting doubt that easily controlled another. She doubted Mannus could even control his own body, let alone his mind.

"Of course." He was a simple man with simple words. Maybe she could mold him into being something more. She needed him and his closest allies on her side. They'd been a tool in her plan to get rid of Nicholas, but perhaps tools so useful should be kept close. "It will be done when my bidding is done. I have one last request." She held up a single finger.

"Our deal has already started and ended." Mannus inched closer to her and she looked back to the Guard but they were distracted by a street fight.

Alexandra took a deep breath and repeated the digits in her head. "Then I have a new *proposition*." If Mannus was impulsive enough to get horns sewn on his head years ago to please a woman, then his curiosity could be manipulated again. And after all, Alexandra was more than just any woman, she was a God.

"I'm listening." He lowered his tone and took a step backwards.

She held up her finger again. "You will be the first of New Petersburg to experience the full Evolution."

"The Cure?" His eyes glistened and it reminded Alexandra of the power that the Flare still had over everyone. The man in front of her was strong enough to kill a God with his bare hands, but his voice weakened to that of a child when asking about the Cure.

"Yes, the Cure is the Culmination of the Evolution. We'll remove your horns at that time, for a full transformation both inner and outer." She allowed her words to linger, dance around Mannus

"When?" he asked with a look of honor.

"As soon as humanly possible."

She smiled at her use of the word *humanly*. Mannus and the other horned Pilgrims were about as odd looking as the half-Cranks. Some, with tattooed faces and necks, wearing hardly any clothes, looked more like animals than people. They were still human, but they could become more human-*like*, to humanity's truest form. Their DNA needed to open up, to re-create all possibilities. She watched as Mannus walked away, his horns bouncing with every step. For far too long the world had veered off course. Humanity had given up on itself. But this turning point in history would be a sharp one.

As sharp as the tip of a horn.

CHAPTER NINE

The Infinite Glade

I
MIKHAIL

Nicholas had known better than to trust Alexandra completely but it turned out that their beheaded God hadn't trusted Mikhail as much as Mikhail once thought, either. Was he as unhinged and as assumptive as Alexandra suggested? Why didn't Nicholas tell him what he'd done with the real vials of Newt's blood? The only thing Mikhail could do was walk the path of the Maze, amongst the stone ruins and rampant ivy, and try to decode where Nicholas had deposited the Cure. There were a hundred places he could have hid something if he meant for Mikhail to find it, but none of them were checking out. And Nicholas had been the telepathic one—not Mikhail. The best he could do was sit and meditate and hope a vision of the Cure's concealment would come to him.

The blood in his body still boiled deep with anger and a heat that reminded him of the sweltering inflammation he'd endured when he had the Flare. He breathed in for three seconds, held his breath for three seconds, and exhaled for a long three seconds to enhance his calm. He couldn't get visions of information if he were angry; only being calm and centered—or asleep—would allow his intuition to flow.

He leaned against prickly vines and mossy rocks. He closed his eyes and put his hands in his lap in the position of the first Mudra, something Nicholas had shown him: the gesture of knowledge. With his forefinger and his thumb joined, the other three fingers on his hand extended, together. Nicholas had compared it to the Godhead, to always standing together. His rage curled up inside him once again and he reminded himself that it was always supposed to be this way, he had prepared for this. Maybe not without Nicholas, but he had prepared nonetheless. For the uprising of all uprisings.

For years Mikhail had prepared without fully understanding why—until Alexandra's own Evolution became out of control. Nicholas had once quipped that he hoped he didn't live long enough to see the aftermath of Mikhail and Alexandra's love; they were once each other's moon and stars. But Alexandra's star in Mikhail's world became too much like the sun. Volatile flares, scorching all those around her. He breathed deeply. He concentrated on nothing except clearing his mind like the clearing of the Glade. He breathed in, held his breath, and exhaled. In the open, empty, vast space of nothingness and everythingness, he entered the place in his mind where anything was possible and all was revealed.

The Infinite Glade.

Colors and shapes seemingly swirled around as if to ask him *what would you like to know?* He focused his thoughts on the vials of Newt's blood and the Cure and waited, but nothing appeared. The only time this happened—when he wasn't able to see anything in his mind's eye—was when he tried to conjure conflicting ideas.

Was Newt's blood not the Cure? he tried to see where the Cure was, the same Cure that had changed his blood and body back to humanity from the Gone. In the Infinite Glade of his mind, only one word grew bigger. The word was in itself a vision, big white capitalized letters growing in a sea of blackness: ISLAND. What in Crank's breath did that mean? There were over 2,000 islands in Alaska alone.

His mind itched with the unlimited possibilities. The frustratingly limitless. He had no reason to question the same man who had saved his life and raised him to power, but Mikhail often wondered if the power was worth it. Part of him still felt like a Crank inside and the pressure of being a man of Godliness clashed against the parts of him that still screamed with madness.

Show me the Cure. He hoped for a vision that held something, anything of detail. And with another slow inhale and another deep exhale, the Infinite Glade opened up to show a rack of vials, hundreds of variants of the Cure. And within the room of his vision, Alexandra walked around, smiling and directing scientists. The future was changing but the constant of his fellow God obtaining the Cure for the Evolution remained the same. How could he let her be the one in control of others when she lacked so much self-control, herself? With the anger rising up in his chest, almost a comfort, the vision evaporated before his eyes. It didn't matter. He had seen all he needed to see.

With no clear path, he would plow his own. And it would be a war path.

A war like Alaska had never seen before. Maybe the world.

2

He walked toward a patch of light that shone down into the dark, damp tunnel. The light. Where the outside world leaked in just enough to guide Mikhail toward the exit. Some people believed that a light awaited them at the end of life. But he imagined only darkness. That's why it was better to be a God in this life.

His feet sloshed through an inch of water along the stone tunnels. Water that held a stagnant stench. Sewage and mold permeated that smell, but this was a path he knew as well as the veins tunneling through his own body. Besides the entrance to the Maze and the paths that were sacred within the Glade, Alexandra knew nothing about these secret tunnels, especially the one through which he walked, now. *Alexandra didn't know what she didn't know.* He lifted the vines and moss that camouflaged the end of the current trail and he crawled up onto the Alaskan ground. He was outside the city limits, the sun moving toward dusk.

SQUUUEEEE...

The sound sent a cold wave through Mikhail's body. It sounded like a knife or an ax being sharpened across metal, ready to strike in battle, but once his brain caught up, he realized it was just the pig traps he'd set. A wild boar squealed at him again.

"Oh. Hello." He shivered with the good fortune. He'd take the poor animal to the Remnant Nation as an offering. A feast meal. He dragged the trap along, the thing kicking up dirt as the pig wrestled with the moving ground below it.

SQUUUEEEE! SQUUUEEEE!

He couldn't blame the pig for crying. Emotions were what made animals and humans alike. Fear. Terror. The will to live. Mikhail understood that better than most. In a way, Mikhail felt like crying too, not just for the loss of Nicholas, his most trusted ally, but for the future. The future looked about as worthless as Nicholas' body without a head.

Heaving with the effort, he pulled the wild pig and the trap closer to the Berg, hidden just beyond the pine trees. "Juuust a little further." He too felt like kicking and screaming. It brought him no joy to unravel the plans that awaited. The boar snorted and snotted and blew an attitude that made him question if he shouldn't do the same. He could throw a Godly fit. Abandon his plan. Stop Alexandra in a way that would be less violent. Less death. Less destruction.

But for nearly thirty years Mikhail had known his part of the New Alaska would end everything that Alexandra and Nicholas had built. Removing Alexandra would be easy, but her cultlike followers of the Godhead might take generations to deprogram. Death and destruction were a shortcut for humanity to thrive.

He lifted the wild pig onto the Berg with a mighty groan. "Just a few hours in the air, and we'll be there," he told the pig, and the animal squealed back as if it knew its fate, already. Mihail would enjoy having company on the flight, even if it was a crying, squealing, smelly mess of an animal.

Once he arrived at the Remnant Nation, he planned to do what he'd done every month for years— meet with the Grief Bearers and instruct them on the coming war. But this go-around, there'd be an escalation.

Time to end the Godhead once and for all.

CHAPTER TEN

Library of Secrets

I
ALEXANDRA

S he wrapped a scarf around her mouth and nose, but the material was too thin. The smell of rotten flesh and spoiled meat filled Nicholas' apartment and seeped through. She'd do her best to get what she needed and get out, even if she wasn't exactly sure what it *was* she needed. If she found something to answer even one of the hundreds of questions she'd had over the years, the foul-smelling visit would be worthwhile. Even though Nicholas' body was no longer physically in the room, the weight of his stench hovered over her like spoiled mist.

Dear Alexandra, what you search for is already within you, he'd say if he were there watching her rummage through his belongings, and even the thought of the man's voice caused tension throughout her body. Her shoulders scrunched and her head pounded. The buzzing in her ears started again. *Dammit.*

She thought death had freed her from Nicholas' control, but instead it seemed to allow him to be everywhere at once. She pictured his smug face reading her thoughts now. She recited the digits, but even *those* reminded her of Nicholas' teachings. His words. His rules. His power. The only way she could disconnect from the bit of control that still remained was to visualize his head removed from his body. His bulging eyes that no longer could blink. She pictured that and it brought her peace. The buzzing in her ears steadied, and she continued on through his library.

She flipped through books upon books. Nicholas was a hoarder when it came to publications of old, and rarely did he ever share the good ones. The ones she could have used to enhance her gifts. Books on history, books on psychology, books on telepathy and the invisible sciences. She set aside a pile for herself and stopped at a large leather tome of a thing. She opened the cover to find the book itself had been hollowed out. Her mind went straight to the Hollowings.

Had Nicholas been responsible for the town rituals and emptying bodies? She had always assumed it was Mikhail and his remaining animalistic instincts that kept madness in its every form right at the tip of his brain. She ran her fingers along the roughly cut pages that left an empty space in the book. *What did Nicholas hide in here?* She frantically flipped open each and every book in Nicholas' entire collection. A storm of paper and board flew through the library, but none of the others held a compartment within them.

When he was alive, Nicholas had always invaded her space, and for the first time she felt as though she could return the torture. Being inside his room in the tower was like being inside his head. But even then, she found only the things he wanted her to find. How could one man keep so many secrets?

She counted the digits. **The Flaring Discipline** helped her to hone into what she needed. *Patience, dear Alexandra*, she could almost hear Nicholas say as her eyes landed on his workspace. She hated his lessons in patience that felt like lessons in torture.

She walked over to his mess of a desk, where he wrote letters and reviewed the needs of the Pilgrims, but the contents held nothing more than written prayers. She stopped reading the letters of the people decades ago. Why Nicholas still bothered to read and reply to them was beyond her. The single solution to all of the problems within the city could be solved by the culmination of the Evolution. Not everything was complicated.

A plea for more rations. Wild pigs outside of town, no plea or prayer, just a letter of useless information. Of course there were wild pigs outside of town. There were wild animals, wild Cranks, wild *everything* outside. She threw the letters back on the desk but from within the center of the stack fell out a page in Nicholas' handwriting. One of his unsent replies. She held the letter in her hands. She started to open it, but as she did, pain surrounded her. Her ears started to buzz. Her head vibrated with noise.

Was Nicholas torturing her from beyond with these headaches and buzzing? She almost hoped for it, because if it wasn't him influencing her now, she was surely going mad. The buzzing grew louder and she lowered herself to the floor. She couldn't allow any more of his words into her head. Whatever advice he had written to the Pilgrims, she didn't need it. She opened the center desk drawer from the floor and shoved Nicholas' letter into it, slamming it shut. And as if the drawer talked back to her, it bounced off its track, collapsed onto the chair, and emptied its contents on the floor.

"You're a mess of a God!" Alexandra screamed, as if Nicholas were standing right there. She sifted through the pile of pens, envelopes, rubber bands, for something—anything of value—but it was clear to her that Nicholas had gotten caught up with the day-to-day of power and lost clear sight of the greater picture. *How did he still call himself a God with such lost focus?*

Nicholas may have had the time to respond to all the people to silence their fears, but Alexandra refused to be a Goddess who held the hands of her people—she would be a Goddess who taught her people how to hold their own. Under her, the people could rise. They'd be stronger, and smarter, and not send in weekly written complaints. The people of Alaska would be the opposite of victims, become the problem solvers of the world.

On her hands and knees, Alexandra shoved the rest of the clutter back into the desk, but once she did so, felt a false bottom to the drawer. *Dear Nicholas, always the secret keeper.* Under the lining of the drawer she pulled the wood free to reveal a small, pathetic, folded piece of paper. She didn't expect riches or gold, but surely more than a simple note. She carefully unfolded the aged parchment and despite her gentle effort the paper nearly ripped in half. *How old was this thing?* Every fold went so deep into the paper that she could only see the creases within the document until her eyes focused on the picture as a whole. *Could it be?*

A map to the Villa.

The mythical place Nicholas often referred to but never breathed a word more. *He brought the Villa to her,* he'd say. She half-expected the Villa to be some private room beyond his library with a secret passage. She looked closer at the map and the placement of the secret location. She never imagined it to be on the most remote island of Alaska. In fact, whenever she searched her mind of ever-expanding knowledge, she sometimes pictured the Villa along the California coast. Sometimes she pictured it within the city limits of Crank Palace in Colorado. But never did she picture it in Alaska.

On St. Matthews Island.

Marked with an X.

How quaint.

CHAPTER ELEVEN

Rash Decisions

I

SADINA

She kept the fire going that night and let Old Man Frypan rest on the rock closest to the flames. When it was just the two of them left, awake in the middle of the night, Sadina could finally ask some of the questions she felt too silly bringing up during the day. "If Newt wasn't immune, what makes his family blood so important? Why not Thomas, or Chuck, or . . . you?" She snapped a thin piece of firewood and tossed it onto the flames.

"That's a good question." He stretched his back and looked up at the stars. "Newt was always special. The kind of special you didn't need to look at nobody's blood to see."

"They chose everyone they studied back then for a reason, right?"

"They had their reasons." The ancient man rubbed the back of his neck. "We're all our own curse and we're all our own cure. I don't pretend to understand science, but if you ask me, humans are a lot like these trees . . ." He looked to the woods and then pointed to the cut branches in Sadina's hand. "Trees have a root system that goes down deep into the earth as wide and vast as their branches above the earth. Often, the roots branch out to weave into other trees. Deeper and more complex than the palms on our island back home."

Sadina looked around. She had never thought about roots being intertwined underground. "Ah. There's too many of them planted here so they fight for their space underground?" She was proud, thinking she'd figured out Frypan's latest parable, that being overcrowded meant there wasn't enough room for everyone to grow as tall and strong as they might if they had more space.

"No, it's quite the opposite."

Sadina felt deflated a little, then proposed the opposite idea. "So . . . the more trees around, the stronger and better they'll grow?"

He gave a single nod. "Exactly. See, out here, the more trees that grow together, the better they protect each other from the wind or a big storm. And forests with different types of trees grow better than a forest of just one species." He pointed across the woods behind them as if to count the variety. Other than the times on the island when storms had blown through hard enough to uproot a couple of palm trees, Sadina hadn't thought much about species of trees or their roots. It wasn't her thing. She almost felt bad stacking the cut firewood onto the flames but the colder nights required more warmth. Plus, the fire *kept the riff-raff away,* as Dominic said. Ever since his bee sting or ant bite, he'd gotten a little soft to the elements.

"How'd you learn so much about plants?" Sadina asked, but as soon as the question left her mouth she knew. She shook her head. "The Glade."

"Yep. There were a lot of trees in the Glade." Frypan nodded and the fire popped. "And from watching the trees we could see that when one got cut or sick, it healed itself. But it wasn't truly healing itself. The other trees connected underground to send nutrients to the one in need. The root systems are complicated."

Sadina watched Old Man Frypan speak. She was in awe of how much he knew about so many things. Living in the Maze must have been awful—truly awful—but she appreciated him sharing what he had learned there with her.

"Why didn't we learn about this in school?"

He let out a sigh with just a hint of a laugh. She liked that, even if it was because she asked a dumb question. "Island school is for island life. Not enough variety of topics to expand your horizons."

"Only in the Glade." She examined the forest and imagined all those trees connected underground, sharing nutrients with each other as if they held hands through their roots. This made her think of Trish. Maybe she just wanted connection, to fix the parts of her that needed healing. Not every person, or tree, had a love like that—Sadina was lucky. She studied Frypan, who didn't seem tired at all. "You know what, you're the smartest person I know." Sadina smiled.

"Well, that doesn't say too much with the characters around here," he joked. "Nah. A lot of brains in these people. I've just had more life experience being my age." He handed Sadina another block of wood.

"My mom is educated. But she's also very stubborn. And her stubbornness gets in the way sometimes." Sadina still thought about that night when they left the amphitheater and poisoned everyone on the island to escape. Why couldn't they just tell them the truth, that it was Sadina's choice to leave and to donate her blood for whatever higher purpose? She loved her mom, but if Sadina were on the town congress she'd have done things much differently. It felt like only damage could result from how they'd left things on the island, like the flames that grew in front of her.

"Smart people tend to be stubborn," Frypan agreed. "They know what they know and they don't want to know what you think you know." He chuckled. "But that's why I think the trees can teach us a thing or two. Nature doesn't need science. Nature does what it does. It's people who need science to *understand* nature."

She thought that people needed science to understand nature. If her blood was something special that Kletter had searched the whole world for, then maybe she didn't need to understand all the *hows* and *whys* of it. Maybe she just needed to trust in nature and let nature do what it was going to do. Could it be that simple?

2

Jackie, Trish, and Miyoko helped carry armfuls of palm leaves and branches aboard the ship. If they'd learned anything from their first adventure on the boat it was this: Jackie did not have the stomach for ocean travel and they could have used something to work the boredom out of their days. Miyoko had the idea to braid and weave palm leaves into mats, blankets, hats, and bowls. Or for Jackie: a puke bucket. Not like they planned to show up in Alaska looking like a bunch of islanders wearing palm hats, but something about the idea of weaving while sailing put Sadina at ease. At the very least, it might keep her hands busy to distract from her anxiety.

The closer they got to boarding the ship, the more intense Sadina's nerves got, because despite Minho's drive to find the Godhead, he actually knew very little about who made up that trio. Every time she asked him, he just repeated the same thing, *The Godhead is not what you think it is.* Whatever that meant. She didn't have enough thoughts about what made up the Godhead to even have an opinion about what it was or what it wasn't—that's why she asked. Letti and Timon had seemingly known just as much about the Godhead as Minho—absolutely nothing.

WHOOMP . . . the horn of the *Maze Cutter* blew louder than any noise Sadina had ever heard a man, animal, or machine make. Except maybe the Grief Walker. The vibration of sound shook her bones as it reverberated within the ship's deck.

"Dominic!" Miyoko turned to look for him, but he stood right behind her, a little dazed, himself.

"Wasn't me!" he protested.

"Sorry everyone . . ." Minho poked his head out of the Captain's room. "I'm just adjusting everything to get all the knobs and whistles figured out."

Miyoko glared at him. "Yeah. Take your time. And make a note, that one you just hit was the horn." Dominic laughed.

"Thanks." Minho looked around at those on the deck and the disassembled camp on the beach below. "Everyone ready to go soon?"

Sadina carried her last sack of belongings down into the cabin. "I'm ready." She handed her sack to Trish. It was the original pack she'd brought from the island plus a few items she'd collected along the way. Rocks that were sparkly, a stick she used to poke the fire every night, and the special piece of wrapped metal Isaac helped her create on the temporary forge.

"You're ready?" Trish asked as she set Sadina's pack beside her own on the cot.

"I'm not *ready* ready, but that's the last of my stuff." She wasn't looking forward to the seasickness and the cold nights out on the ocean without a fire to keep them warm. She knew the road—or the waters—ahead were bumpy. They went back up to the deck.

"Ready as I'll ever be," Dominic patted Minho on the back. "Captain."

"Where's Isaac?" Sadina asked. She didn't see him in the cabin or on the deck. She looked over the railing and found him still on the beach with his pack standing next to Sadina's mom and Old Man Frypan. "Isaac, same sleeping spots as before! You're downwind of Dom. Sorry." She waited for a laugh but he only looked to Sadina's mom as if it were up to her what he should do.

"Can everyone come here for a moment?" her mom asked. Trish followed Sadina off the boat.

"Stricter rulers for the trip," Trish whispered, but Sadina had no idea what her mom was doing. Some kind of proper bon voyage send-off or prayer on land? One by one Jackie, Dominic, Miyoko, Orange, Roxy, and then finally Minho—a little peeved—walked off the ship and joined them on the beach.

"What?" Sadina asked her mom. Everyone had gathered now but she still wasn't saying anything. Something was off. She looked at Isaac. Was he sweating?

"We need to talk about the trip."

Minho adjusted the gun strap around his shoulder, and for the first time Sadina felt nervousness coated in *fear*, not anxiety. Something was definitely about to happen. Sadina looked to her mom for support but she appeared more tired and defeated than when Wilhelm and Alverez died.

But she finally stepped forward and stood straighter. "I have an announcement. I wanted to wait to share until we were all . . . ready."

"What are you talking about?" Sadina snapped at her mother, like only a daughter could. Her mom's stance and body language only added to the fear. "What's going on?"

"I'm so sorry, Sadina." Her mom looked at her as if she were supposed to know what that meant. Sadina turned to Isaac but he just stared at the ground. "I won't be traveling to Alaska with you all." She avoided her own daughter's eye contact.

Sadina froze, top to bottom, with a stunned sickness. Then she began to tremble with anger and hurt.

Words poured out of her. "What's the point of a vote if you're going to make your own rules as you go, Mom? We voted. Majority wins. We're going to Alaska. *All* of us." She tried to be verbally cutting as she spoke.

"It's not because I don't want to go, but Isaac and I have decided—"

"*Isaac?*" Sadina's torment shifted to her old friend. *What in the hell was going on?* Isaac's only response was to look at Sadina's mom as if he wanted her to give an excuse. But no excuse could settle the fire in Sadina's stomach.

"We're going to the Villa," Isaac said unapologetically, and that hurt more than the rest of it. As much as it had hurt to see his hand fly up for the Villa when they voted all those days ago. She searched for answers to make this make sense, but she couldn't. Even the way Isaac and her mom stood five or six feet away from the group seemed like an ill omen, like they had already split apart. Why didn't they show any emotion? Regret? Remorse?

She tried to use reason. "Timon and Letti said the Villa was bad. They saved our lives to get us away from the Villa!" She was yelling by the end and turned to Trish for support.

"Yeah, we all promised we'd stick together," Trish said, somewhat pathetically.

"It's our only chance," Isaac said to the ground.

"Chance at what?!" Sadina stepped forward, demanding that they tell her their full plan, and in the moment she completely forgot the others were standing there. They were all so quiet, all anticipating the same thing. Answers.

"I'm so sorry, sweetie," her mom said, tears in her eyes as she pulled the scarf from her neck and revealed the nastiest, reddest rash Sadina had ever seen. She trembled with disbelief.

"Oh good God," Roxy sputtered.

"Ms. Cowan!" Miyoko cried.

Sadina felt her whole body shake as if Minho had blown the horn of the *Maze Cutter* again.

"It's not the Flare. It can't be." Her mom rambled on, trying to reassure her that everything was okay, that they'd meet up again soon, but Sadina heard none of it. She knew the truth. Her mom's eyes looked hollow. Everything was far from okay.

3
ISAAC

The knife that he'd forged wasn't sharp enough to cut skin or kill a slug, but it was sharp enough to carve something into tree bark. He traced the point of the blade across a downed tree while the others gathered around Cowan and Sadina. He didn't need to witness the long goodbye and he didn't know what to say, anyway, so he just sat back.

Cowan's rash looked worse than it did two days ago. Even that morning Isaac had still held out hope that maybe it would fade. But no, it was worse. There was no other plan, now. This wasn't going to be some breakaway adventure where Cowan and Isaac just waited behind for everyone to rejoin them later. This was a rescue mission. He needed to figure out how to get Cowan to the Villa.

Minho kicked up sand with every step as he walked over to the downed shore log. "If I knew saying goodbye could take a whole day

I'd have made you do this announcement yesterday." Minho sat down next to Isaac.

Isaac never felt jealous of Minho, not until this moment. There they were, around the same age, with the same goal: to go to Alaska and protect Sadina, but only one of them would be getting up off the log to do so. He hated thinking of all the things he'd miss out on, and what awaited him on his new path, and he felt empty. "She just needs some time to process." He gestured at Trish consoling Sadina by the remnants of last night's campfire. "It's not easy saying goodbye to a parent when you might never see them again." He wasn't sure if Sadina was lucky for the chance to say goodbye to her mom, a chance he'd never had, or if that made her unlucky.

"I wouldn't know," Minho said as he looked out at the ocean.

Isaac pushed his knife deeper into the log and removed chunks of bark in a specific design that would last long after he was gone. "Sorry, life doesn't always make sense." He didn't know what was worse: never having parents to miss like Minho, or Isaac having the best parents in the world and knowing exactly what he missed when they left. "If you did know, you'd understand . . ." He waited for Minho to say something cold and soldierlike, but he just looked out at the small waves as they crashed against the boat. The soft clapping sound reminded Isaac of life back on the island and how he used to watch the waves hit the rocks along the cliffs. He wasn't just missing home, he already missed everyone who reminded him of home. Dominic, Miyoko, Jackie, Old Man Frypan, and of course Trish and Sadina.

Minho picked up a stone and began sharpening his own knife. "The rock has to be porous for this to work." He looked up at Isaac and his newly forged blade. His pathetic attempt. "I don't know if it'll work with yours."

"Any other advice?" Isaac meant it sarcastically but it wasn't received that way.

Minho used quick short strokes of the rock. "Watch for Cranks. Don't trust anyone. Always assume the person you come upon is going to try to kill you. Because out here, they will."

Isaac looked down at his carving and thought about everything.

He'd miss Old Man Frypan's cooking. He'd miss Roxy being snarky. He'd miss the group campfires.

"Here, take this." Minho handed his freshly sharpened knife to Isaac. "I know you're not good with guns, but you'll need something out here more than an art tool."

Isaac took the better blade. The weight of it felt like a force to be reckoned with. It sure beat the one he'd tried to hammer up on the fly. "Thanks." Isaac sat with a sense of disbelief and something like grief. Emptiness and loss watching the others. He was losing everything he'd ever known all over again, and that's its own kind of grief. "If things don't go well for you in Alaska, will you promise me something?"

"What's that?" Minho asked.

"If things turn sideways, promise you'll come back down the coast and check this spot right here for me. I'm not sure about the Villa, and if something happens to Cowan I'll be . . ."

"You'll be fine," Minho said.

"I don't know about that. We could get to the Villa and it could be empty. Or worse, it could be filled with Cranks."

Minho leaned over to see what Isaac had carved into the log. Isaac used the sharper knife to improve it. Now his message could stay marked in the tree forever. Minho motioned to the left side of his neck with one finger. "You go for this spot, here. Any man, Crank, or animal will be gone in a second."

"And what if I can't get a good go at the neck?" Isaac thought about the half-Cranks he and Jackie had faced.

Minho stood up from the log and walked around to Isaac's back, tapping spots on the lower back to the left and the right of his spine. "Then you get him here," Minho dug in with his knuckles, "or here." Kidneys. They're full of blood. You hit that spot, either side, and they'll be dead within minutes."

Even the knuckles had hurt in those two spots, so Isaac couldn't imagine getting stabbed there. He committed it all to memory. "Okay, so if things don't work out for either of us, we'll meet back here?"

"Sounds fair." Minho sat back down on the log. Although it wasn't a promise like Sadina had made Isaac, he'd take it.

"Thanks for this," he said as he tucked the knife into his pocket.

"No problem." Minho leaned over again to see Isaac's fresh carving. "Now, what the hell is this supposed to say?"

Isaac traced the deep grooves he'd made into the wood with his fingertips. He didn't expect Minho to understand the symbol of water below a sun, with an arrow pointed in both directions *from the sea to the sky*.

"This is my promise," he said.

CHAPTER TWELVE

Words of Wisdom

I
XIMENA

N*o hay dos sin tres.*
Ximena's Abuela had sayings that became like prayers to their small family. Always repeated with an urgency that felt like a stern, ominous warning. And even though her grandmother was far back at the village now, Ximena heard the wonderful woman's words echo in her mind as she stopped in her tracks on the desert. Heat rained down on her and Carlos like hot, invisible rain.

No hay dos sin tres.

There is not two without three.

Something can happen once and be not of worry, but if something happens twice, it will surely happen a third time. All bad things happened in threes. Ximena wondered if good things were the same— if maybe good things happened in a sequence of three *all the time* but we were too distracted or too unimpressed to notice. Ximena looked for the good and the bad in everything, but the echo of her grandmother's adage at the sight of another dead and bloated jackrabbit landed the omen square in her stomach. Within the next day or two of walking, she'd surely stumble upon another one.

"Shame we didn't get here sooner, we could have had supper." Carlos jabbed at the tiny corpse with the pointy end of his walking stick but she'd have rather eaten rat meat. She could never eat rabbit without thinking of its pounding heartbeat. Anytime she managed to catch one back in the village, the poor little thing's heart raced faster than it could hop.

"What do you think is killing them?" she asked Carlos.

"Could be anything. Snake. Bird of prey." He continued walking, but Ximena stopped to examine the rabbit on its back, moving it to its side with a rock. No visible blood. No holes or cuts to its body. Just dead. *Muerto.*

"A snake or a bird eats its prey after they kill it. Looks like it's been here for maybe two days." She shook her head and wondered what her Abuela might say about two dead, blackened rabbits. All things in nature held a language, a symbolism that her grandmother seemed to have memorized. Ximena stared at the ratty fur waiting for some bit of information or wisdom to come to her. *Was this a warning from Creation?*

"Sometimes animals kill just to kill," Carlos said from ahead and Ximena pulled herself back to her feet to catch up. She hadn't minded not having kids her age to play with growing up, and even now Carlos as her *only* friend didn't bother her, but her only friend was often wrong. It wasn't that he was stupid, it was that he let hope outweigh his critical thinking. He *hoped* nothing mysterious had killed these rabbits, leaving their carcasses to rot, so he reasoned it away.

"Animals kill to eat. They kill out of instinct to survive. Killing just to kill—you're thinking of *humans.*"

"Ah, Ximena, always the wise one." He smiled as if neither of them knew how truly murderous humans could be.

"People are inherently evil. You know that." Carlos was trying his best to ignore reality, but she couldn't let him. Not anymore. Not while they were out in the middle of the desert all alone. She pushed him to confront what those in the village tried so hard to cover up. "The *Hollowings*." Ximena insisted, "People are doing that, not animals."

She waited for Carlos to reply, but he only responded with the same rehearsed thing that all the adults seemed to love repeating. "The Council of Elders said it's wolves. Wild wolves."

"Wolves are wild. You don't have to say 'wild wolves,' it's redundant. And I think you know wolves couldn't slice a human open with a clean square cut. *Wolves* don't have thumbs to pull out organs. And they wouldn't leave all that meat behind." Ximena waited for Carlos to respond, but he didn't. He walked like a man on a mission, and she hoped he was just trying to protect her. She had enough doubts without having to distinguish the truth from the lies. She didn't need protection. She needed the truth. "Do you really think we'll find them? It doesn't feel in my heart as though we're getting any closer to them."

"You and your feelings. Of course we'll find them." He added no additional reasoning.

Ximena had thought that once they started the search for her mom and Mariana that she'd feel better. Like all of Creation might play a game of Hot or Cold with her and shout through various signs, *caliente, caliente.*

But their search was not a game of *Frío o caliente.*

Even if it were, surely two dead rabbits in two days were a sign from Creation that they were cold. Very far from finding her mother and even further from finding out the truth. And just then, Ximena's entire will to take one more step in the hot desert sank to the bottom of her feet. *That's it. ¡Dios mío!* . . .

The reason she didn't feel any warmer, any closer to finding her mom and Mariana the more they traveled up the California Baja Peninsula could only mean one thing and it wasn't good. She thought back to when she first told Abuela about leaving to look for her mother. The old woman hadn't been shocked or scared, just serene. Ximena hadn't understood the calm reaction at the time, but it all made sense now. Just like how the adults responded to the Hollowings.

As if Abuela already knew, deep in her own bones, the dark truth but wanted to protect her granddaughter from pain.

Two dead rabbits.

Not being able to feel her mom's presence, her existence.

Ximena knew the truth already.

Her mom and Mariana were dead.

CHAPTER THIRTEEN

Wild Animals

I
MIKHAIL

The animal was a beast.

Mikhail carried the wild pig on his shoulders, bound by its feet with a rope that wrapped around his right hand so tightly that it rubbed his skin raw. The boar wiggled and squirmed like one might when they were about to die. Understandable.

Mikhail's back already panged from the quickened pace. He needed to arrive at the Golden Room at true noon, the same time he always entered the Remnant Nation's most important site. Consistency created trust with the Grief Bearers. The Great Master would appear at the same time if he decided to grace them with his presence. The Grief Bearers collected each day to see if he might show. Mikhail never showed his face, his presence cloaked in dark wool.

Mikhail shifted the pig's weight to distribute it across his broad shoulders, and the pig squealed right in his left ear. If those squeals could have been words, they would have been, *STOP! Put me down!* But there was no stopping what Alexandra had put into motion.

Mikhail walked the abandoned tunnel underneath the Remnant Nation. A tunnel system none in the Nation knew about. A tunnel that allowed Mikhail to sneak in and out of the Nation's path, past the prisons of Hell and into the trapdoor within the Golden Room of Grief. Above ground, the infamous Orphans lined the walls of the fortress exactly as trained, ready to shoot without warning. Without question. Without explanation.

The Orphans he collected.

The Orphans he trained.

He stopped to shift the weight again and to tighten the rope before continuing down the tunnel. Mikhail needed the wild pig alive as a sacrificial offering. He'd offer it to the Grief Bearers who would then offer it as a sacrifice to the Flare. It didn't matter what sense it made. Rituals didn't make a lick of sense to him.

The Remnant Nation had spent its entire existence preparing for battle, and now that the long-awaited time was here, it needed to be marked with a sacrificial feast. Ancient armies of old had sacrificed animals before a battle, smearing their blood on the altars of their worship, on their walls, on their faces. Mikhail would show the Remnant Nation how to do the same. And then he would march them all to war, where many of them would die a death far less dignified than the pig's. What a vicious cycle. A truly tired cycle. Men feasted on the dead flesh of animals only to become the dead flesh on which the animals later feasted.

War didn't make sense. It didn't need to. All Mikhail needed to do was to overtake New Petersburg. End the Evolution once and for all. He couldn't worry about the amount of death that lay ahead: animals, men, half-Cranks, and Orphans.

"Almost there," he said to the pig, and the wild animal quieted down. With every step closer, Mikhail felt a sensation of finality. In an infinite world with infinite possibilities, few things felt final. Even fewer things felt final to Mikhail since coming back from The Gone. A miracle. A curse. How could something be both things?

His life was his own but at the same time it was never his own. He saw everything in contradictions. His brain worked differently than Alexandra's, whose mind only allowed her to see what she wanted to see. *Mikhail is erratic, he can't be trusted.* It never offended him because he knew her brain and her intuition battled each other. Mikhail wasn't *erratic.* He wasn't an unpredictable mess without any direction or consistency. He was quite direct and consistent with his plans for the Remnant Nation. His plans were to *eradicate* the people of Alaska.

She, the Goddess, obsessed with correcting him on his mis-use of vocabulary, was at the fault of her own assumptions. Her ego made her intuition less powerful, and her ego was the exact reason the Evolution would never work.

She only heard what she wanted to hear. She only saw what she wanted to see. And she didn't know what she didn't know. It was Alexandra's war within her own mind that made it possible for Mikhail to sneak away so often to the Remnant Nation. To build an army of Orphans solely for the purpose of defeating her and wiping the Flare from the Earth for good.

As Mikhail walked closer to the connecting tunnel to Hell, he smelled fresh blood and all the scents of stress. Sweat. Urine. Tears. Hell had all the worst smells. The wild pig on his shoulders wiggled and squealed. *SQUUUEEEE . . . SQUUUEEEE . . .*

Mikhail shouldn't have brought the pig with him alive. He'd have had an easier time carrying the beast and sneaking past the tunnels of Hell without the added noise. But then again, who would hear him other than the Orphans banished to Hell for punishment? And they'd be close to death.

A creaky tunnel gate opened in the distance. Or closed? In all his trips, in all his passages through the tunnels, Mikhail never heard sounds from Hell other than the moans and groans of children trapped inside the dark, dank prison, wishing they were dead.

He heard—and felt—the pounding vibration of footsteps behind him. Quick, small, footsteps. But the wild pig shrouded on his shoulders prevented him from turning his head. Before he could turn his body, before he could even wonder who was behind him, he felt the screaming stab of a knife in his lower back. Three inches to the right of his spine. A pain so great he could only collapse to his knees.

He dropped the pig from his shoulders with a thud, and grabbed at his right kidney. One of the first lessons of defense for the Orphans, learned at a young age, was how to render a man useless and dead within minutes by stabbing him in the kidney. Mikhail knew, because he was the one to teach the Grief Bearers, who taught the Orphan soldiers. The pig squealed and flailed its hog-tied legs. Mikhail rocked on his knees and breathed in deeply for three seconds, held his breath for three seconds, and exhaled for three seconds. Then he watched as a young boy, barely a soldier, used his knife to cut the hog's ties loose. Mikhail's prized pig and the wild Orphan ran off, together through the tunnel, not looking back.

Breathe in. Hold. Breathe out.

Three seconds each.

CHAPTER FOURTEEN

Destiny Awaits

I
SADINA

In a matter of seconds her entire life had changed.

Sadina sat next to her mom and squeezed her hand tight. She went from hating the people at the Villa to hoping they could save her mom. For the first time, she understood just a tiny amount of what it must have felt like when Newt and Sonya were pulled away from their families—except unlike them, Sadina would remember every painful thing. She couldn't help but look at the scarf that covered her mom's rash.

"It doesn't hurt," her mom offered without prompting. Sadina had so many questions, but deep down she knew they weren't worth asking because there were no answers. *How had her mom gotten sick? Why wasn't she immune?* And then something worse crept into her mind. Doubt. If her mom wasn't immune, how could her own blood hold any Cure?

"I'm sorry I was being so . . . I just, I thought . . ." Sadina felt like apologizing for the entire trip. They should have never left the island. "I'm sorry I was so mad. I just . . . I didn't want us to split up and now we are. Maybe forever."

"Stop. It won't be forever." Her mom squeezed her hand, but Sadina was old enough to know that sometimes parents said things that they hoped were true as if they were true. Or even if they knew they weren't. She looked over as Isaac hugged Dominic goodbye.

"You're going to leave me with Happy?" Dominic pulled on Isaac's shoulder as if to twist his arm into staying. Good thing Minho wasn't paying attention to them.

"You'll all be fine," Isaac replied. "And Happy isn't so bad. Try not to annoy him too much."

Sadina couldn't let her mom and Isaac just slip away down the coast. What if she never saw them again? "There has to be something the Godhead can do to help? You both should just come with us to Alaska. We can quarantine you on deck and create a makeshift—"

"We can't sail with that." Minho motioned to Sadina's mom's rash as if it were a bomb that might go off at any moment. "It's just not safe." His voice was just loud enough to circle the whole group back together.

"We could make it work," Miyoko said. "We should stick together."

Dominic piped in. "We've all been together and not quarantined this whole time and she's already been sick. What's another week or so?"

Minho shook his head and palmed his gun. "Things on the open water are different, the ocean makes every problem you have harder. The sick get sicker. The weak get weaker."

"Then we don't go on the ocean. We can stick together on land." This came from Trish. "We'll all go to the Villa, then." Sadina looked to Jackie for her to chime in, but she was sullen, silent. Old Man Frypan just looked down at the sand.

"I'm not going to the Villa," Orange said.

Minho nodded. "You all can decide what you're doing. Orange and I have business in Alaska and—"

"Me too, you're not getting rid of me that easily." Roxy elbowed

Minho. "I'll miss you all but you have to do what's best for you." She motioned to Cowan and the islanders.

What even was best for them? Their mission got so mashed up after the kidnapping, and now with her mom being sick and the thought of losing Isaac, Sadina didn't know what would be best. She wanted to stay with her family, but all the other islanders had left *their* families to come help in some willy-nilly quest to find a cure. "We can figure it out . . . we just need to figure something out." She didn't know what the solution was, but she panicked at the thought of Isaac and her mom leaving the group.

Old Man Frypan stuck his walking stick deep in the sand. "Sadina's right, we should think this through. If something happens to Cowan, Isaac will be all alone. Not only that, but there's strength in numbers." Sadina thought about the trees and the forest as Frypan had described them. How they were more likely to survive storms when there were more of them in a group. *They all needed to stick together.*

"Yes, he's right," Sadina said aloud.

"At least one of us should go with them," Frypan continued, and Sadina felt the pain in her chest spread out further in all directions. "I'm volunteering to help make their group stronger. I've seen Isaac's fire-making skills and I know they'll be living off raw slugs if I don't go along." He was right—for a blacksmith apprentice, Isaac wasn't great at cooking fires.

But she couldn't take the thought of losing Old Man Frypan, too. Sadina felt as though all the pieces of her heart, all her favorite people were leaving her when she needed them the most. Except for Trish, who pulled at Sadina's hand and squeezed it. She'd still have Trish. She'd always have Trish. Sadina looked at her, deep into her eyes as if to say *thank you* and squeezed her hand back.

Frypan put his hand on Sadina's shoulders. "You know I'll miss you, kid." The look in his eye reminded Sadina of the promise he'd made not to step foot back in Alaska. His soul couldn't take the Alaskan adventure any more than her soul could take losing her mom, her best friend, and her mentor.

"I'm gonna miss you, too," she said through falling tears. Isaac's face had relaxed into relief, probably for having someone else join him —but Sadina couldn't hold her emotions in. She knew Frypan wasn't looking forward to Alaska, but she thought he'd do it for her. This whole journey was supposed to be to support *her* and now it felt like almost everyone she loved most was bailing.

Frypan hugged Sadina. "Maybe it's like the trees. Maybe it's me who can help your mom?" She squeezed him hard, hoping this wasn't the last time she'd ever see him. "I want you to have this." He reached into his coat pocket and pulled out his copy of *The Book of Newt.* "Read it. Keep it safe."

"But it's yours." She couldn't take his most prized possession. His only connection to his friends from the past. "No way. You need it to help you sleep."

"Nah. I got it all up here." Frypan tapped his head with his index finger. "And in here." He tapped his heart. He placed it in her hand and pressed his hands over hers. "I want you to have it in your heart, too."

Sadina held *The Book of Newt*, a copy written in Old Man Frypan's handwriting that chronicled the journals and last thoughts of her great uncle Newt. She doubted she'd ever held anything more precious and meaningful. "Thank you," she whispered as she hugged the dear old man again. Then she looked at Isaac and her mom. "We'll just all stick together, we have to. It doesn't make sense to split up like this." Anxiety filled her core.

"Whatever you decide, can we do it before sunset?" Minho asked impatiently.

Sadina's mom cleared her throat and everyone got quiet. Ms. Cowan was the elected official back home and island laws or not, the group still listened to her and respected her authority. "You're going to go to Alaska and meet the Godhead. You've still got big things to do, and I can't let myself get in the way of your destiny."

And with that, the anxiety in Sadina's stomach finally settled. Because deep down, the call to Alaska was just as strong as it had been the day they'd left the island. She felt it in the center of her bones. Her life had a purpose. She needed to help end the Flare for good.

She didn't know *how.*

The only thing she knew was *where*.

Alaska.

2

MINHO

Orphans never had goodbyes.

And they certainly didn't have long goodbyes.

What Orphans did have was patience. Minho stood alone on the deck of the boat eating almonds from a nearby tree. No matter how long he observed the group below, he didn't understand the time it took to part ways. And why all the touching when the risk of infection lingered? Once Old Man Frypan announced he was staying behind, all the goodbyes and hugging started all over again. Minho thought about blowing the horn to get everyone's attention, but he thought that was something Dominic might do. Orphans had patience and Minho would be patient.

"Ready?" Orange joined him on the boat's deck.

"Just waiting for the rest of the crew." He tossed another almond in his mouth.

"Well, you called it," she said with raised eyebrows and a smile. Minho rarely saw her this impressed. At the same time, he wasn't sure what she meant. "The stock of food for seven people," she added. "You knew someone else was going to stay behind."

He shrugged. "Just a feeling." In truth, his feeling was that Sadina might stay behind. But she didn't. The Orphan named Minho still struggled to understand what family meant and how they behaved. Turns out he didn't understand the relationship between a daughter and her mother at all.

"What a crazy day, huh?" Roxy boarded the ship and joined them, leaning against the railing, looking at the islanders' long goodbyes below. "Gonna miss those three, especially Frypan's cooking."

"Your cooking is better than Frypan's. Maybe *your* nickname should have something to do with cooking, too.".

"Roxy is just fine." She laughed, "or Rox. My dad used to call me that."

Orange let out a noise that sounded like it came from a wild monkey. "What?" he asked her. Whatever she thought was so funny was only funny to her.

"I was just thinking, Rox sounds like *rocks*—like the potato rock I gave you to cook for breakfast. You really could make rocks taste good enough to eat!" Orange giggled again, so unlike her, and Roxy smiled. Minho felt a little jealous, wishing he could lighten up.

He handed Roxy some almonds while the islanders slowly started to board the ship. Dominic nodded at him and said something about being happy that Minho didn't quite make out but he nodded right back. A happy crew was a good crew.

Roxy leaned into Minho, "You don't have to ever worry about me getting sick or infected. I'd just end it all myself. I wouldn't put that on you."

"Don't say that!" he snapped before he could stop himself.

"You don't think a Cure is possible?" Orange asked.

"Oh hell, no. Don't you think if there was a Cure they'd have found it by now? Maybe 50 years ago?" She wrapped her arm around Orange's shoulders. "This is all we have: what's here and what's now." They both looked out at the ocean that awaited them.

Minho nodded. *The here and now*, that was something the Orphans could understand.

There was no past and there was no future in the Remnant Nation. Only the here and now. He looked up at the sun in the sky and wondered about the tide; they needed to set sail. He leaned over the railing and in his kindest tone possible, asked, "Can we hurry this up?" They were still waiting for Trish, Sadina, Miyoko, and Jackie.

Ms. Cowan waved from the shore. "Yes, he's right, we have to get on our way too. At least now with Frypan we'll have a better dinner." Ms. Cowan, Isaac, and Old Man Frypan separated to the left of the ship to allow everyone else to get on their way, and to Minho's surprise more hugging ensued. It was like an execution line but instead of bullets, Cowan, Isaac, and Frypan lined up for hugs from each one as they climbed the deck. At least the sick woman had her neck covered up. Minho watched closely as Trish reached for Sadina's hand and Sadina shook her touch away.

"You'll all be safe." He didn't know what else to say. He nodded a goodbye to Isaac, feeling like they had an understanding he'd never really experienced with anyone else. He turned to pull the anchor up and get the engine started, but a commotion erupted on deck.

"No! Please!" He turned around and half-expected to see Cowan dead on the sand and another change of plans, but there was no visible reason for any of the commotion. Who'd shouted?

Cowan, Isaac, and Frypan all looked up from shore with wide eyes. "What? What happened?" Minho held his gun tight to his chest and looked around the perimeter. Trees. Water. Sand. *What the hell was it now?*

Dominic was the one to explain. "Jackie's not coming. She can't take another boat ride. Barfed nearly twelve times a day on our way here and almost barfed now walking across the deck."

Minho watched as Jackie threw her pack off the boat to the dry sand. Trish stopped the girl and hugged her. "Are you sure? We'll all miss you."

"Sorry. I just can't. Land seems like a better option for me and I can help Isaac if any Cranks show up." She apologized for changing her mind, but Minho didn't understand all the *sorry this* and *sorry that*. Orphans never apologized.

Dominic went up to Jackie and wrapped her in a hug that looked like it hurt. Miyoko squeezed Jackie's arm. Minho didn't understand these things of *holding onto someone* when they wanted to be let go, and he watched in shock as Orange went over to hug Jackie, too.

He took a deep breath as Roxy followed suit.

Another goodbye would take another hour at least. He looked over at the sun's placement in the sky and then at the ship's deck that was now empty again.

It felt like a failure to stay another night, but in order for Minho to have a successful chance at sailing the boat, he needed all his senses, including sight. He couldn't wait around another hour for goodbyes and needed his crew alert to help with the journey.

"What do you think, son?" Roxy shouted up at Minho from below. "One last fire here, we'll catch some fish?"

His shoulders tensed before they relaxed. What choice did he have? "We'll set sail at first light." The islanders cheered as if Minho was a God that had just granted them their one wish. He never wanted to be like the Grief Bearers of the Remnant Nation who enforced rules just for pain. Rules just for rules. If he was going to join the Godhead, he needed to first understand the balance of power and people. His first lesson: *People needed time.*

PART THREE

Direct Observation

Every day I change my mind about going back and finding my friends for a proper send-off. But would one long goodbye ever be enough? Nothing ever seems like enough, does it?

So today, I'll decide not to go back and find them. Today I'll decide goodbyes are rubbish.

Who knows about tomorrow.

Maybe tomorrow I'll change my mind again.

—*The Book of Newt*

CHAPTER FIFTEEN

Sound the Alarms

I
ALEXANDRA

The small fishing boat puttered to a stop and Mannus slipped into the icy water and pulled it ashore to sit on top of the crunchy snow-covered bank. If he hadn't had horns for brains Alexandra would have smacked him in the head for the rough ride. But she needed his muscles.

"Are these the people who'll remove my horns?" Mannus asked as he pulled the boat farther onto the bank of land. Alexandra didn't want to make any specific promises. She didn't know what the people of the local Villa were capable of and if horn removal was a practiced skill set. The remoteness of the island led her to believe Mannus wasn't going to get his wish. She just might have to find another way to fulfill her promise and keep him quiet about Nicholas' murder.

"Have the Hollowings worsened since Nicholas' death?" She stood up to climb out of the boat. Somehow, the boat was more wobbly on land than it was on the water.

"I told you, I'm not one of those crazy Pilgrims that believes in rituals and sacrifices to the Maze." Despite the gruff tone, Mannus held out his hand to Alexandra. She thought twice before touching him but climbing out of boats wasn't something she did every day. Both her feet hit land and she straightened out her cloak.

"Have they increased?" she asked again with patience. "You see the bodies when you walk by the entrance to the Maze, do you not? Have they spread outside of town?"

"They're the same. Maybe a little more since your speech about the Evolution."

More bodies Hollowed out since she had given the people hope? How could being on the precipice of the Evolution create more sacrifices among the people? And human sacrifices at that?

"More? You're sure?" Her ears buzzed with anger. Were the people she led no more than half-Cranks? She sloshed through the snow a few yards before stopping. She had no sense of intuition when she held this much anger inside. She needed to recite the digits and clear her mind.

"The Hollowings—"

"Silence!" she snapped. She went through the digits as her feet grew numb in her boots. The island was so desolate that even the sun could barely find it. Shivering, she cleared her head and connected to the infinite knowledge of the universe. Mannus' horns may have looked like antennas, but he received no information from the Infinite —except infinite stupidity, it seemed. She closed her eyes, took a deep breath, and exhaled. When she opened her eyes, she saw a path of trees ahead that stood out from the rest. There was no sign of any Villa, no signs of fresh footprints or even animal tracks, but it was the way.

She moved in that direction with a swish of her cloak and Mannus followed her lead. His loud, nasally, stinky breathing chipped away at her patience. Time passed. Trees passed. The brisk air seeped into her depths.

"Goddess?" Mannus moved in front of her and pointed ahead, where sunlight reflected off the surface of a window. She smiled before quickly controlling herself.

"Be on your best behavior and do not speak." It might have been better to have him wait by the boat, but she didn't yet know what help she might need carrying things back from the Villa. With any luck, she'd return to mainland Alaska with armfuls of the Cure.

Her foot stepped through something barely stronger than a spider web but too thin to see. A single *CLICK* accompanied her pause and Mannus tackled her from the side. Her mouth was suddenly full of snow, something she hadn't done since she was a child; it tasted no better now than it did back then. She spit it out and tried to push herself to stand but Mannus' entire weight was atop her.

"Don't move," he whispered. Not a moment later, an ax flew out of nowhere, thunking into a nearby tree. The very same tree to the right of where Alexandra had been standing. Her ears buzzed, her vision flashed with fire, a vision so real that she couldn't help but gasp for air. Mannus drew his knife and stated the obvious. "I guess they don't want visitors."

An alarm sounded from a two-story building of stone, only slightly louder than the buzzing in her head, and three women emerged from the upper-level balcony doors.

"Show yourself," the tallest of the three commanded; she held a gun on them, and even from the ground Alexandra could see it was enormous. In New Petersburg, they had banned guns years ago, and when the Evolution was complete there wouldn't be a need for such weapons. No more Hollowings. No more rituals. Humankind could finally re-advance itself to the builders of old. New technology. New systems. New life.

"I told you it wasn't a bear." The shortest of the three women's voice traveled clearest through the Alaskan air to Alexandra's ears. Something in the woman's voice struck her as trustworthy. The mist in the air seemed to amplify the words spoken.

The tallest woman fired the gun in the air as a warning, as if the ax wasn't enough. She then shouted in an extremely formal manner. "On behalf of the Godhead, we demand that you return to that which you came. This isn't an area to trespass."

Nicholas had obviously employed three misfits parading as scientists. Alexandra had no patience for such a show. "I *am* the Godhead!"

She pushed Mannus off of her, then climbed to her feet and brushed the snow from her cloak. She'd never been so humiliated and insulted. Apparently, her trip to this remote island was a day of firsts:

The first time she was tackled to the ground by a Pilgrim.

The first time she had been threatened with a gun *and* an ax.

And the first time that anyone in greater Alaska didn't recognize that she was indeed one of the Godhead.

"You must recognize me!" She straightened her cloak and forced a smile. She had only ever been idolized and recognized as she walked through the crowds of Pilgrims. They not only recognized her but begged to touch her. The three women on the balcony exchanged nervous, doubtful looks between themselves and Alexandra grew impatient. "Well?"

"Forgive us, but we do not." The shortest of the three had answered.

Alexandra tried to remain stoic but the buzzing in her ears increased and her head spun. *MADNESS!* She couldn't lose it, not now, not when she was this close. She recited the digits within her mind. "Tell them, Mannus."

"You're speaking to the Godhead." He motioned to Alexandra with the slightest bow.

The three women didn't move. They didn't say anything. Alexandra couldn't blame them for wanting proof. In fact, it encouraged her. The Godhead's cloak would speak to her royalty once she cleared it of mud and wet snow.

She spoke in a careful but commanding voice. "Please, make us some tea, and I'll show you."

2

After the short one made Alexandra a cup of lukewarm green tea, she displayed her Godhead "powers" by opening a door in the Villa with a wave of her arm. She knew Nicholas would have used the same

Godhead technology as the security doors in New Alexander and the chip in his hand matched that of hers. Had, anyway.

Alexandra was once naive enough to think the red-leather Coffin that held Newt's blood could only be opened by the three Pillars of the Godhead when they were all three present, but Nicholas and Mikhail had opened it without her. Opening one of Nicholas' doors without him there now brought a smile to her face. "You'll assist us now, I presume?"

The three supposed scientists looked at Mannus and each of his horns as if something didn't make sense. They exchanged glances before the tallest one asked, "Is this Mikhail?"

Alexandra wondered for just a moment if she should lie and say yes. Perhaps the presence of two members of the Godhead would be more persuasive. But one look at Mannus and anyone could see he was nothing more than the bottom rung of society. The way he breathed. The way he smelled. The way he stood right now in the presence of so many women but didn't bend to show the slightest respect.

"I'm Mannus. The horns were a bad idea."

The fact that they'd asked about Mannus meant that Mikhail had never made it to the Villa either, at least not this one. Whatever his plans were that took him on pilgrimages hopefully had nothing to do with her plan of the Evolution. She didn't really care what the man busied himself with. It was probably just killing season for him when he left. The Cure that reverted his DNA could only change Mikhail so much; it couldn't patch up the cracks in his soul or tame the madness he housed within.

Alexandra walked around the room and carefully traced her finger along the glassware of pipettes stored there, test tubes, petri dishes, beakers, until her eyes found a unit which she could only assume held what she came for. The Cure Nicholas had used on her.

"Goddess . . . ," the tallest woman stuttered, "we're sorry for the confusion, but Nicholas did not tell us of your arrival. We're not—"

"You needn't worry about Nicholas." Alexandra gently placed the red-leather box Mannus had brought onto a stainless-steel lab table.

"We're here on a separate accord." She opened the Coffin. "Five vials of Newt's blood. You'll use this for a new batch of the Cure."

Surely, they'd be elated at this discovery, but instead she watched as their faces morphed into confusion. They asked for a moment and huddled, whispering fiercely . . .

"Say it. What's going on?" Alexandra demanded.

The short one answered. "These . . . these can't be Newt's vials. We already have those placed in the safe . . . the ones Nicholas sent over not that long ago." Her voice was suddenly coated with a condescending tone. As if she knew Alexandra had made a huge mistake and could not go back.

How could she have known these weren't Newt's? How could Nicholas have replaced them? She pivoted to Mannus. She looked back to the Coffin; the scientists had to be mistaken. They didn't even look that closely at them. How could they know?

Time to recover the situation. "No. You're wrong. Nicholas instructed me that these vials, Newt's blood, would be needed."

Alexandra watched the tall scientist pick up each vial and examine the labels. Alexandra wondered if Nicholas had ever trusted her with any truth, or if Newt's blood being the Cure was just yet another lie. But it *felt* true, known to her the way other information came through her senses, through her cells. Everything in her body vibrated at this confusion, and the three women stood just as confused in front of her. Alexandra wanted to scream and toss the Coffin against the glass window, but she restrained herself, embracing the Flaring Discipline and the Principles. She recited the digits in her mind.

"A4?" The shortest of the women nosed her way into an old scientific log. "That test subject of the Maze trials was Chuck if I'm correct." She looked up with blank, questioning eyes.

Alexandra's ears rang with anger and she spun around and slapped Mannus as if he was responsible for the buzzing alarms within her head. All the anger that trembled within her needed to go somewhere, and it went out of her palm into Mannus' cheek. She had slapped him so hard that he spit something onto the floor. "You idiot! You brought the wrong case from the study!" Mannus looked at her with surprise and genuine hurt feelings.

"Apologies my Goddess . . ." he half-heartedly said.

"Nicholas is feeling under the weather . . ." Alexandra closed the red-leather case and latched it shut. "So he must've forgotten that he'd already brought them and given Mannus the wrong . . ." She was scrambling for a solution and quickly looked around the small lab. "But while we're here—"

"Nicholas was supposed to be back here for our report last week."

"He didn't show."

"What illness does he have?"

All three of the scientists spoke at once. Alexandra searched her mind for another lie. *What illness did Nicholas have?* She had never once in thirty years known Nicholas to be under the weather.

She replied with the utmost confidence. "He has symptoms of dizziness. Vision black-outs. Shaking, a loud buzzing in his ears." She spelled out her own growing symptoms. "And his thoughts are foggy. Clearly." She pointed to the vials of Chuck's blood labeled as Newt's.

It was the middle-sized woman's turn to speak. "All mild symptoms of Ascension. Although . . ." She exchanged doubtful glances with the others. "I thought Nicholas was well beyond them. Perhaps the northern lights are affecting his inner brain chemistry the same way a full moon does for those who are sensitive."

"Yes," Alexandra said, but what did they mean by *sensitive*? What was all of this? "I can attest to the full moon causing more disruptions within the village since the full spectrum of the northern lights returned." She placed her hand on her heart. "The Hollowings have increased, you know?" She waited for the women to react but they didn't. Of course, they didn't have fears of being hollowed, they were too far removed from any society. Alexa had to find what they *did* fear and play into that. "The Hollowings are a sign of the end of days. Nicholas believed that once the ritual increased in frequency, we would be out of time to change the fates."

"He did say that there wasn't much time." The short one's turn.

Alexandra latched on to that. "Which is why you must help me share the Cure now."

Tall spoke next. "We can only release the vials to Nicholas, and dispensing the Cure is still being worked out by Villa One. They're using the—"

"Shhh . . ." Short elbowed Tall.

"I am the Godhead. Nicholas is not well. I will dispense them." She said it with a motherly tone but they looked at her as though she were the one with the horns sewed to her head.

Tall replied. "It's out of no disrespect, Goddess, it's simply the protocol, we do not answer to you, we answer to Nicholas. You don't have the clearance here."

Alexandra smiled her last fake smile of the day. Nicholas had taught her patience, but even this was a stretch of what she was capable of entertaining. She had been tackled, shot at, and drank the worst tea of her life. It was time to get what she came for. She threw all her powers of persuasion and command into her voice.

"Enough of this. You'll begin answering to me as of right this minute, because Nicholas is dead. He was murdered." Alexandra waited for the apologies and groveling, for them to correct their course, to serve Alexandra Romanov as their one true Goddess.

But they didn't.

Alexandra watched in stunned disbelief as each woman scurried to a different part of the lab and began packing instruments. *What was going on here? What was it they feared more than her?* She tried to command them. "Stop this at once!" But she and Mannus helplessly watched as they poured beakers full of liquids down drains and smashed other glass collections. "What are you doing? You're destroying it!"

Tall replied. "Yes, matter of safety. We have a plan in place for such a thing, and with your news of the Godhead's assassination, that plan is now in effect."

This was absurd, Alexandra thought. *What the hell was going on?*

Middle spoke up, now. "This is an offset experimental lab, and Villa

X was never approved by the greater coalition to be doing any of these tests."

Alexandra had no choice but to roll with the punches, now. "It's okay, the Evolutionary Guards can protect you, you'll be safe." Her offer didn't slow down their panic. "You can't just give up and walk away from thirty years of research."

Small responded. "We're not walking away. We're destroying it. In the event that anything happened to Nicholas, this Villa was to be destroyed. . . . And Goddess . . ." Short walked over to a safe in the wall. After typing in a code, she reached in and, instead of pulling out a vial or a collection of manuals or journals or studies she handed Alexandra a single envelope, "This is for you."

Alex, stunned into the most unusual silence of her life, looked down at the envelope. Her name had been scribbled across the front in a very familiar handwriting. Nicholas.

3

Alexandra held the envelope tightly in her hand.

She could already feel the vibration of the letter, some *I Told You So* from Nicholas about Newt's vials not being in the case, about switching the labels. Something about how she should have had more patience. But she wouldn't let his words control her anymore. She folded the envelope into three and put it in her cloak pocket.

The women continued to pack up what was left of "Villa X" and Alexandra looked to Mannus with a desperate plea. His hand inched closer to his knife. She had no more time for games and counted on the fact that he had killed for his Goddess before and that he might do it again. True to her wishes, the horned man grabbed the tallest woman and held his knife against her throat.

But his words surprised her. "Stop the emergency shutdown, and inject me already." His voice was just as rough as the way he handled the woman's life in front of him.

Alexandra could work with this. "Not so rough, Mannus, these faithful employees of Nicholas are our new friends and perhaps they'd like to be employed in a *new* way." She held her palms open, faceup, showing she had nothing to hide. Her power of persuasion only needed to work long enough for one of the three women to trust her. "Every end is indeed just a new beginning, and while this ends the reign that Nicholas had over your studies we can begin to now make history together. Don't you want your hard work to be a part of the turning point of humanity?" She fed them a gentle smile. "We can bring you to New Petersburg and—"

Mannus went off the rails. "We can't fit five people in that boat. You'll inject me now. Here."

Alexandra stepped up to him. She squeezed his elbow with two fingers, just between the bones where it pinched him enough to lower his knife. *Would all the Pilgrims of the Maze be so selfish?* She needed to remember that there would be ways to sort out the worthy from the unworthy. Alaska would be seen as the great frontier once again, ahead of the rest of the world and guiding the way to the future.

"We can't just inject you." Tall rubbed her neck where the point of the knife had been just moments ago.

Alexandra wasn't leaving without getting what she came for. If she couldn't take the vials and the science back with her, she'd settle for taking it in the veins of Mannus. She walked backwards to the balcony where the woman who'd greeted them to the island had set her gun down. Her heel slipped for a moment on the tile and a white odd-shaped marble rolled from under her boot as she bent down for the gun. She picked up the weapon with strength.

"Listen . . ." She commanded everyone's attention. She didn't want to kill three people today, but would pull the trigger if it meant igniting the final stages of the Evolution. No, that was madness. But perhaps she needed those mad thoughts to drive her forward? Every person in power since the beginning of days had at one time or another done something they thought they'd never do, made a choice they wished they hadn't needed to, and this responsibility was now in Alexandra's hands.

"I don't want to hurt any of you. I want us to work together. To help the world evolve further than what has been possible. The Cranks can only be Cured physically but their souls can't be saved. They will always have a monster within them even when their DNA is reconstructed." She needed to look no further than to Mikhail for that example. "But for those of us who are able-bodied, who are ready for more—we can have it. We can have the Cure and the Evolution within one. A whole new generation without the Flare. Can you imagine what the coming generations could do without the fear of the Flare holding them back and with the advanced DNA sequencing?"

She almost laughed at the pureness of her vision. Everyone in the world living up to an infinite potential. How beautiful the world could be if they would just embrace the Cure. The three women stood there and said nothing. Alexandra lowered the weapon to reason with them. "What will you do and where will you go if the other Villa isn't supposed to know of these studies? Where will you live and work?" Again, silence from the women, so Alexandra answered for them, "In New Petersburg alongside me. With the Godhead."

"Enough of this bullshit. Give me the Cure already." Mannus cleared away beakers from a lab table with his hand. Glass shattered on the floor in a million pieces as he laid his arm on the table for an injection.

Short responded with surprising confidence. "No, we can't."

"You will," Alexandra demanded, and with the gun still in her hand, the scientists obeyed.

"Do you have the Flare? Before The Gone?" Tall asked as she inspected him with her eyes.

"Do I look like I have the Flare?" Mannus replied.

"What about fevers? Have you had any fevers lately?"

"No."

Middle, who was neither good at making tea nor taking orders, and who said the least of any of them, walked over to Alex. "This isn't perfected. He's got a sixty percent chance of falling over dead before the day is over." Alexandra didn't understand what she was talking about. "The horns," Short said. "He's got . . . predispositions."

Alexandra laughed and shook her head. "The horns aren't from his DNA, you idiot, he had those sewed on by choice."

The soft-spoken scientist looked back at the others before explaining to Alexandra, "It's not the horns, it's the DNA sequences visible in those who typically make . . . such rash decisions."

"He'll be fine." Alexandra couldn't care less if Mannus lived or died at this point. As long as they left right after his injection, he'd steer her back to the city and he would either make it back onto shore or he wouldn't. If he lived, then she'd share his story as an example for the Pilgrims of the Maze to see the potential in the Evolution, and if he died, then she would have to regulate the Cure accordingly.

Short insisted. "I will not be responsible for what will happen. If you want to end your life as you know it, fine." The woman readied a syringe and handed it to Mannus.

"Yes. I want a greater life!" Mannus shouted and spit flew from his chapped lips. Being on the precipice of mental power had already changed relatively mild-mannered Mannus into something Alexandra did not quite recognize.

The short woman had an incredible amount of patience. "Whatever happens is the result of your own hand. Good or bad. We don't have enough studies of how your specific DNA will change, and we should really first take your blood and then. . . . Evolution needs to happen in steps, in slow methodical steps. Creatures on Earth who've evolved have done so slowly, over time, like the environment, and this need not be any different if you want it to be successful. Because this," she motioned to the lab's contents, "this has infinite possibilities based on blood type and genetics for each person, and we simply don't know its full effect until we have a catalog of every possibility and those possibilities are as infinite as the human race."

Alexandra shifted the weight of the gun in her hands. Infinite possibilities was not something to be afraid of, it was something those of the future could embrace. "If thirty years of studies isn't enough, then what will be? It is time. The Evolution is ready." She motioned with the gun for Mannus to go ahead, to become a part of *her* evolution.

Mannus uncapped the syringe and hesitated for only a moment before injecting himself in the crook of his elbow, even as he stood in the middle of all that broken glass and spilled chemicals.

Alexandra watched for any change in his face. His jaw muscles tightened and his shoulders twitched. The other women seemed to hold their breath collectively as they observed and waited. His face relaxed, his jaw softened, and Alexa imagined his body cooling from the Cure. She remembered the sensation of her own Cure way back when, the way her body had felt cold and just a bit tingly before a warming band of fireworks traveled through her veins, tickling her from the inside out. Cleansing her.

And as if Mannus could hear what she was thinking, he turned to smile at her, his right cheek still red from where Alexandra had slapped him. His bottom, middle tooth was missing, but he certainly didn't seem to care.

CHAPTER SIXTEEN

War Path

I

MIKHAIL

The Remnant Nation held only one secret: the identity of the Great Master in the Golden Room of Grief. The Great Master who gave commands, rewards, updates, and promises. The Great Master whom no one had ever seen—until today. All of it a practice in pretension.

Mikhail walked along the crimson-red wall of the empty Golden Room of Grief with his hood cloaked over his face, as he always did, but he planned to reveal his full self to them today. Well, maybe not the little part about him being with a member the Godhead that they were trained to kill, but he did want the Grief Bearers to see the fire in his eyes when he spoke of the war. The flames within Mikhail needed to spread to their souls and filter down to the hearts of the soldiers. Flames of anger and justice.

His fingers shook as he hovered them over the alarm that alerted the Grief Bearers of his arrival. Pain radiated from his right kidney and he wiped the sweat from his forehead. The human body was capable of regenerating and repairing almost any cell, but the human body was also capable of eating itself alive from the inside out. A wonderful fact.

Mikhail never knew which path his body might take.

One of obedience. Or one of betrayal.

He depended on his body to regenerate healthy cells, but he'd learned after breaking his ankle in the Glade years ago that the body stored trauma in different ways. Nicholas forced Mikhail to spend to six weeks on his couch for constant observation as he explained that sometimes trauma was processed as expected: the body healed. But at other times, the impact of *one* trauma caused an explosion of multiple side effects.

The body and the mind are interlinked, Dear Mikhail.

Nicholas insisted on testing Mikhail's memory and levels of anger each and every day, worried the broken bone might trigger his mental state back into the comfort zone of a Crank. Mikhail hated the tests. He hated the time it took to heal. He loathed it all.

Mikhail breathed deep for three seconds, held his breath for three seconds, exhaled for three seconds, then hit the alarm. He tried to relax as he moved to the exact center of the room, holding his body in as normal a posture as possible, but the stab wound in his right side weakened him. His legs buckled and his breath labored. Even so, he felt better than he should have. Shock. Like the broken ankle on which he'd walked three miles to reach Nicholas, he remembered that shock could last for hours or days before the true impact of an injury presented itself.

But enough time had passed since the boy stabbed him that Mikhail was sure the kid had missed his main organ. Probably why the little bugger was in Hell. Weak strength and poor execution. The Remnant Nation had no room for such weakness. The men Mikhail awaited to join him were twelve bearers of knowledge but they were even weaker than the boy who'd stabbed him. He needed the armies of the Nation to be strong while keeping these most senior leaders of the Nation weak. It was the secret to any successful government: Power was one thing, strength another. As he waited for the Grief Bearers, he closed his eyes under the shadow of his hood.

Mikhail entered the place in his mind where anything was possible and all was revealed.

The Infinite Glade.

And he exhaled.

He conjured in his mind a single, simplicable, proposal: to give the present and the future one last chance to change its course before he revealed himself. Before he started the war. What was about to be done could not be undone.

Ever.

He asked the Infinite Glade, *Is it time to execute the war?* And in a flash the word YES, in all white, glowed within the blackness of his mind. Still, knowing this was what he'd prepared for, Mikhail felt conflicted. A similar feeling had come over him when the boy cut the wild pig loose and he watched it run and squeal into the far distance. This confliction between anger and relief mesmerized him, because it meant he was—at least for today—more human than Crank.

A shuffle of footsteps. He opened his eyes and the colors of the Golden Room of Grief flooded his vision. A room with red walls and golden accents that almost blinded. He'd created this war room, with the red a shade somewhere between the color of bright bloodshed and that of darkened, dried blood that stained weapons. The gold accents were crafted from pyrite found alongside deposits of gold. And along with the pyrite there was sure to be arsenic, because as great as gold was, it was always mined alongside clusters of poison. A lesson he'd never forget, no matter how muddled his mind:

Anything of value was equally toxic.

Mikhail straightened his legs and steadied his breath as the footsteps drew nearer.

"The Great Master!" one of the Bearers of Grief exclaimed upon entering.

"Oh highest of high!" Another Grief Bearer bowed. Mikhail quickly counted six of them, but that wasn't enough. Not to ignite the flames of war.

"Where are the rest?" He spoke low and slow from the shadows of his cloak, careful not to let on to his pain.

"Griever Glane and Griever Barrus are missing. Along with a Priestess." One of the Grief Bearers stepped forward. It had been decades and Mikhail still failed to learn their individual names. He didn't care who Glane or Barrus were, he just needed the numbers.

"And what about the Orphans from the cliffs? You haven't promoted anyone in their absence?" It had been his plan for years to promote stronger Grief Bearers by the time they went to war. He had systems and plans, and the faces of those before him were ones lacking competence. His anger raced through his wound and pounded at his back.

One of them continued. "Griever Haskin and Griever Clarence have sped up the pilgrimages for the Orphan soldiers, even starting the rituals at sixteen for some of the stronger ones."

"Then why are there only six of you right now?" He emphasized the word *now* as if it were a command and not a question, but he was met with only silence. He'd once again overestimated the Bearers to be more than what they were. Just like he'd underestimated Alexandra. And now he was in the middle of this mess of Evolution without a solid Nation to stand before him. "Say something!" he demanded.

"They . . . they . . ."

A skinny Bearer stepped forward. "The Orphans have not been . . . coming back."

Mikhail breathed his routine. The cloaked men in front of him were merely tools. Nothing more. The entirety of the Remnant Nation, a box of tools that he would finally use today. Tools that could break and be thrown away after the war.

The men before him did not deserve the sacrificial ritual of war. They didn't deserve the feast of a pig. And they didn't deserve to see Mikhail's face. He fixed the hood of his cloak tighter. "You have more problems in the Nation than I have time for. Missing Grief Bearers, holes in the tunnels of Hell, allowing Orphans to flee. Never mind the missing. This war has begun." He paused as each Grief Bearer lowered to their knees. At least he still had their will to bend to his own.

"Gather the Orphan Army and the Crank Army at once." The Bearers looked at each other with great hesitation. "What is it?"

"The Army of Cranks oh, Great Master . . ."

"What about them?" He slowed his speech to increase his patience, another trick taught him by Nicholas. He may as well have been talking to Cranks.

"They are . . . not well."

It had been months since Mikhail visited the Crank Army. Was his memory already failing him? He thought of Nicholas' tests for memory loss after trauma. The pain from his back amplified with his anger. "Take me there, now."

2

Within walking distance of the Golden Room of Grief was an unassuming plot of land, stretched within the walls of their fortress. On the surface, it was empty and sparse, but ten feet below, a bunker held over a thousand Cranks. Within the underground was a complex tunnel system, filled with safe rooms and areas for supplies. Mikhail let the six Grief Bearers walk before him so they wouldn't see the tear in his cloak. They walked like cowards, their backs stiff with fear.

"You're sure we all need to go down there?" the skinny one turned to ask.

Mikhail simply nodded and motioned to the moss-covered hatch. One by one, the six men lowered themselves into the bunker's entrance, as if they were lowering themselves to certain death. The Grief Bearers of the Remnant Nation were no better than the starving Orphans in Hell, but the cloaks made them think otherwise. Cloaks of power. None of the Bearers actually held any power, no, Mikhail made sure of that. They only knew as little or as much as he deemed to share during his masked visits to the Golden Room.

He climbed down the hatch, into the tunnel, walked to the lift.

"Sir. The Crank Army is very hungry." The skinny Grief Bearer followed too closely.

Mikhail's loss of blood made him dizzy. "Hunger for war is a good thing." He shouldn't have needed to tell the Grief Bearers that.

"No. They are not, how do I put this . . ." The Bearer stepped forward, ahead of the entrance to the bunker's shaft. ". . . Satisfied."

"Then feed them more." Mikhail moved past him and into the small elevator but one of the men stopped him from pushing the lever to descend.

"I saw one eat their own arm yesterday, Sir." The Grief Bearer let go of Mikhail's cloaked arm.

Mikhail didn't believe it. Self-cannibalism. Autosarcophagy? Cranks were cannibalistic, but they weren't going to eat themselves for Flares-sake. No animal would. He lowered the lever of the lift once all six Grief Bearers were inside; the elevator clanked and grinded down, gears shifting and turning until they arrived at the bunker level. The others collectively took a deep breath as the gated door of the lift opened. The wound caused a clammy heat to coat Mikhail's body and he welcomed the cooler air from the mine shaft. The smell, however, he could have done without. It smelled of stomach acid and bile. *Had the Grief Bearers not been keeping up with maintenance of the Army?*

"They're chained in groups of eight?" Mikhail asked. Eight was a sacred number. Part of the digits Alexandra recited. She clung to those numbers for her sanity, and soon he would deliver her an army of eights.

"Yes, sir." A Grief Bearer who'd brought a notepad and pen cleared his throat. "For the most part." He clicked the pen nervously. *Click clack. Click clack. Click clack.* The sound of it made Mikhail's eye twitch.

"What the hell does that mean? They're either shackled together, ready to fight, or they're not." He stepped out of the lift, onto the bunker floor, suddenly assaulted by the sounds of chains, dragging. Metal on concrete. *CLANK CLANK CLAAAANK. . . .* Noises that somehow seemed both loud and quiet at the same time. Harsh and angry sounds, coming from back hallways out of view.

"Soldiers report!" a Grief Bearer shouted, but only the dragging and clanking answered him. "Soldiers report!" Still no answer. Mikhail had never come down to the bunker without one Orphan soldier being at the lift and another one standing guard in the hallway. Every entrance point to a path within view should have had a soldier standing near it.

"Something's not right." The skinniest of the Grief Bearers positioned himself at the back of the elevator, ready to return to the surface. Not a chance, Mikhail needed to know what was going on with these Cranks. Maybe the Orphans were already moving them to the Bergs.

He started to walk toward the loudest of the sounds, coming from a hallway off to the right, and realized he was walking alone. He turned to the Grief Bearers behind him. "If you're going to be cowards, I'll feed you to the army as a sacrificial war feast. How's that sound?" Mikhail hid his own pain and doubt. Slowly, five Grief Bearers stepped forward. The skinniest, the weakest one, pulled the lever to go back up. The gears clanked as the mechanical sounds lifted him away.

Some people might call that dastardly.

"Griever Banks!" one of the men shouted at the elevator shaft.

"Long live the Cure!" The skinny, scared, Grief Bearer said as he rose from view.

Mikhail seethed. The Cure would live, yes, but the Bearer who turned his back on the Remnant Nation would not. One way or another that idiotic coward would die a painful death, reserved for those who betrayed the Nation.

Mikhail grimaced with pain as he walked from the main lobby of the bunker to the hallway. "Get both armies together. Make note of the coordinates," he said to the incessant pen-clicker. "56.8125 degrees North and 132.9574 degrees West."

"Wait, say it again?" The man scrambled to keep up.

Mikhail took a slow, deep breath. "56.8125 degrees North and 132.9574 degrees West." He walked toward the sounds of dragging metal. "Pack the Bergs full of Cranks. You'll land on the exact coordinates and send them to march in on foot from the south. The Orphan Army and the air strikes will happen from the north, and the two will meet in the middle to destroy the city of Gods once and for all." The Grief Bearers looked to each other with something that could only be described as dark excitement, all wide eyes and suppressed grins. "Do you have any questions?" The clanking noises got louder. There had to be at least one group of Cranks loose from the pits.

"We have the coordinates. We have the orders. We just need to know the target day for the attack."

"Sunday." He hid his own smile. "The holiest of days. The Goddess will address her people in the square after Mass. When you see a woman more beautiful than Alaska herself, that is the Goddess." He never wanted Alexandra hurt, just destroyed, and there were several ways to destroy a person without physical harm. But the way she'd boasted on and on of taking Nicholas' head, he couldn't afford a second thought. "Kill her however you see fit."

"Long live the Cure," the Grief Bearers said in unison.

Mikhail turned a corner in the hallway and saw an unnatural sight: a group of Cranks shackled together in a line of eight, working themselves out of chains . . .

By chewing at their own limbs.

It took his mind a moment to wrap around the situation in front of him. He had never feared the Cranks before, but the wound in his back made him weak. Vulnerable. In counting the Flare-ridden, bloodied bodies before him, he only counted six still attached to their wrist and ankle shackles. Two gaping holes in the link—loose chains dragged on the concrete. Two Cranks were loose in the bunker.

"Get to the armory room!" Mikhail shouted as he stumbled backwards, not able to take his eyes off the sight of their madness, their desperation to be free. Like caged animals, they would rather chew off every limb than stay enslaved. The armory room had a full supply of guns, knives, ammo, and hand grenades, but his right leg suddenly gave out from the spreading pain. Like something poked him from inside the wound. He screamed despite himself.

"Great Master!" one of them exclaimed, but the cloaked men didn't have the instincts of Orphans who'd trained their whole lives. They were organizers and politicians, didn't have the minds of soldiers. To guard. Protect. Kill. Mikhail spun around and within an inch of his face was a snarling Crank, ripe with rage.

Widened eyes with no soul behind them. Only bloodlust.

Such smells. Every bodily fluid combined into one. Spit. Bile. Blood. The Crank lifted his half-chewed wrist toward Mikhail but he grabbed it, held it back, held it tight. The Crank gargled a scream.

"Give me your pen!" Mikhail shouted. He reached for it, grabbed it from the hapless Grief Bearer, *clicked* it, then stabbed the Crank in the neck. Right in the artery.

The monster dropped to its knees, Mikhail still holding its wrist. Detached from its body.

"Great Master, you've been hurt!" a Grief Bearer cried from behind, finally observing Mikhail's wound. But he wouldn't allow this to weaken his plan.

"Pack the Cranks into the Bergs. Now!" He forced himself to his feet and moved swiftly toward the armory.

3
MINHO

"One time, Skinny found an Orphan all the way out in a field. Dead."

Minho appreciated company while he steered the ship, but Orange was not going to convince him that one dead soldier in a field meant there was an army of Cranks. "He saw the Crank Army?"

"Well, no. The guy was dead. Skinny never reported it, he wasn't supposed to be out there."

"Then how does a dead soldier in a field equal a whole army of Cranks?"

"*Because*." Orange took a deep breath. "Skinny said the body was hollowed out."

Hollowed out? He shrugged. A single Crank could have done that, or a pack of Crank-wolves. Minho didn't know if Crank-wolves existed but if they did, it would make more sense than an army of trained Cranks. "Don't go telling her all these crazy stories, okay?" He nodded toward Roxy, approaching the two Orphans at the captain's bench.

"Stories about what?" Roxy asked.

Orange shook her head. "Nothing . . ."

"Everything working okay?" Roxy asked as she looked over the controls. Minho nodded. He'd figured most of them out. Steering a ship on water was a hell of a lot easier than steering a Berg in the air, but still, being out in the ocean made him nervous. He kept the *Maze Cutter* within sight of the coastline so that he could anchor in at night. The Orphan found that being behind the captain's wheel required only one thing: Focus. Like watching the distant tree line from the walls of the Remnant Nation. Patience. Balance. Watching the surface of the water. Listening for the sounds of the ship to change.

He tried to ignore the things he didn't know, like why the rudder of the ship kept pulling to the left, but it was getting worse by the hour. "The alignment's off. It wasn't this bad when we started. Something's making it pull." He steered slightly to the right in order to go straight. "Think you can take over while I look at the mechanics?" Orange nodded.

"I can help, too," Roxy said.

Minho scoffed. "No offense, Roxy, but I've seen you in a truck. I don't need you finding every bad wave and hitting every whale."

"Heyyy." She almost sounded offended. "I'll have you know my grandpa taught me how to canoe. Yeah, that's right. It's a little different, but his first rule," she held a single finger in the air, "was to respect the water."

"That's a good rule," Minho replied. "You can help Orange 'respect the water' by keeping watch for anything ahead of us."

"Ain't nothing in this water but water." Roxy looked out at the gentle ocean waves. "No other ships, no whales, nothing to look at. Kinda boring, gotta be honest."

"Wait." Orange took over the captain's wheel. "You knew your parents? And your *grandparents*?" Tiers of soldiers and generations of Grief Bearers were about as close to a family tree as Orphans from the Remnant Nation ever got. Minho wanted to hear the answer.

Roxy nodded with pride. "I knew my grandparents and my dad. Although I wouldn't exactly say I knew him. I met him and we spent lots of time together, but I never got to really *know* him." She stuffed her hands in her pockets. Minho thought about what that meant, for Roxy to have had someone like that in her life but still never really know them. "My mom, she died some horrible death that no one loved me enough to talk about."

"Oh." Orange turned the captain's wheel to the left as she glanced at Roxy. "I'm sorry."

Minho remembered Roxy telling him about her mom before, but it must have really bothered her. Never knowing the truth. "Maybe . . . they loved you a *lot* and that's why they didn't tell you. You know, if it was horrible." He stepped over and corrected Orange's steering back to the right to overcompensate for the pull to the left. "Sometimes, what we know. . . it changes what we *knew,* and maybe they didn't want that for you." He **understood** this by how much he'd kept from Roxy and the others about himself, his *true* self—because he knew it would change what they thought about him.

Roxy was lost in thought. She may not have been his real mom, but he wanted to get to know her—really know her as much as he could before they got to Alaska and things changed. He could look at the rudder later. "Tell us about your grandpa." He sat on the captain's bench. "He taught you about the water, what else?"

Roxy sat down next to him and pulled her legs up to her chest as if she was about to tell a proper yarn. "He collected stories from all over. Books, pamphlets, almanacs, whatever he could find, and he'd memorize those stories. He'd travel the country and towns on horseback to find more." She laughed.

Minho couldn't picture it. "Your grandpa went around on a horse? Just to tell stories?"

"Why is that so hard to believe?" She scrunched her eyebrows.

Minho didn't mean to offend her, he just didn't get it. Traveling to give a warning he understood, because he'd killed many people doing so. Traveling to give aid was another excuse he'd heard often before shooting arrows at trespassers. But traveling to share fairy tales seemed less . . . respectable. It seemed like an unworthy reason to die.

"What, spit it out. Whatever you're thinking." Roxy frowned.

He wasn't sure how to share all that without telling her how many men he'd killed who had been traveling with greater missions. He looked at Orange but she was only watching the ocean. As she should when at the wheel, but it didn't help him find the right words. "Because there's no honor in doing so."

"Honor?" Roxy spat it out as if she'd never heard the word before.

"The reason. The purpose. A need that's greater than your own." The Orphan explained as best he could. He didn't want to say that telling stories wasn't worth dying for. He knew Orange would understand his perspective.

Roxy shook her head back and forth. "*Connection* is the purpose. Without stories, we're all just barely living. Stories help us understand life so we *can* live. Stories are the glue that hold our bones together. Stories of family. Stories of Old. Stories of make-believe. Didn't that Nation of yours ever teach you anything?"

"We have rumors in the Remnant Nation. They're like stories, right?" Orange asked, and Minho tried not to make a face. "Tell us one of yours." She didn't take her eyes off the small waves ahead.

"Oh, there were so many." Roxy tilted her head back as if looking to the cloudless sky might help jog her memory. "People used to come from many towns over just to hear his tales. The ones about the ancient Gods were the stories people loved the most."

"What ancient Gods?" Minho asked.

"The Elohim."

He gazed lazily at Orange but she looked just as confused as he did. "What is that?"

"You know, the God with the Angels and the Devil?" Roxy waved her hands in front of her as if that could help them place it. The only God they'd ever heard of while growing up was the Godhead, and those weren't stories about how to worship them. No. Only ways to *kill* the Godhead.

"The Flare was our Devil," he said. "And our God was the Cure."

"Still is," Orange agreed.

Roxy huffed. "The Cure is just a thing. You can't worship a *thing*." Minho knew plenty of people who did just that.

She continued. "Most people of old worshiped a God, but not everyone had the same one. Different names, different origin stories, different lands and planets the Gods came from, but one thing that never really changed was the Devil. Evil remained a constant in all tales of old."

Orange steered the ship, and Minho watched to make sure she continued to favor the right side. To him, evil was evil, no matter what shape, body, or thing it possessed. The Flare would always be his Devil even after he joined the Godhead. And the Evolution was needed to stop that Devil. "This guy have a name?" he asked to appease Roxy.

"Iblis." She paused. "God commanded all the spirits to bow before man, which he'd created from his own breath, but the spirit named Iblis refused. He wouldn't bow to anyone but God. He didn't believe man could be a God."

"Kinda like the Godhead," Orange contributed. "People who think they're Gods and can control the Cure." What would she think of Minho when she found out his personal mission in Alaska was to join the so-called Godhead? To become one of them, despite the rank he was born into? "I agree with this Iblis fella. Men aren't Gods."

Roxy seemed pleased with the conversation. "But by not bowing, Iblis offended God. So much so that he was cast into Hell."

Minho and Orange looked at each other with wide eyes. They both understood Hell long before these grandpa stories. They had *been* there before. It was the lowest level of the Remnant Nation fortress, a place of torture and cruelty. A place to which Minho vowed never to return.

"Oh, we know Hell," Orange said.

"Yeah," Minho added. "We've both been there."

"No, no, no." Roxy laughed. But if she had ever been to their Hell, she wouldn't have. "Hell is a place you go to *after* you die, where the Devil rules his little scary kingdom. I don't believe in it, not literally anyway, but some people do."

Roxy could say Hell was a made-up place all she wanted to, but it was real.

All too real.

"So . . ." Orange thought out loud. "This Iblis guy. He's in charge down there?"

"Sent there, then ruled it." Roxy paused. "Still does, I suppose?"

Minho stepped in to correct Orange's steering again. "I got it, I got it," she said. "Go check the rudder, already."

He nodded. Yeah. He'd check the rudder. Anything but this Devil nonsense.

He thought about everything Roxy had said as he walked toward the other end of the ship. It seemed like every generation on the Earth had a different idea of God, and every generation their own idea of a devil. He had his own beliefs and would stick to them.

Men *could* be Gods, no need for a Heaven or Hell.

Maybe those left back in the Remnant Nation already thought of Minho as a devil for not returning. They'd surely think it when he joined the Godhead.

It didn't matter if they did.

He'd never go back to find out.

CHAPTER SEVENTEEN

Blind Luck

I

ISAAC

It had been over a day since they watched the *Maze Cutter* disappear beyond the horizon, but Isaac couldn't stop thinking about everyone on board. His only solace lay in the fact that he trusted Minho more than he'd ever trusted Kletter.

"Think they'll be okay?" Jackie asked quietly as they walked south along the coast.

"Yeah . . ." Isaac rubbed the grass-braided bracelet around his wrist that Sadina had made him. "They'll be okay." He wanted to fill the silence that Cowan and Old Man Frypan left open. Isaac didn't blame Frypan for not wanting to go to Alaska. To everyone else, the stories of old were just stories, but to Frypan they were memories. Painful, terrible, memories.

"They'll be something." The old man added, "Long as they don't come across any Grievers, they'll be fine."

Isaac couldn't tell if he was joking.

Cowan coughed. "They'll come back to join us soon. Once they reach the Godhead, we'll be their next stop."

"You think it'll happen that quickly?" Jackie quickened her step with this news.

Isaac wondered if Ms. Cowan was going to tell the others what she'd told him—that everyone from the island was a test subject, not just Sadina. Well, except for Isaac and the old man, who were last-minute additions. It made sense now why Cowan had hesitated to let them come on board. Surely Frypan didn't look at manipulation kindly. Not about test subjects, at least, with the infamous tattoo still visible on his neck.

"What do you think will happen when we get to the Villa?" Isaac directed his question to Cowan in an attempt to invite the whole truth to the rest of their group. He'd kept the secret of her infection and he didn't want to carry another one.

"We'll introduce ourselves and our lineage and we'll ask them for help," Cowan answered matter-of-factly, as if it would be that simple.

Frypan chimed in, "Nobody's going to help us if they don't see any help in it for themselves." The trees on the path started to look weak the farther they went, more and more bare. Something was eating their leaves. Or infecting their leaves.

"We don't have to go in the Villa, you and me," Jackie said, turning to Frypan. "We can just stay in the woods until they—"

"Nah, we'll go in. If there's something in my old blood that can help you recover Ms. Cowan, I'll help."

This brought an honest smile across Cowan's lips. "Thank you."

"It doesn't look like the Flare." He added, "A new variant, maybe, but it's not the Maze-forsaken-Flare, that's for sure."

Isaac's shoulders relaxed at hearing that. He had nothing to compare Cowan's symptoms to in his mind, but the rash looked *bad* and the woman's face had begun to droop, as if the sickness in her body pulled her down in every possible way.

"Anyone need a rest?" Isaac asked, looking back specifically at the adults. If his legs were tired, then Cowan's and Frypan's had to feel twice as worn.

"I'm good," Cowan said.

"A little farther," Old Man Frypan added.

"How is it that I'm ready for a break and you two aren't?" Jackie blew out a heavy sigh and laughed. "I'll walk all day if it means I'm not swaying on that stupid boat, but I don't think I'm in quite the shape as you two."

Frypan flexed a bicep. "Back home I walked four miles every morning. Up the coast and back around." *No wonder he had so much energy.*

"When we get back home, I'm doing that walk with you," Jackie said. "Every day."

"Me, too." Isaac smiled thinking of home. He wasn't sure they'd ever make it back to the island, but he was relieved to have the others. Even if something happened to Cowan, Isaac wouldn't be alone. Jackie might not have the stomach for a boat ride, but in Isaac's opinion, she was the strongest islander of the group, even stronger than Dominic. If they ran into Cranks again, he'd trust Jackie to kill them with her bare hands if needed.

"What *is* that . . ." Cowan pointed to a brown lump on the dirt path up ahead. Isaac squinted at the strange blob. He walked ahead to investigate and leaned over. It was a dead bird.

"Just a sparrow." Jackie joined him and bent over to touch the bird.

"Wait, don't touch it," Isaac said, "it might have a disease."

"I'm not touching the bird, there's a little someone I wanted to say hi to." She motioned to the tiny, wiggly, red and orange thing crawling on the dirt behind the bird. An amphibian. Cowan had started another coughing fit and took the opportunity to stop and rest. "Hi little guy, what's your name?"

Old Man Frypan took a look. "That there is a big ol' Salamander."

Cowan coughed and coughed to clear her throat. "This is silly, but maybe it's a sign . . ."

Isaac looked down at the dead bird and then back to Cowan. He didn't want her to think she'd soon be dead on her back, beak to the sky, too. "No. Everything will be okay."

"Exactly. It's a *good* sign." She managed a smile, but her forehead creased like a frown. Isaac had no idea what she was talking about.

"We have these old books in congress, written accounts by the immunes, sharing their knowledge and memories. And in one of those books, someone called a Salamander a Newt. Said not to eat them."

"I'd starve before I ate this cute thing." Jackie pet the creature on the top of its head with the pad of her finger.

"Little Newt," Isaac said, and it earned him an honest smile from Old Man Frypan.

"That's a fine name for anyone," he added.

"Hear that?" Jackie asked the tiny salamander. "You're a newt, Little Newt." She stood up and placed the new pet on her shoulder.

Their group had just added another member, one that made each one of them smile. Maybe the little guy even had a bit of luck in him. Isaac wasn't superstitious, but he'd welcome any good fortune they could get, especially since the brown sparrow was the second dead bird they'd found in as many days.

2

Their days had found a routine, and that helped Isaac's mind from going completely bonkers—or *wonky bonky* as Trish would say if she were here. Cowan's rash was getting wider and its red rawness peeked out from behind her scarf. Their plan was to retrace their steps to the house where Isaac and Sadina had been kidnapped, where Kletter was killed, and then to follow the streets and houses up the hillside until they saw people.

"Kletter never told anyone what the Villa looked like, did she?" Isaac asked.

"No, that woman had way too many secrets," Jackie said bitterly.

Isaac looked over at Cowan for her answer, but as a woman with too many secrets herself, he knew she wouldn't say anything. "Ms. Cowan?" he prompted her. "Did Kletter say anything to you about the Villa? Before we got on the ship, maybe at your meeting?"

Cowan blinked more slowly than usual, like her body and muscles were exhausting their strength to keep her legs walking. "I don't know

. . . I don't think so." Isaac wasn't convinced. If Kletter had told her about needing control subjects and more people than Sadina from the island, then he was sure Kletter had revealed something else. Things that Cowan either didn't remember or chose not to share.

Jackie picked up another wiggly insect. "I think he likes worms the best."

Isaac watched Little Newt slurp up the even smaller creature. "He definitely is not a vegetarian."

Jackie rubbed her mouth, "Ew, plhhhpt!"

"What happened?" He stopped as she spit something out and scraped at her tongue.

"A bug just flew right in my mouth. Gross."

Frypan looked concerned. "Did it sting you?"

"No," Jackie said, still scraping.

"Here." Isaac handed over his canteen. "Wasn't a murder hornet, was it?"

"Probably, with my luck." She spit again then took a sip of water.

Frypan stole away their attention. "Hey, look. I remember that up ahead, that building." He pointed, and it only took a second for Isaac to recognize it, too. It was the first building they'd seen upon arriving from the island. A true skyscraper, surrounded by many others. Only a short journey now to the house where Letti and Timon had slit Kletter's throat.

Thinking about that put Isaac on edge. He couldn't let his guard down, and as they walked on, toward the same place where everything had gone wrong before, he reached for the knife Minho had given him.

This time around, if someone taunted them from a creepy house, Isaac would be ready.

3
XIMENA

Gastar saliva.

A waste of saliva and a waste of breath, as her Abuela would say. There was no use in telling Carlos what she felt to be true about her mom and his wife. Dead. His poor, young, beautiful wife who he'd hoped to have children with someday. Carlos' measure of hope would always outweigh anything else in his mind, and their trip was already depressing enough. Eating snakes, sleeping in the desert, moving camp every morning. The heat. The unbearable heat.

"Do you want the snakeskin to make something?" Carlos asked as he packed up their cooking tools. Ximena declined with a quick shake of her head. There would be plenty more snakes on their path if she wanted to fashion something. "What's the matter? You've been quiet."

"Nada. Nothing's wrong."

Up until the clear feeling she'd had about her mom being dead, Ximena had spent every single day in the desert looking at the horizon, hoping she'd see her mom and Mariana walking toward them. Then they'd walk faster, then maybe they'd run. But she should have known that it wasn't hope which brought them out here. It was her intuition that something was wrong. *Manera de ver,* as her Abuela would say. Her way of seeing.

"You having a vision and not telling me?" Carlos asked as he flicked the snakeskin aside.

She shook her head and kicked a rock, then started walking north again on the worn path. "No." It wasn't a lie. She had a *feeling*, not a vision. They were two very different things.

Carlos nodded as he joined her. They had a map to the Villa if needed, but so far, the path was clear enough.

Many people back home in the village had intuition in various forms. Carlos might, too, if he wasn't so clouded by hope.

Hope. It had a way of blanketing all things as some big, glorious lie until they morphed into what a person wanted them to be. Seers, on the other hand, embraced the pain of truth, and saw things how they *weren't*.

Ximena looked over at Carlos as they walked. He was a strong enough man to protect her from almost anything that came along—anything but the truth.

"There's something bothering you," he said when he noticed her gaze. "You're never this quiet in the morning." He was right; typically, she thought out loud.

Ximena softened. "Just thinking about what will happen when we get there, is all."

Carlos stopped. "Don't be all mad at Annie when we see her. She can't help it that these missions go on longer than expected."

"She *can* help it. She's the lead on the team. She's literally the only one who can help it." Carlos picked up his feet again, but she wasn't letting him leave this behind. Her mom and Mariana were two months past the latest point in time when the group had assured they'd be back. But Absent-Minded-Annie always conveniently forgot the promises she made to those back home, like when their mothers, daughters, and wives would return. Ever since Ximena was little, her Abuela had taught her how to trust herself and why she *shouldn't* trust 'Annie from the Villa.'

Despite this, Ximena never actually thought Annie would get her mom or Mariana killed. So why was she feeling that way now? *Ellas estan muertas,* her gut whispered, as her mind searched for any feelings that came with names from home who'd left at the same time as her mom. *Fransico, Manual, Ana* . . . she concentrated on each name as she and Carlos walked but no imprint came to her. *Dónde estás?* But she got nothing. Not even colors of their auras came through.

There had never been a time in Ximena's childhood when she'd been separated from her mom where she couldn't at least *feel* her, out there, wherever she was. Ximena didn't know how to explain it to anyone else, but she couldn't feel her mother anymore.

If something was killing the rabbits, something could be killing people. Half-Cranks. Or healthy humans who weren't Cranks but might as well be. Humans evil enough to annihilate her whole village.

Or, there could be another virus.

One that her homeland couldn't withstand.

A virus that started with dead black jackrabbits in the desert.

"Annie isn't—" Carlos gave a big sigh. "She's not to blame for everything." He looked back at Ximena to make sure'd she heard the last part.

She had, but she didn't believe it. It was painfully obvious that Annie had been responsible for every last thing that went wrong in their village in the last twenty-five years, and Ximena had only been alive for sixteen of those. If Carlos wanted to ignore it, she would let him continue to ignore it.

"You're so much like your mom right now."

"What? Why?" Ximena hated that it had been so long since her mom agreed to work off-site for the Villa that she was already starting to forget things about her.

"She always thought she was smarter than everybody else." Carlos shook his head as if being intelligent in a world full of half-Cranks was a bad thing. So what if her brain was more . . . *human* than most humans. Better that than the brain of an animal. A monster. Or a liar like Annie.

Ximena itched at her neck. The mosquitoes were terrible in the desert. "Sorry." She didn't know what else to say. It wasn't that she *thought* she was smarter than others, she simply just *was*. She almost always knew things before they came to fruition, especially when it came to her family and their village.

A storm that came unexpectedly, out of season, and wrecked the roof of the south station.

A sick elder on the west end who went blind from eating berries.

And the most important one of all: her mom foresaw an "Eagle" coming to the land and bringing with it truth and awareness. An eagle moved itself into their village two years ago, perched on the highest of trees. No one else understood its importance as deeply as Ximena's mom. Ximena was still trying to figure out what the prophecy meant, but the big beautiful bald eagle hunted in the field across from her house every day and watched over her village every night.

Ximena's mom sewed the design of an eagle into everything she laid hands on.

And she made her daughter promise that she would do her best to sew truth into the world for the rest of her days.

4
MINHO

Orphans certainly weren't Gods, but Orphans were no devils, either.

Minho struggled to give himself a place within Roxy's grandfather's story but it was difficult to do because he didn't know his creator—he'd never met his parents.

"You fix that steering issue?" Roxy asked, motioning to the wheel.

"Maybe," Minho said. He'd tinkered below for an hour or so without knowing exactly what connected to what, but something might have worked. He let go of the wheel to see which direction it favored, and the ship slowly started to veer left again. "Nope."

"That's okay. You've been blessed by the Gods." She pointed to the sunset.

"What're you talking about?"

"They used to say *pink sky at night is a sailor's delight.*" She laughed. "Are you getting tired of all these stories of Grandpa's yet?"

Minho smiled, something still relatively new to him. He liked that she called him *Grandpa* and not *my grandpa.* "Never." He kinda liked hearing someone's family history even if it wasn't his own. And he especially liked knowing that more than just pain, torture, and disease could be passed down from generation to generation.

"Well you've had just about the best sailing weather possible and this sky promises you another good day tomorrow." Roxy put her arm around his shoulders. "Want me to take over?"

"Not a chance."

"You're finally getting me back for not letting you drive the truck?"

"I'm getting you back, and I'm getting us there safely." She wasn't wrong; he did like being in control. Roxy nodded and handed him some water. He let her hold the captain's wheel while he took a sip. Maybe he shouldn't ask the next question, but he couldn't help himself. Something about seeing the boat make wave after wave, ripple after ripple, made him realize that every action had a reaction. He needed to know. "How did Grandpa die?"

Roxy's face wrinkled up, like a berry that hung on the vine too long. "You soldiers get a little morbid, don't you?"

"No, I mean . . ." He paused, tried to ask what he really needed to know most. "Did he die at home, warm in bed?" The Orphan set the water down. "Or did he go for one of his travels one day and just never come back?"

Roxy didn't respond for a moment.

"I need to know," he said with a shrug. "Just like you needed to know about your mom. I just do."

Roxy let go of the captain's wheel. "Are you worried you killed him? All the way out in that Remnant Nation of yours?" She shook her head as if it were impossible, but she didn't know just how many men the Orphan had killed.

He swallowed hard. "We've shot lots of trespassers." He hung his head, couldn't bear the thought of it.

"Grandpa died long before you were even born." She put her hand on Minho's shoulder, but it didn't make him feel any better. Someone in the Remnant Nation still could have killed him.

"At home?" Minho asked.

Roxy shook her head slowly. "He died while traveling." Minho knew it. He took the controls back over and she stepped aside. "But his life wasn't just his. His life was also in each and every one of those books he read. He lived hundreds of lives, and he died hundreds of deaths every time one of those stories ended." She took a deep breath. "He lived a long, good life."

Minho couldn't let it go. "But it's possible he wandered near the fortress . . ."

She finally gave in. "I guess anything's possible." He stared at the ocean ahead. The vast, empty, ocean. The water went on so far that not even something as big as the Remnant Nation could control it. "Minho?"

The Orphan looked at her.

"Why's this bothering you so much?"

He wasn't sure exactly. Something about being on the other side of the wall made life feel different. Waves. Ripples. The more days he spent training himself not to kill people, the more he started to regret the times he did. "Anyone who touched our borders. . . . We were instructed to not let them say more than three words before shooting." He'd always broken that rule. He'd let them say a sentence or two, because every man deserved to speak before they died.

"Why only three words?"

"Just a rule. Lots of rules." Minho looked over his shoulder to make sure Orange wasn't on deck to hear. "I'd always let them say more, though." Trespassers would either insist they weren't infected or they'd beg for the Nation's help for someone who *was* infected. Someone they loved. "Everyone. . . . They all had a story to tell."

Roxy sighed. "At least you were different enough to recognize such a thing."

Minho wanted a change of subject. Anything to stop Roxy from picturing him killing trespassers. "What about the books? Your grandpa's books?" he asked awkwardly.

"Oh, I still have them. Well, *had* them. Most of them are back at the house where you found me."

The Orphan remembered seeing lots of books on shelves when she welcomed him in for a meal. Somehow, thinking of Roxy leaving all of her grandfather's stories behind felt like more of a death than all of the intruders he'd killed put together. "You left all his books behind to come with me?"

"Of course!" Roxy said. "Those stories will be there. I know most of them by heart, anyway. But in this story . . ." She hugged Minho tighter than anyone had ever put their arms around him before. She hugged him like Minho had seen Dominic hug Jackie before they left her behind. His reflexes tightened. He fought the urge to twist her wrist and flip her to the ground. "In this story, it's a true adventure. And in this adventure, I get to have a son."

The Orphan named Minho would never get tired of hearing her say that.

And instead of flipping her and breaking her arm, like every instinct within him screamed to do, he did the exact opposite.

The Orphan hugged her back.

CHAPTER EIGHTEEN

Losing Grip

I
MIKHAIL

F lying the Berg back to Alaska was more difficult than he'd imagined. The stab wound near his kidney had stopped bleeding but the wound in his mind only grew. Gaps of time were missing. Memories. Lost. Second-guessing everything. *Madness,* as Alexandra would say.

Complete Crank-filled Madness.

The shock was wearing off.

He swerved the Berg and took another swig of the canteen he'd filled with turmeric water. He choked down the pain-killing and bacteria-stopping concoction. It tasted like armpits, as bitter and pungent as the rust-colored spice looked. A warmth within his mouth and throat made him cough, but Nicholas had taught him long ago that the spice aided in calming inflammation. *Always keep a jar of turmeric on hand, Dear Mikhail,* Nicholas would say.

Mikhail could not remember if the spice was meant to be used on open wounds or just internally, so he did both. Maybe it was neither. Who the hell knew? Not Mikhail. He guided the Berg back to the edge of the mountains outside of New Petersburg. As long as he kept the wound from getting infected, he'd live despite the loss of blood. *If* he could remember his landing path. *Where was his landing path?* He needed to get to his very own safe haven. The cabin in the woods that no one, not even and especially Alexandra, knew about. The one he'd built high enough above sea level to watch the war unfold.

He took a deep breath, tried to think hard, but he had so many questions still. What did Nicholas mean when he'd said that trauma could affect his brain? His personality? *SQUUUEEEE . . . SQUU-UEEEE. . . .* The squeals of the pig echoed in Mikhail's mind.

But there was no pig on board.

Madness.

SQUUUEEEE

Mikhail was going crazy. Nicholas warned him that could happen. Infected trauma. *Inflicted?* Inflicted trauma. That was it.

The war would continue. The Remnant Nation had the coordinates and the time. As long as the Crank Army held itself together, literally and figuratively, the Evolution could still be stopped. He laughed to himself as he swerved the Berg back and forth. *SQUUUEEEE.* The pig in Mikhail's mind, his own wild boar of a soul screamed to be freed. The future of the world depended on Cranks. Cranks! Laughable. Complete Madness. He should have shot every single one of them deadie dead dead back in the bunker, but he couldn't. He didn't shoot them deadie dead dead because he'd have been killing himself. All he'd worked for. Gone. *The Gone.*

Where was he going, again? *The cabin.* He had to land and get to the cabin.

He steered the Berg like a proper captain and took another sip of turmeric water.

2
ALEXANDRA

The Goddess stirred her tea, staring deeply into the tea leaves as if they held some sort of answer, but there was nothing there that could calm her mind. Mannus had survived the boat ride. Of course he did. Those women at the Villa may have known more about creating the Cure than her, but Alexa knew more about living it.

She knew the Evolution was good.

It was already inside of her.

She recited the digits in her mind. She'd been able to keep the women at the Villa from destroying everything, but only temporarily.

"Goddess?" Flint opened the door without a knock. Maybe he'd knocked and she just hadn't heard it over her mind's buzzing. Regardless, the man made it far too easy for her to take out any small frustration on him.

"What is it, Flint?" She enunciated every word so he knew to be quick about it.

The man stood in the doorway, tapping the handle of the door. "The speech is set for Sunday. After Mass."

Alexandra watched him as he nervously tapped the door. "What is it? What else?"

"Nothing, Goddess Romanov." He paused. "Nothing that requires your attention right now." He backed from the doorway.

Alexandra pushed her tea away. "But you'll bother me with whatever's making you nervous later? What is it?"

Flint nodded and stepped one foot back in. "The Pilgrims are . . . they're just starting rumors about Nicholas' death." He sighed. "You know how the people get when they don't see activity."

Alexandra had given the people *activity* in the biggest way possible. She'd had Nicholas killed so that the Evolution could culminate. But they'd never thank her for that because they'd never know. Even if they knew, they would not understand. "What actions do you suggest?" She walked toward Flint in the doorway.

His hand shook. "I think sharing the details of the investigation into Nicholas' death would quiet their fears."

She tried hard to control her face to not roll her eyes. Before Nicholas' death, the Pilgrims had been afraid of the Northern Lights. There was no fear out of reach for their feeble minds. "You understand I've been grieving. The people will—" She was stopped by shouts outside, but more than that was Flint's expression—his reaction to the voice. Complete terror. His eyes grew wide and he held his breath. She knew the servant well enough to know that he didn't want her hearing whatever that woman was shouting.

She walked to the window and flung it open.

"It's nothing, Goddess, the Pilgrims will—"

"Shhh!" Alexandra waved him off. Below her on the street, a Pilgrim in a mustard-yellow cloak flailed her arms in madness. Alexandra squinted. This Pilgrim looked familiar. She was one of the women—without horns—who'd met with them when Alexandra revealed her plan to Mannus. One of the devout followers that she'd taken down to the Maze.

With whom she'd shared sacred ground.

With whom she'd shared the title of murderer.

The woman ran through the streets, screaming words that Alexandra did not quite understand because it was something that never should have been spoken aloud. Like the sacredness of the Maze, this was to stay a secret. But the woman below her window shouted of Nicholas' death and shouted of the murder. Alexandra went through the digits as her ears buzzed. Her vision went red.

"One of the Godhead murdered their own!" the Pilgrim yelled, her voice screeching and raw.

Alexandra turned to Flint as calmly as she could after softly closing her window. "It's a shame when they reach for rumors like this." She shook her head as if the Pilgrim were nothing more than a sad case of madness. "Take that woman off the streets for her own good." She walked back over to her tea, surely cold by now. "I'd hate to see anything happen to her."

3
SADINA

Despite leaving her mom, her best friend, and her favorite late night fire companion behind, Sadina didn't feel alone. Trish made up for their absence. She'd try to get Sadina to hydrate and eat more—like a mother. She'd let Sadina poke fun at her—like a best friend, and she tried to listen and offer wisdom like only Old Man Frypan could. Still, it wasn't the same. It would never be the same again. And despite all of Trish's best efforts, Sadina needed time with her thoughts to process everything that had just happened. She needed time alone.

She walked up to the ship's deck and sat against the trunk that held the anchor. Minho nodded to her from the captain's wheel and she waved back. Sadina wanted to feel okay, and to be okay for Trish, but it wouldn't happen overnight.

She pulled out *The Book of Newt* and ran her hand over the wear marks from the journal living in Frypan's pocket for who knew how many years. She didn't know why, but she sniffed it, half-expecting the stench of sweat and armpits, but it smelled like leather and his famous stew. That made Sadina miss him even more.

She flipped through the book and let her finger land on a single passage.

I feel the peace of a certain knowledge. I have had friends, and
they have had me.
And that is the thing.
That is the only thing.

She shut the book to keep from crying. She would read the entire *Book of Newt*, because she'd promised Old Man Frypan, but she wouldn't read it today. The loss of Lacey and Carson still stung, and never knowing if she'd see Isaac again, or her mom, or Frypan. All of these things sent Newt's words even deeper into her heart.

"Hey, you okay?" Trish walked across the deck with a frantic look on her face.

"Hey. Yeah." Sadina took a deep breath. She knew she needed to talk to Trish about how she felt, *she needed to*. But she was so emotionally exhausted that it seemed an impossible task. At the same time, she knew nothing would change unless she communicated her feelings. "Can I talk to you for a minute?"

Trish's eyes moved back and forth, quicker than Dominic playing ping-pong with himself across the makeshift net he'd made below deck. *Nervous.* "I don't like the sound of that."

"Trish. Just sit." She motioned next to her and Trish plopped down. "Listen . . ."

"Nothing good happens when you say *Listen* to someone . . ."

"Listen," Sadina repeated firmly. She needed Trish to get past her own insecurities to really hear what Sadina was about to tell her. Trish nervously cracked her knuckles and Sadina reached for her hands. "When you're nervous, you need *this*." Sadina bounced Trish's hand in her own. "You need touch, and reassurance, and words of affirmation." She paused to think of how best to explain the next part. "But when I'm nervous, or scared, or I don't know how I feel . . ." She let go of Trish's hand to point to herself. "I don't need that. In fact, when you do what makes *you* feel better to me—it can feel uncomfortable sometimes and . . ."

She took a deep breath when Trish's eyes started to tear up. "Look, I know you went through hell when Isaac and I got kidnapped. I know it was harder than hard and it was for me, too. I thought about you every single second. And when I came back you were just so relieved, but you haven't let me out of your sight for more than five minutes, and I need—"

"I know. I'm sorry, I just—I fell asleep and then Dominic shouted something and I got startled and you weren't there and—"

"It's not just today, or right now. I need you to know that when I'm going through something, the kind of support I need is space. Even though I love you more than anything in this universe. But we're all on top of each other down there and I don't always need to be—"

"So you're saying you want . . . space . . ." Her voice lowered.

"I'm saying that what comforts *you*, can be overwhelming to *me*. Touch comforts you, while it can feel suffocating at times to me." Sadina was trying so hard to be slow and gentle with her words, but no matter how it was said, the word *suffocating* had just come out of her mouth. Formed itself into a weapon and stabbed Trish in the gut.

"You're suffocated . . . ?" Trish stood up and walked to the railing of the ship. *Shit*, Sadina thought.

"Trish, let me finish." She caught up to her.

"No. I don't want to *suffocate* you. I'll just stand over here and cry by myself since my girlfriend needs space."

"I'm not breaking up with you."

"Sadina, that's exactly what *I need space* means!" Trish gave her a cutting look.

"I know, but it's not what I mean." She took another deep breath. "I want you to know how I feel in case anything happens. Anything could happen to us in Alaska, and if they need me to go into some weird place without you, I need to know that you're okay and not going to lose your shit because I'm not there. And if something *bad* happens . . . like losing my mom . . ." Sadina swallowed hard and tried to tame the tears that appeared like dew at the thought of her mom. "What will comfort me more than anything else in bad times is just helping me create space. I need more alone time than you. I need time to . . . reflect and gather, and sometimes being touched makes me feel even more scattered and overwhelmed and anxious. It's not that I don't like your touch because I most certainly love it, but when things are going on all at once that I need to process–it's too much for me. It's overstimulating. Does that make sense?"

"Overstimulating?" Trish repeated. "I guess?"

"Yeah. Like . . . when you reach for my hand, or touch my arm when I have too much going on in my head, it doesn't feel like a normal touch . . ." She tried her best to explain by taking Trish's hand in hers and tapping all of her fingers across Trish's skin. "It feels all zippy-zappy." She stopped the tapping and squeezed with love. "Even though you don't mean it to. And even though I don't want it to."

Hell, Sadina was still trying to understand all these feelings, herself. She'd never been more stressed than the night of the amphitheater back home and every day since had just kept compounding onto the day before it.

Trish chewed her lip.

"But," Sadina added excitedly, "it's not all the time. Not even close. Just lately when there's been so much craziness. When we're relaxed, swimming by the cliffs or taking a walk, it's not like that. Stress and anxiety just make it—"

"All wonky bonky."

"Totally wonky bonky." Sadina smiled and that made Trish smile.

Trish slowly nodded. "I get it. I really do. And please don't ever say zippy-zappy again. Only I'm allowed to make up stupid words."

"Now that's a deal." Sadina reached deep into her pocket to what she had made back on the coast. "Thanks for listening and understanding. I know I'm weird."

"You are." Trish kissed her on the forehead. "But you're my favorite kind of weird."

Sadina smiled. "Here." She handed her the gift. "I made this for you before we left on the boat. Again." She watched anxiously as Trish slowly opened the small palm leaf–wrapped gift that Isaac helped Sadina forge. Trish lifted the necklace in front of her, wire wrapped in metal, soldered, a chunk of wood dangling from the chain. "It's a piece of driftwood I found when Isaac and I were kidnapped that I kept. I don't know why. I guess it was something I could carry to comfort me when we didn't have anything. It was something that I could say, *this is mine.*"

"It's . . . beautiful." Trish examined every intricate part of the necklace with her fingers. "Thank you . . ."

"Just like this piece of driftwood was something that I could hold on to and say was mine, when I had nothing—I want you to know that our love is *yours.* You have it. And just like the driftwood floating itself back to the shore from wreckage, I promise to always find my way back to you. No matter what." Sadina reached over to help Trish fasten the necklace. "The same storms that might pull us apart will also pull us closer together. Okay?" She looked at the necklace on Trish then hugged her, hard.

"Man, that's cheesy as hell and I loved every word. And this." Trish fingered the chunk of wood dangling from her neck. "So sometimes you need space, and I'll give you space. Sometimes you need *not* to be touched so your nervous system doesn't go wonky bonky. And sometimes you make me freak out that we're breaking up but then give me the most romantic thing ever. Thanks for talking." She hugged Sadina again and whispered, "I love you."

"I love you, too." They kissed, and Sadina squeezed Trish even tighter, and the cheese-fest might have lasted forever if Dominic didn't race up to the deck shouting like the cabin was on fire.

"You'll never believe what I found!" He ran over to them, flapping his arms with a book in his hand.

"What's that?" Trish asked, finally breaking up the hug.

"The captain's log!" He was shouting every word and went looking for Minho. "I found Kletter's captain's log!"

4

MINHO

Chaos. Commotion.

The yelling from Dominic and everyone suddenly flanking the captain's area caused the Orphan to tense up. He turned from the captain's wheel and visually identified each crew member: Sadina, Trish, Dominic, Miyoko. Everyone but Roxy and Orange who were untangling a mess of ropes. No one had fallen off the boat, at least.

If Dominic had truly found a captain's log, it might help him figure out the problem with the ship's steering. "Here, let me see." He reached for the small book in Dominic's hands.

"Good luck reading it."

"What, she had terrible handwriting?" Trish asked.

"No, it's written in some kind of secret code," he replied.

Miyoko punched him in the bicep for some odd reason. "You let Happy look at it before me?"

"Huh?" The Orphan asked, but no one answered. *Happy?* "Where'd you find this?"

Miyoko actually answered. "Behind the wood panel of the steps. Dominic slipped and crash-landed." That made sense. Minho had heard a thud a few minutes earlier and figured they were just horsing around. Miyoko continued, "When we looked to make sure the steps were okay—"

"I'm fine by the way, thanks for asking," Dominic added. Miyoko ignored him. "There was this little book squeezed in between the paneling."

Minho flipped through the pages and saw the English alphabet, but all mixed up, nothing he could read. He recognized a word here and there, but wasn't sure. *Colección, científico observación, extraordinario, reacción, exploración,* and then one word in particular that would be clear to anyone on the planet: *infección.* "It's not a code. I think it's Spanish."

"Spanish?" Dominic repeated, as if he'd never heard the word.

"Yeah, Spanish. You know, another language? Let me see if Roxy can read this. Somebody watch the wheel for a minute."

Sadina stepped in and took over. Minho started to walk away but then turned back to Dominic. "Don't spin it."

"How did you know I wanted to spin it?"

Minho glanced at Sadina, "Don't let him spin it."

5

On the south side of the boat's deck, Minho found Roxy and Orange sitting amongst a jungle of knots. Different colors and thicknesses of ropes draped over them, a mess of white nylon, yellow cord, orange twine, and blue anchor rope all tangled together. Fishing lines wrapped around thicker sailing ropes and Orange used her knife where needed. They were so mesmerized by the task at hand that they didn't even look up when Minho approached. "That Kletter lady who sailed before us, she left a notebook behind," he said.

"What'd the note say?" Orange asked, still not looking up from her knots.

"Not a note, a notebook. A captain's log, but it's in Spanish." He bent down to their level. "Can you read Spanish, Roxy?"

"A little, yeah."

Judging from the upkeep of the boat and its poor condition, the Orphan wasn't sure how helpful any advice from the last captain might be. Still, he was curious. "Can you take a break and see if any words stick out to you?" He handed Roxy the book.

She looked back at him as if he was a knotted mess himself before she flipped through the pages of Kletter's notes. "I don't know. I mostly learned Spanish from posted warning signs."

"Here." Minho found a page with some of the words he'd recognized. Words about experiments and expeditions. "Even I recognize some of it." He pointed. "The word infection is repeated on almost every page. *Infección.*"

That finally perked Orange up. "She documented the Flare?"

"I don't know. Something."

"Let me see." Orange dumped the pile of rope from her lap and leaned over. Roxy pulled it closer to her face and then farther away. "I know this word. Sure as canned beets will stain you, I know this word." She tapped the handwritten text. "Caducado."

It wasn't anything the Orphan had heard before. "What's it mean?"

She handed the book back to Minho. "It's on every canned good I've ever seen. Tells you when the food will go bad, expire."

Expire. That didn't sound good. "Could it also mean something else?"

Orange shrugged.

Roxy sighed. "Well, let's see . . ." She looked to the sky. "A time limit, a length of time until something will go bad, oh, and—" She stopped talking.

"What?" Minho asked. Roxy didn't say anything, just made that same disapproving expression she pulled whenever Minho talked about the Remnant Nation. Her eyes got a little bigger and her mouth a little tighter. "What else does it mean?"

"Well, sometimes . . . in our language at least, people might use the word *expire* when they talk about a person dying."

Dying. Now that made sense. Not just from the Orphan's past and all the death he had seen and delivered, but from Isaac's stories of Kletter arriving on the island. "Those people on Kletter's crew, who Isaac said were shot in the head when the boat first arrived. . . . Maybe she wrote about them." He carefully examined the text around the word 'Caducado' until his eyes locked on to *infección* again. "What if they were infected?"

"Why would she have brought infected people to the island?" Orange asked.

Minho agreed it didn't make much sense. They must've caught the disease en route.

No captain would kill their entire crew for the fun of it.

"Maybe that's why she murdered them. They got infected on the journey and she had to shoot them." Minho thought about how many times words like *reaction* and *infection* showed up in Kletter's notes. "Or maybe . . ."

That was it.

It had to be it.

He looked behind him to make sure Dominic, Sadina, Miyoko, and Trish were still at the captain's wheel. "Maybe the islanders have something to do with it." Sadina's blood. Cowan's rash. "Maybe they're not immune after all?"

CHAPTER NINETEEN

Haunted Houses

I

ISAAC

There it was. The house where everything changed and their adventure became an escape mission, then a survival mission, then a rescue mission. There was something about the house even before it all went bad that creeped Isaac out. The windows broken and dusty, the paint peeling, the burnt siding from some long-ago fire. Once he walked past this awful place where he and Sadina had been taken, where Kletter had been viciously murdered, he hoped they could all reset their future and forget Letti and Timon had ever mentioned evolution and extinction.

Isaac wondered about Letti and Timon, if maybe they hadn't been half-Crank when he met them. Then he wondered if Kletter's body was still decaying somewhere. He picked up his pace and decided it best not to find out. He twisted the grass-braided bracelet around his wrist. Every day that passed, the bracelet got drier and drier. He hoped

Sadina and the rest of the crew were doing okay. "You think they're getting close to Alaska?" he asked the group.

"Closer every day," Old Man Frypan replied.

"What do you think, Ms. Cowan? Think Minho threw Dominic overboard yet?" He liked the challenge of trying to make Cowan laugh.

"No, I'm sure Dominic is on his best behavior, but Sadina," Cowan coughed, "now she can be stubborn. I hope she and Minho don't have any differences."

Isaac hadn't even worried about that. Cowan was right, they were two strong personalities, but he'd count on Trish and Miyoko to keep them in line. He knew the islanders would stick together. "It may be hot out here, but at least we're not seasick." Isaac waited for Jackie to chime in, but she didn't. She'd been awfully quiet the last mile or so. He turned to her. "Right, Jackie?"

Her walk slowed.

"Ithaac . . ."

"Jackie?" He stopped, tried to catch her eyes, but her distant gaze was unfocused. She looked right through him. "What's wrong, Jackie?" Isaac knew she was prone to nausea, but the path had been smooth and straight. "Do you need to throw up?"

"If you gotta blow chunks, blow them over there." Old Man Frypan pointed to a bush of clover weed. But Jackie wouldn't make it that far. Her knees buckled, then her legs folded beneath her like an island hammock cut by a storm. Isaac rushed to her side and caught her weight in his arms, lowering her to the road. Newt fell from her shoulder and scampered off into the weeds.

She reached for Cowan. "Myth Cowan."

Cowan took Jackie's hand.

"What's going on?" Cowan asked. Jackie felt heavy, almost lifeless in Isaac's arms.

"I can't feel my lipth, or my thongue, or my legth."

Jackie's voice was slow and slurred. Isaac looked at her and then back toward the *house*, as if it held some kind of curse. It was probably haunted by Kletter's spirit.

"What's happening?!" Isaac looked to Old Man Frypan, their most trusted source of wisdom, but his face didn't hint at any answers. Isaac frantically searched her skin for a rash. Nothing. No sting marks. No rash.

"We've got some bad luck going on around here," Frypan said.

Isaac, in a panic, looked up at Cowan. "I don't get it, no rash, you're still standing but she's not?" He could feel the warmth radiating from Jackie's skin. Whatever this was, they had to get to the Villa even more quickly.

"Ithaac . . ."

"It's okay. We're going to get you help. The Villa can't be that far. I'm gonna carry you, okay?" With one big lift Isaac hoisted Jackie into his arms. "You're okay." He tried to reassure her with a forced smile but she wasn't looking back at him.

She was looking right *through* him.

"Ithaac," she slurred, "I can't thee."

2

Isaac walked as fast as he could through the endless neighborhood, Jackie in his arms. His biceps burned, tendrils of flames leaking through his muscles, but he wouldn't stop to rest until they found someone, anyone, who could help. He'd run if he knew where they were headed, but the uncertainty only aided to the panic in his chest.

"The houses are getting bigger up here, we have to be close," Frypan offered. They reached a mansion rimmed with circular columns in the front. Something moved.

"There!" Cowan pointed at a person near the front door, but Isaac knew it could just be a wandering Crank. The knife Minho had given him was strapped to his boot, but his best Crank killer lay limp in his arms.

"Please, help!" Cowan shouted; the figure ahead stopped and turned. As they walked closer, Isaac, sweating profusely, breathing with labored heaves of hot air, could see a woman with blonde hair.

Despite his weak condition, he started to run, Jackie bouncing in his arms.

"Stop! Don't come any closer!" The stranger's voice trembled and cracked, as if she weren't used to talking so loudly, or talking to other people.

"Please, we just need help." Isaac slowed down, but he didn't stop.

"We're scientists, not doctors. We're not resetting bones and we sure as hell aren't a Crank Palace. If she's got the Flare, you take her there. Hear me?" The woman turned her back on them and opened the door to what Isaac hoped was the Villa.

"Is this the Villa?" he asked in desperation. "Kletter told us about you."

The woman stilled. Then slowly turned back around. "Kletter? Is she with you?"

"She's not that far behind us." *Just a bit dead, but you don't need to know that*, he thought. Isaac made eye contact with Cowan and Old Man Frypan, hoping they understood.

The woman looked each of them up and down and eyed Frypan as if she had never seen anyone so old. And maybe living out here among the half-Cranks, she hadn't. What did Kletter mean to these people to change the stranger's mind so quickly? "What's wrong with the girl?" she asked.

Isaac answered, wearily, almost to the absolute end of his strength. "We don't know, she just started to slur her words, then lost feeling in her legs, and then sight. I think it was in that order. I don't know. It all happened so fast."

The woman released a heavy sigh. "Okay, we'll bring her in. But you all need to stay *out here* until I get clearance. We can't compromise our lab."

"We don't have the Flare," Frypan said.

"It's not the Flare I'm worried about. It's Evolution. Come on. Lay her down right here, in the doorway. In the next thirty minutes we'll know if she'll make it."

Evolution? Isaac wondered. What was that supposed to mean?

"Wait," Cowan spoke up, "I need help, too." She pulled down her scarf and revealed the rash. The woman started shaking her head back and forth so vigorously Isaac thought it might pop off.

She shouted at them, "Let me see all of your necks. Now!" She pointed vigorously at Isaac, then Frypan.

"It's only the ladies who are sick," Frypan said as he lifted his chin and turned in a circle, as did Isaac, Jackie still in his arms. The woman walked completely around Frypan to look at his neck again.

"You're . . . tattooed . . ." She said it in a tone that was somewhere between worship and fear. Probably in disbelief that he could actually be a Glader of Old.

It was Frypan's turn to sigh. "Yes. I'm a subject from the original Maze trials." Isaac had never heard him say it out loud like that, but perhaps the scientist would appreciate it being put so formally. *More like a hero*, Isaac wanted to add. *A survivor. A legend.*

The woman again appeared conflicted. Honored one moment, horrified the next.

Isaac couldn't hold Jackie another second. "Can you help us or not?" he asked.

The woman slowly nodded, obviously still stunned. "Come in. All of you. We'll take the cellar entrance."

She led them down a gravel path that wrapped behind the building, finally to a door in the rear that was painted black, like the pupil of an eye.

3

XIMENA

"Getting close?" she asked Carlos. Abandoned houses lined both sides of the crumbled street.

"Yeah. Maybe twenty minutes."

"You keep saying that and then we walk another hour." Sweat drenched her shirt.

"If I keep saying that, then one of these times I'll be right." He smiled, always so genuine from him. "Give me a break, it's been two years since I walked this path."

A heaviness hung inside Ximena's chest. One she knew well and had learned not to cling to. Anxiety in and of itself was sometimes a premonition. She tried to focus on each of the passing houses and imagine what bright colors graced their walls when they were first built.

"Lookie, Ximena." Carlos picked something from the ground. A small bush of weeds. "Mariana loves these. Well, no, she actually hates them, but she'll laugh if I bring her some." He gave Ximena a single weed to investigate. "She grew these right after *you* were born."

"Me? Why?" She looked at the little pink flower on the end of the red clover, but she didn't understand Carlos' excitement and her face must have shown it.

"Because your mom said she'd been drinking red clover tea before she got pregnant with you. So, Mariana ripped out and collected every last clover in the village, no matter what color it was." Carlos chuckled. "Eventually she planted a whole garden's worth of *just* clovers." He continued gathering a bouquet of weeds for his wife.

Ximena nodded. The whole village did a lot of weird things after she was born. "What's clover tea taste like, anyway?"

"Terrible. Exactly like a weed should taste. But if she wasn't tending that garden or drying the clover, she was busy drinking the tea, day and night. Hot tea, iced tea, making tea cakes from it. She wants a child so badly. Doing something you hate for someone you love is, well, that's unconditional love."

"She would've been a great mom," Ximena agreed, before realizing she'd said it in the past tense. She hoped Carlos didn't notice.

"There's still time." He laughed. "I know to a teenager like you I must seem ancient, but we're not that old yet."

Ximena looked at the house behind the patch of red clover and wondered if the woman who'd lived there before the Flare ever needed to drink fertility tea. Her eyes focused on an unusual deterioration pattern on the house. Burnt siding.

"Do you see that?" she asked Carlos, but he was too busy trying to make weeds look like flowers. "The side of the house got burned. You think that's from a fire or an explosion?" She walked closer to the melted siding of the dusty haunt.

Carlos stopped picking. "I know you think people used to walk around throwing hand grenades every day. Probably not."

"I think they're a revolutionary weapon of defense and more people had them than you think." She was so focused on possible evidence of her favorite weapon from history that she didn't pay attention to the ground below the burnt siding.

Once she did look down—she couldn't look away.

"Carlos . . ." She had a hard time catching her next breath. The anxiety from before found its reason to spread. Her heart pounded all the way to her eardrums. "Carlos, quick!"

She didn't actually want him to look. He had a weak stomach, but she *needed* him to verify that she wasn't just imagining the clothed skeleton at her feet.

"Oh jeez, get away from it." He waved her closer to him, but she couldn't take her eyes off the bones. The knife sticking out of the pants pocket looked oddly familiar.

"Wait, Carlos?" She bent closer to the dead body and reached into its pocket to free the knife.

"Ximena you'll get a disease. Come on." Carlos said it as if he'd forgotten for a moment that she couldn't catch the Flare; no one in their village could. And no disease was as great as the Flare.

"This is from our village!" She held up the knife so that Carlos could see the embroidered outline of an eagle, with a circle around it, on the weapon's sheath. The same design that Ximena's mother sewed into everything. To symbolize truth. She traced the white and brown thread of the eagle's head, sewn directly into the leather. "My mom's design . . ."

Carlos stepped forward and Ximena gave him the knife to see for himself. He looked at it with dismay, as if its blade had just popped his entire balloon of hope. "Oh, shit." He suddenly looked like he was going to throw up.

"What?"

He took a deep breath and looked away from the body. "Does the left hand have a snake ring on the second finger?" He asked as if he already knew the answer was *yes*.

It took Ximena a few moments to distinguish what was and wasn't a part of the skeleton, but a shiny sterling silver ring reflected the sunlight. "A snake eating its own tail? What's that mean?"

Carlos avoided Ximena's eyes. ". . . A symbol for the eternal cycle of destruction and re-creation. Or some such mumbo jumbo."

"No, I—what's that mean as far as the person the ring belongs to? *This* former person. Who is it? Who *was* it?" Not anyone from Ximena's village, she knew that much.

"It's . . . Kletter." Carlos looked at her as if she was supposed to know who that was. Everyone who visited their village had three or four names. Birth names. Middle names. Surnames. Town names.

"Did they work for the Villa with mom?"

"It's *Annie* Kletter."

Ximena's shoulders tensed; all the air in her lungs whooshed out of her. "*This* is Annie?" She looked down in disbelief. Anger. Absent-minded Annie. Dead. Like a black jackrabbit in the desert, right here on the way to the Villa. Ximena would have rejoiced at the thought days ago but now it only made the anxiety in her chest grow to a monstrous size. "Mom and Mariana . . . they wouldn't have just left her here. They would have given her a village burial. Why . . . why didn't they?" She paced, gripping the knife in her hand.

Carlos didn't answer. He just held his bouquet of weeds.

Ximena let the anger surge through her body to block the tears from coming. Not that she would have cried for Annie's death, no. She was glad that woman was dead. *Ellas estan muertas.* But the tears she wouldn't let come were for her mom and Mariana. Something was wrong. They wouldn't have left someone they worked with for so many years behind. Her mom wouldn't have let the animals feed on Annie's dead flesh without any sign of ritual or prayer. "They wouldn't have just left her here!"

"Maybe they . . ."

"There's no reason. This close to the Villa?" She shook her head.

"Maybe that's why your mom and Mariana stayed behind for so many extra months. The lab needed extra hands." Carlos turned back to the road. "Come on. They're at the Villa. We'll find answers. Maybe Kletter left for a different trip and they have no idea she's . . . gone."

Ximena followed Carlos up the road.

Her feet pounded the cracked pavement. She wanted answers. Justice. She hoped Carlos was right. She hoped for . . . Hope. But the anxiety in her chest said that Hope was a Devil, luring her to a false reality until both the lie and the truth killed her.

A circular object in the road caught her attention. She bent down to pick up a grass-braided bracelet.

"What's that?" Carlos asked. "Is it fresh?"

"Yeah," she said as she wrapped the bracelet around the handle of Annie's knife. "Might be a clue. Someone had to kill Annie Kletter and I want to know who."

4
ISAAC

The woman at the Villa had never told them her name. Isaac wished he'd asked as he sat impatiently in the quarantine room with Old Man Frypan. They were there to be 'observed' but it had started to feel more like a prison than a safe place to wait. Frypan sat quietly against the back of the glass pod. Isaac wanted to believe that Jackie would be okay. He wanted to believe that he'd see Sadina again and reunite Sadina with her mom and that Frypan would live to be a hundred years old. But the truth was rarely better than what you wished for.

Isaac thought he couldn't have been more emotionally drained until he looked down and realized his grass bracelet had broken off somewhere. Must've been when he was carrying Jackie. He rubbed his bare wrist. That was it.

"Hey!" He knocked on the glass wall of his room and got another scientist's attention. He had counted five total people since they'd stepped into the building. All of them wore black clothes under white lab coats. Seemed almost like a cult. Did all scientists do that? He tapped the glass again, and a man at the back wall of the lab looked up at him. "Can you tell me what's going on?" Isaac shouted. Despite the guy looking right at him, he said nothing and returned to his work.

"They're not gonna level with you because they don't think you're on the *same level as them*." Frypan sighed.

"But she brought us *all* in because . . . we're unique. We're immune. Sadina and—"

The old man interrupted him. "Ever wonder if the truth ain't really the truth?"

Isaac paused. "What do you mean? You don't think we're immune?"

"Things change. Isn't that what evolution means?" He closed his eyes and settled further against the glass wall. "When a stew gets too salty, you don't throw it away. You've got to add a potato."

Isaac shook his head. "Seriously? What does *that* mean?" The mention of food made his stomach growl.

"You can add a peeled potato and it'll soak up the salt in the stew, but you gotta remember to take the potato out. And if you get clever and chop a potato up and *leave* it in, you can solve the problem that way too, but then you'll end up with potato soup rather than a stew."

Isaac truly loved this man and his lessons. "Are you talking about the Evolution? With a capital E?"

"I'm just saying that we're in a salty situation, here." He looked around the lab as if he were afraid the scientists wouldn't like what he was saying. "We came in to help Cowan and Jackie, but we gotta make sure these two potatoes," he pointed to himself and then to Isaac, "get the hell out of this pot as soon as we can." His eyes motioned to a glass pod way in the corner of the lab, which had a black curtain hanging on the outside. Black curtains like black uniforms. Everything in this place had a sense of mystery, cloaked.

"What's in there?" he asked, and Frypan pointed to the bottom corner of the glass pod. The curtain was flipped up just a bit, slightly revealing the contents of the room.

But Isaac couldn't really see anything.

"Just wait . . ." Old Man Frypan whispered and watched.

Isaac waited.

He didn't know what he was looking for, but nothing happened.

Until a flash of metal moved within the visible space. Something like Isaac had never seen before. Brighter than any metal he'd ever hammered on the forge. Sharp. Jagged.

"What is that thing?"

"That is something I never wanted to see again." The fear in Frypan's face highlighted every wrinkle and every age spot. "That, my friend, is a Griever."

Isaac turned back to the pod but the Griever's leg or arm, whatever it was, had moved on. He could only reach into his imagination for the stories Frypan and the elders told of the Glade and the Grievers coming after them, stinging the Gladers with a variation of the Flare. Nightmares come to life. *Could that really be a live Griever in there?* Seemed almost impossible, like a fairy tale. He turned to Frypan. "What's the longest you think two potatoes can simmer in a stew before they get mashed?"

He didn't hesitate. "Maybe a day at most."

5

MINHO

"Whether they're true immunes or not, this Kletter lady sounds a lot like the Grief Bearers. I don't trust any of it." Orange was sitting on the captain's bench and flipping through the captain's log. Minho had spent two nights looking at the book in detail but couldn't string enough words together to form an opinion, other than the same conclusion that Orange had just come to.

"You never trusted the Grief Bearers? Even before that crazy stunt on the Berg?" Minho focused on the waters ahead. It wasn't long ago that the Grief Bearers of Remnant Nation had sent him away so that he could become one of them, one of their peers, but he'd known before they shoved him off a cliff that he didn't want that. Not only did they torture children for the sake of rising up one day to kill the Godhead, but Minho didn't *want* to kill the Godhead—he wanted to join them and help the world evolve. But of course, he couldn't tell Orange that. Evolution—even the mention of the word—was blasphemy within the Orphan Army.

"Something about them never felt right." Orange handed over the captain's log and picked up her binoculars.

Minho relaxed behind the captain's wheel.

Unlike everyone else on the boat, Orange could watch for whales and other ships ahead without trying to fill the space between them with words. It was just like they were back on the wall guarding the Remnant Nation—except no one would die. Hopefully. Meanwhile, Minho could decompress in silence. He didn't have to work so hard to understand the dynamics of the group or to fight his soldier instincts. When it was just him and Orange, he could be himself—the Orphan named Minho.

He watched the horizon as he steered North-East. The sounds of the ocean grew on him, like the wet scraping the bottom of the ship made as it cut through the water. The whoosh of the wind over the deck. Even the way Dominic's cheerful voice carried up to the deck like an echo from the cabin below.

Minho would miss all of this when they got to Alaska.

Orange lowered her binoculars and turned to him with a confession. "Skinny and I never said anything out loud because we didn't want to get reinforced, but . . . once you left, we knew you wouldn't come back."

"Really?" The notion brought him peace, like an affirmation that he'd made the right decision. He wondered if the Grief Bearers had known, too. If that's why they'd fastened his cordage so tight. Why they'd pushed him so hard off the cliff. Why they came after him.

Orange nodded. "Yeah. We were jealous."

He'd never dreamed that anyone would even notice his absence, let alone be jealous of it.

"Have you thought about how you're going to do it?" she asked. "Kill the Godhead?"

"No." It wasn't a lie. He looked at her for a reaction, but she didn't have one. Maybe it was the number of days they'd spent on the open ocean, but Minho decided to test Orange. "What do you think Evolution is really about?" Her eyes got big with surprise. "Sorry, it's just something I think about sometimes . . ." He returned his attention to the ocean ahead of them.

"I don't know . . ." Orange wasn't accustomed to having permission to think on her own about the subject. But if she had time to think about Crank Armies, surely she would have thought about the Evolution and what it was or wasn't. "I guess it could be what we were told, or it could be something completely different. I only know one thing for sure. I'm never stepping foot back in that place."

"Me, neither." The walls of the Remnant Nation were ones he'd never see again. Ever. But as soon as he said it, he felt a pang in his gut. *Kit.*

"What's wrong?" Orange asked. "Your face just did a thing."

"Nothing. Just remembered something I left back there."

"Minho, no weapon, artifact, or internal organ is worth going back for."

"How about a person? A little boy named Kit." He couldn't believe he was telling this story to Orange but if anyone could understand how he felt, it would be her. "One night I was walking through the tunnels of Hell and heard something that sounded like a dying dog. I saved him, I think." Minho wasn't sure how long the boy would have lived after such a beating; maybe he should've just put the kid out of his misery. What the Remnant Nation called "reinforcement" was just another version of death, beating their will and subordination far below the surface. Saving Kit was the first time Minho went against the things he'd been taught.

Leaving the Remnant Nation and never going back was the second.

Orange seemed genuinely impressed. "Wow. Can't believe they didn't kill you on the spot for that."

"I don't think it was a Grief Bearer that hurt him. Whoever it was ran away."

Orange set her binoculars on the bench. "You should feel proud of that memory, not sad."

The Orphan shook his head. Pride had nothing to do with it. "When I asked the boy his name he said, *Kit*. But when he asked me back, I told him I didn't have one." Shame. In the same moment of his life where he'd shown the most courage, he also displayed the most cowardice.

He took a deep breath.

"You couldn't have, and he shouldn't have told you his name. That's probably why he was beaten, for giving himself a name. You know that." She crossed her arms at this and shook her head. Minho knew she'd understand. He needed to stop berating himself for it, but not telling Kit his name lingered as his one regret. "Gotta just try to forget about it. When I was a kid, I got reinforcement real bad like that."

"You did?" He looked her up and down for visible scars, but she was pretty spared.

He shook his head. "Not beat like this kid was."

"No?" Orange turned away from Minho and lifted up the bottom of her shirt. Across her lower back were three-inch-thick scar lines that looked like she'd been nearly cut in half. "I was ten. They heard me sing." She lowered her shirt and faced him again.

"Damn, Orange. You're tougher than I thought." That image would be impossible to get out of his mind. Slashes. *All for singing? But if Orange could survive that, then there was hope for Kit too.* Minho tried to move on. "Even so, as the captain of the ship, I give you permission to slap Dominic across the head anytime *he* starts singing again."

Orange smiled, leaned into the captain's wheel, and whispered, "He's awful, right? Like a seagull squawking over a dead fish."

Minho shook his head, his face pained. "I can't believe we've listened to him hum and holler this whole trip and you've been holding back on us. *You* should sing. Over him, with him, but preferably instead of him."

"Eh, maybe." She shrugged, not quite able to move on.

The Orphan understood. He once had a beating so hard he didn't talk for a month. Minho felt intrusive even thinking about it, but he had to ask her. He slowed down the ship. Orange deserved his full attention for this next question.

"What's your name?" His eyes focused on hers.

Orange tilted her head in confusion.

"Your name?"

She trembled slightly, as if a Priestess could slap her right now for even thinking about it, but the Remnant Nation had no hold over them now, out here in the middle of the ocean. They were free. She had to have a name.

"You know my name. It's Orange."

"Orange is a nickname, not a real name." He wanted to know what this girl, standing in front of him with scars from singing, called herself inside her own mind.

"Yeah, but nicknames are better than real names because only *friends* call you by your nickname." She nudged him. "Which means I have friends."

Minho took it in like the slow-moving waves ahead of them. He wondered if having a nickname was the one true measure of friendship—and if he'd ever have a true friend. Orange interrupted his thoughts, "Just like Skinny and I always called you *Happy*."

Minho searched his memory for a time when Skinny would have called him that.

He could only vaguely place it.

"Happy?" It wasn't anything he would have called himself.

"Yeah," Orange squinted at Minho, "Everyone calls you Happy." She cupped her hands around her mouth and shouted across the boat to the others climbing on deck from below, "Hey Dom, what's Minho's nickname?"

Dominic was all too enthused to answer. "Happy!" He waved from across the deck. "She told us on the Berg. Took actually meeting you for me to really get it." Then, completely unprompted, unwarranted, and unwelcomed, Dominic started singing a song about being happy while the others clapped along.

Minho couldn't help but smile. He moved the lever to pick up speed. Roxy and Miyoko clapped enthusiastically, letting out hoots and hollers to go with the song.

Minho, the Orphan with no name, now had two names.

One he chose. And one he just might grow into.

Happy.

6

SADINA

Anchoring close to shore before sunset helped the *Maze Cutter* stay safe while Minho and Orange rested, but Sadina hated how much the ship rocked back and forth from the incoming waves. She leaned against a bunk and closed her eyes while the others prepped dinner.

"Can't you do that on deck?" Miyoko asked Dominic, "You're getting fish slop everywhere and it smells terrible. Worse than you."

"Jackie would be vomiting if she were here, that's for sure," Trish added.

Sadina tried to block out the noise and commotion, but thinking about Jackie made her think about Isaac which made her think about her mom and Old Man Frypan. Her heart ached.

Dominic was never fazed. "I cook them down here so it makes more sense to prep them down here. I like the smell! Plus the deck is extra windy today."

"Oh that's right, Dom gets cold," Miyoko teased. Sadina opened her eyes.

"Hey." Dominic stood tall with a fish head in his hand. "I didn't know when we packed for this adventure that we'd be freezing our asses *and* our heads off." He put the fish on his own head, mouth down, like a hat.

"Gross. Stop." Miyoko waved.

"What? I'm the Godhead of fish."

"You're the Godhead of nothing." She swatted the fish from his head.

Trish laughed and looked to Sadina, but Sadina, worried about her mom, didn't feel like laughing. Today, for some reason, she felt like something bad was about to happen. She kept telling herself that they likely made it to the Villa safe and sound, but not knowing what was really going on only made the feeling worse—it gave that bad feeling room to spread out and take over.

"You look like you're going to throw up," Trish said as she came over to Sadina.

"I'm not seasick, but I don't feel good." She wasn't nauseous. But she wasn't *right*. It came from a different place in her gut. "I think I'll go up for some air."

"And I shall honor your space." Trish smiled and blew her a kiss. She was taking their talk particularly well, which Sadina was thankful for. It seemed like the farther the *Maze Cutter* got from her mom, the sicker she felt and the more space she needed.

Sadina climbed the steps to the deck; her eyes squinted at the change in brightness. The sun setting off the water was blinding, a brilliant contrast to the dim cabin below. And Dominic was right; it was cold. She walked over to Orange and Roxy along the railing.

"Hey," Orange said; her fair skin looked redder by the day. "What's wrong? You going to be sick?"

"No, just. . . I don't know. I have a bad feeling that something might happen to my mom." Sadina unloaded this before even thinking that something had most definitely happened to Orange and Minho's moms —and dads. "Sorry, that was insensitive."

"It's okay. We grew up knowing our moms were prolly dead in Flare pits somewhere. That's why this sunburn doesn't bother me. It could be worse." At times, the things Orange and Minho said felt dark —and this was one of those times.

"I just can't shake the feeling that something's really wrong," Sadina said again as Minho walked over carrying ropes in his arms.

"Why didn't you stay behind then? Stay with your mom?" Minho always caught Sadina off guard. He was so direct with his questions in a tone that sounded like he judged her. Truth was, his comment hit her so hard because she hadn't even considered staying behind. The pressure of their mission, the call to Alaska was so great—it didn't feel like *not* going was an option. But he was right—it had been. Isaac didn't think twice about staying with her mom so that she could go to Alaska. She could have stayed behind, too.

"I don't know. I mean . . . the Cure and all, I think if we get to the Godhead and we can help them with that, then—"

"But if you're the Cure, shouldn't you have stayed *with her?*" Minho pushed further and tears just about welled up in Sadina's eyes.

"But she doesn't have the Flare, right?" Sadina looked at Minho, Roxy, and Orange. Did they know something she didn't? Roxy took a deep breath and shrugged. *What did that mean?* "Roxy?" She searched the woman's body language.

"It's okay sweetie, you weren't wrong to leave her. You did what you felt you needed to do. Just . . . something that Kletter lady wrote in the log made Minho wonder about things." She put her arm lovingly around Sadina's shoulders.

"Wonder what?" She examined each of their faces for a clue.

Orange didn't say anything.

Minho just looked at Roxy.

Sadina shrugged off Roxy's arm. "What is it? What did Kletter write?"

Roxy sighed and threw her arms up. "Well, I don't know, I can only read a few words here and there, but she chronicled a lot about infection and expiration, and . . ." She looked at Minho and he nodded. "And she wrote a couple pages about your mom."

"She what?" The waves against the boat rocked Sadina extra hard. "What did it say?"

Minho handed her the captain's log.

"We can't understand it, but back here," Roxy pointed, "these pages are where she wrote *Señora Cowan* a couple times next to *infección.*"

Sadina looked down at the journal and Kletter's stupid, sloppy, handwriting. She stared at the words surrounding '*Señora Cowan*' and wished they could have unjumbled themselves to make sense, but they didn't. That feeling deep in her gut, the one that said *something is wrong*, wasn't a premonition—it was regret. She should have stayed with her mom. Sadina handed the book back to Minho and tears fell from her eyes. Roxy wrapped her in a hug. Sadina wished Trish had followed her up to deck and *not* given her space. She couldn't have felt more wrong. She was one big mess. "I shouldn't have come."

"You've got too much on your shoulders, girl." Roxy rocked Sadina back and forth in a hug. "It's okay. You're doing what you believe is right, and Minho didn't mean to make you cry—did he?" She glared at her adopted son, stern eyes held with the necessary pause for an apology.

"I'm sorry," Minho said. "I just wondered why you didn't stay." *What a way with words.* Sadina stared into the sunset and let the tears fall.

"It'll be okay," Orange said. But as sunburned as Orange's skin looked, that's how Sadina's heart felt.

"Just try to do a sniper move," Minho said.

"I don't think shooting anyone is the answer here." Roxy continued to rock Sadina.

Orange nodded her head as if she knew. "No, that is a good idea." She held her hands out. "To stay calm under pressure we did breathing exercises." Roxy loosened her arms around Sadina. "Before you shoot at a trespasser or an animal, you always take in a lung full of air through your nose, and let it out real slow through your mouth. Then the rifle and you are steady enough for a shot."

"But I'm not going to shoot anyone." Sadina shook her head. "No, thanks."

"It's not about pulling the trigger," Minho said. "It's about letting everything go in that breath, out of your mouth so your body can steady. You put every anxiety, every worry, every thought you ever had in your whole life into that exhale. And you push it out of you to somewhere else." He pointed far off into the horizon.

"Go on, try it," Roxy said. "Can't hurt." And they all waited for Sadina to breathe. It felt silly.

She wiped her eyes and took a slow inhale through her nose and held her breath, long enough to think about everything she needed to put into her exhale to let go. Worries about her mom being alive. Seeing her again. Ever seeing Isaac again. Living up to Old Man Frypan's legacy. Living up to her great uncle Newt's legacy. Being a part of the Cure. Meeting the Godhead. All of it at once.

And then Sadina let it out in a slow whoosh. She released all the worries and pressure into the air to float away somewhere else. She pictured those thoughts skimming along the top of the ocean, and pictured the same tide that rocked the ship so roughly, taking them away. Far, far away.

7
XIMENA

"Here we are." Carlos pointed ahead to a building with columns in front, but it didn't look like what Ximena remembered. The Villa seemed so much bigger, and scarier, when she'd been little. The mansion in front of her looked worn down and weak. Concrete crumbled on the steps leading up to the front door. She headed that way.

Carlos grabbed her arm and stopped her. "Not that door."

"Why?" Ximena waited for Carlos to point to another entrance but instead he just looked into the trees to the left and the right. He wouldn't let go of her arm. "What?" she asked again. Carlos pulled her by the wrist to the side of the Villa. Her foot slipped on the knotted roots of a dried-up bush. "¿Qué diablos?" She looked at Carlos for an explanation.

"They have security," he said in a whisper.

"In the trees?" She watched as he scanned the whole property with his eyes, keeping his body tight against the Villa. *He couldn't tell her about this on their long journey?* It would have only confirmed her doubts about the trustworthiness of Annie and the Villa, and Carlos probably hadn't wanted to hear miles and miles of Ximena's questions. "What's going on? You're acting like they'll shoot us for trespassing."

Carlos didn't say anything, which told Ximena everything.

He waved her to follow behind him along a thin path in between more dried bushes. Ximena took the knife she'd taken from Annie and lifted it out of its leather sleeve. "But you worked here, too. Isn't there some sort of password you can give them?"

"It's more of a process than a password." He carefully stepped closer to the back of the building. "I don't know if they still have traps, so we have to—"

"Traps?" Traps were for animals, not people.

Carlos turned to her. "The work they do here is very important, Ximena. It needs to be protected."

She sighed. She'd heard her whole life about how important the work at the Villa was, but she had yet to see the *impact* of that importance. She only saw the ways it affected her own village negatively. She matched Carlos' steps as best she could until they turned the corner of the house and reached a door painted all black. The paint was chunky as if someone had painted over it in layers. Sloppy. If this was a sign of the work the Villa did on the *inside*, then her thoughts about the Villa would stay unchanged. Carlos knocked once, hard. The crack of sound echoed around them as if the door was made of metal. *Why did the Villa have metal doors?*

Carlos rocked back and forth. He only did that when nervous. "Think they already know about Annie?" he whispered as if someone might hear him through the steel door.

"No. If they did, she wouldn't still be there. They wouldn't have left her there, not like that." Ximena steadied herself as the door opened. To her surprise, someone from their village was on the other side. Ximena recognized her features, but couldn't remember her name. "Diena?" she guessed.

"Danita," the woman said without any warmth. She eyed the two of them up and down.

"Hola, ¿Podemos . . . podemos entrar?" Carlos asked, but Danita shook her head.

"Tenemos que hablar con la profesora Morgan ahora." Ximena insisted they speak to Professor Morgan, but Danita started to close the heavy black door. Ximena stopped her with the same hand that held Annie's knife. "Annie Kletter, Ellas están muertas."

Danita paused. "¿Ella esta muerta?"

Ximena nodded.

"Podemos entrar?" Carlos asked again motioning to the door.

8

It had been years since Ximena had seen the inside of the Villa. Danita led them through the lower rooms to the main floor without a word. Ximena would have expected questions about the village and her family back home, but Danita seemed only focused on the task at hand —finding Morgan. Carlos held his bouquet of red clover as if he might see his wife at any moment, but Ximena wasn't even looking at the faces of workers and scientists around her. She was too busy examining the machines and instruments that changed room by room. The Villa had grown in its capabilities, greatly, since she'd been here last.

They reached the main floor and Danita turned to them, "Wait here."

Carlos nodded. Ximena's memories of the Villa came to life when she looked over at the glass-cased room built within the lab floor. A room she knew well. It was the one they'd built for her after her mother insisted Ximena be on the same floor of the lab as she worked, not below with the rest of the subjects. She started to walk over to the glass box but Carlos grabbed her wrist again. He motioned with his eyes to the two men inside. Ximena hadn't noticed them before.

Two men, one old and one young, sat with their knees folded into their chests. They looked tired, haggard. Or maybe it was defeat. She remembered well how the glass box they called a 'safety pod' made her feel the exact opposite.

The young man stood and made eye contact with Ximena.

She quickly looked away.

"Carlos, Ximena, what is this news about Kletter?" Professor Morgan walked in from the hallway, and just hearing her voice made Ximena shiver. Morgan's hair was just as blonde as Ximena remembered and her hands just as boney.

"We found her body, about two miles from here, south. In the narrows." Carlos put his backpack down but still clutched the red clover. "Can you let Mariana know I'm here?"

"Mariana was with Kletter." Morgan said it without emotion, but Carlos acted like he hadn't heard, still holding the bouquet of weeds as if his wife would be there soon. "She took a research group with her to find the descendants of the Immune. You should know this."

Descendants of the Immune? No, her mother would have told her if that's where *she* was going. "Where's my mom?" She realized Annie's knife was still in her hand and she gripped it tighter.

Morgan carefully approached Ximena and helped her put the blade back into its sheath. She hated that her mind and body still followed directions from Morgan so easily. It had been years, but just like that— Morgan had disarmed her. "Your mom was with Mariana and Kletter."

"But we *found* Annie. Mom and Mariana weren't there." Ximena realized they hadn't checked inside the haunted house. They should have. *Why didn't she?* She looked at Carlos, "We didn't go inside that house."

"They wouldn't stay there." But that wasn't what Ximena meant. What she was trying to say was, *they should have looked inside the house for more dead bodies.*

"Well, they'll turn up," Morgan said, as if Ximena's mom and Mariana were just a pair of lost dogs who wandered from the pack. "We have four of the group they found here, from the island." She motioned with her eyes to the two men inside the glass room.

"*Those* are the immunes?" She looked back at the room. Both of the strangers were dirty, sickly. Something wasn't right. "If my mom and Mariana went looking for *them*, with Annie, then how are *they* here and Annie's dead? My mom wouldn't have left a mission." Professor

Morgan didn't respond. Ximena turned to ask the two men herself, but Carlos stopped her again.

"Ximena." His sharp tone reminded her of Abuela letting her know when she was out of bounds. *But why weren't they as worried as she was?*

Morgan finally spoke, quietly. "They told us that Kletter was coming, right behind them." She stepped closer to Ximena and Carlos. "Was she dead long?"

Ximena nodded. She had never seen a body so decomposed. Being out in the open certainly hadn't helped.

"How long do you estimate?" Morgan turned to Carlos as if he knew, but he hadn't seen any more dead bodies in his life than Ximena —and he'd barely glanced at Annie's. He wasn't an elder who conducted burials, had no measure of decomposition. He was just a man looking for his wife, holding a bouquet of weeds and too much hope.

Ximena took it on herself to guess. "The flesh was liquified. Bones." She was no longer a child to be set aside in a glass box.

Morgan nodded slowly, only once. An up-and-down motion that somehow made Ximena feel heard. Respected. "They know more than they've told us. We need to question them carefully." She motioned to the lab techs in the background. Danita walked back over.

"I'll help," Ximena said before thinking. Morgan looked impressed, perhaps seeing potential. But it wasn't about that—Ximena needed to know what these men who'd traveled with Annie knew. She needed to find her mom.

"Join us, then," Professor Morgan said. "Danita, open the door."

PART FOUR

The Limits of Paradox

Are the thoughts that run through my head, again and again and again, the most important or the most meaningless? The less I think about something, the more thoughts and images seem to come along. Even in the darkness of my mind, I see them. I hear them. I feel them.

Where are they coming from?

—The Book of Newt

CHAPTER TWENTY

Flare Above

I
ALEXANDRA

She paced back and forth on her balcony, squeezing the cup of tea to keep her hands from shaking. For the first time in her life, she'd had a dream that was so visceral, so real to life, that it caused her to feel genuine fear. The cold Alaskan night air dried the sweat from her face. She had no doubt in her mind, now. Soon she'd be welcomed into complete madness.

She recited the digits, but she couldn't empty herself of the dark, lingering feelings of the dream. She remembered every moment, as if it had imprinted itself deep within her cells: hunted down by a metal machine, fire falling from the sky, arrows plunging into bodies.

Alexandra took a sip of tea.

It's not fire, it's just the northern lights that have returned, she told herself as she looked out to the sky. But even she couldn't ignore the red parts of the Aurora Borealis that had grown in strength over the last few days. Red was not a calming color. It was not a color of Evolution, it was a color of danger. The color of fire. Of War. *Get it together, Alex.*

The Flaring Discipline be damned, the last thing she needed was going mad like Mikhail with his constant talk of dreams and visions. *Nicholas did this to her.* He must have known she'd try to take over and poisoned her so that she'd slowly go crazy. *That must be it?* She set down the tea and pushed it away from her along with the Crank-headed thoughts. *No,* she thought, *that's just the madness talking.*

Paranoia and fear can turn a person inside out.

That was it. It was simply the paranoia from earlier, the Pilgrim shouting in the streets of Alexandra's guilt. She heard it, Flint heard it, everyone heard it. The war she'd dreamed of was just a war within herself—her subconscious mind alerting her conscious mind of the arrows pointed her way. She needed a plan to calm the situation. She looked down at her tea. She smiled to herself. What calmed *her* would calm the entire situation.

She knew exactly how to put out the flames of paranoia and accusations.

She grabbed her mustard-yellow cloak and what else she needed from the apartment, then left, headed to the Guardroom.

2

Alexandra went through the digits as she walked between bushes and brush in the midnight Alaskan air, timing them with her steps. The sky above helped to illuminate the very plant she was looking for: bog rosemary. It grew from the ground with spiky arms to the heavens. Some of the herbs produced flowers, but despite their bog-ridden beauty, she needed only the leaves. After finding it, she snapped off several arms of the plant until she had more than enough rosemary needles, and shoved them into the depths of her cloak.

She walked quickly back toward the Guardroom as she developed her plan. Would her entry be smoother with a disguise? *No.* The Evolutionary Guard had been on heightened alert since Nicholas' death.

She'd need to enter the Guardroom as the Godhead she was and quell any suspicions for her late night visit.

"1, 2, 3, 5, 8, 13, 21, 34 . . ." She whispered without thinking. The digits were more than just nature's favorite numbers—they constituted the golden ratio, the spiral that held the start and the end of every single life cycle within them. Trees grew their branches to the specs of the digits. Flowers bloomed seeds to the spiral of the ratio. And Alexandra would help the world evolve to its purest sequence, just as nature intended.

Nature was the great equalizer.

In a matter of hours, she'd address the Pilgrims and all those in New Petersburg with her announcement: the official start of the Evolution. Never mind her own evolution or whatever the fear growing inside her should be called; she couldn't give it a name other than what it was: Madness. She'd push this nightmare aside and speak to the people in the morning. Delivering hope and solutions to the Pilgrims would be the easy part; they worshiped her and feared the Flare. Convincing the Villa to get the first round of the Cure dispensed, on the other hand, would take some creativity. She'd worry about that later. One plan at a time.

As she approached the Guardroom—the building in town that most resembled the Maze—she waved at two Evolutionary Guards. Not unlike the Maze, this place held its own kind of prisoners.

"Goddess, are you okay?" They rushed to her side. It pleased her to know she still had their loyalty despite the crazed rumors of the Godhead killing their own.

"I had a terrible nightmare and needed to come before morning. The woman who shouted from the streets about Nicholas' murder? I need to see her." Before she'd even finished, the Guards ushered her inside the heavily fortified walls of the building. They were all too eager to appease her.

"She's in the back," one of the guards said.

The musty air of the Guardroom choked Alexandra. She coughed and coughed. *Mold.* These older buildings were filled with it. "Is it possible to get some hot water?" She cleared her throat from the thick air that the Guards were probably used to.

"Of course." One of them led her back while the other went for the water. Alexandra thanked them and followed the Guard through the intricate paths of crumbling arches. She tried to hide her disgust at the state of the Guardroom. It smelled like a warm toilet. Cobwebs gently swayed back and forth in single strands as she walked under them. She wouldn't be staying long, but she hated that she had to come at all.

"Here you are." The Guard motioned to a woman behind bars, sleeping on a filthy floor.

Alexandra nodded, putting on her best face of grief and desperation. She held her hand over her heart as she studied the woman's sleeping face. The poor wretch had thought it blasphemy to *play out the betrayal of Nicholas at such a holy time*, but there'd never *been* a more fitting time for betrayal. Alexandra woke up the woman with slow, loud claps for her abysmal performance in town. Startled, she snapped to attention and shuffled to the back of her cell.

She had no pillow, no bed, no pot to piss in.

"Wha—what are you doing here?" The Pilgrim's empty hands reached below her.

"I just wanted to applaud your performance. You've got the town in quite a stir over the Godhead turning on their own."

"I—I didn't mention you or Mannus," the woman whispered, trembling from head to toe.

Alexandra met her absurdity with silence. She would remind the Pilgrim of what it meant to be devout. To have faith. Honor. After a full, uncomfortable minute, Alexandra spoke. "I think it's terribly unfair that they put you in here for seeking justice in Nicholas' murder." The Evolutionary Guard arrived with her hot water. She nodded for him to leave her alone with the prisoner.

"What do you really want?" the unfaithful Pilgrim asked, barely lifting her head.

Alexandra mixed the bog rosemary into the water for tea. She stirred it and stirred it until the smell of rosemary needles intoxicated the air. The prisoner's eyes widened when instead of sipping the brew, the Goddess offered it to the Pilgrim. "I want you to return to your faith. That is all." The woman hesitated to take it but Alexandra insisted. "A Goddess is nothing without her people, and you are special to me even if you feel your purpose has been overlooked."

She accepted the cup. "Thank you. They've given me nothing all day." She sipped the bog rosemary tea. "The air in here is very musty."

"Dreadful. That will soothe your soul." Alexa watched as the Pilgrim drank the tea a few sips at a time. She told her the story of the Maze Trials, one she knew by heart. A story of faith and deceit. The Goddess recited all of her favorite parts loud enough for the Evolutionary Guards to hear, and when she was done, she left the Pilgrim and the Guards warmly.

There would be no uprising. No rogue Pilgrim. Not today.

Because within six hours, the bog rosemary would release its andromedotoxin to its fullest effect. The Pilgrim would start to have watery eyes and a runny nose that slowly turned into low blood pressure and vomiting, eventually progressing to convulsions and paralysis. By the time Alexandra addressed the town tomorrow at noon, the woman's physical body would appear as crazy as her mind. Spasms. Slurring. If the woman's tongue worked enough to form any words at all, no one would believe a single thing she said.

3

MIKHAIL

The Berg half-crashed, half-landed in a space well hidden by tree cover, smoke pouring out the back end. Colors spoke to him and sounds took shape as he floated in and out of consciousness. His fever raged. Maybe that little bugger did stab him closer to the kidneys than he'd thought. Everything around Mikhail moved in slow motion. He watched six Bergs fly overhead in war-formation, and the vapor trails spinning out behind them formed into letters, then into words, but in a language that he couldn't read. And then the vapors from the Bergs turned into colors, and the colors hardened into the Alaskan night sky with the colorful Aurora Borealis.

Madness.

Mikhail laid back in the captain's seat. He knew better than to close his eyes with so many physical woes, but he couldn't trust his sight and he could only think of visiting the Infinite Glade. Maybe this time would be the last time.

He took his slow, deep breath, in for three seconds, hold for three, out for three. He listened for the sounds of war as he exhaled.

Destruction was the only way to create.

Death was the only way to bring new life.

The people of Alaska would never truly know *why* the war happened. They might assume the usual—power, control, to stop the Evolution . . . and they'd be right on all three accounts. But if the war was successful, they would never truly know *why* the Evolution needed to be stopped in the first place. The greater destruction it would cause if the world walked the path of Alexandra.

Mikhail entered the Infinite Glade inside his mind and found nothing there. *Did Nicholas have any premonitions before he died?* He must have, but dear Nicholas had no defensive wounds on his hands when the body was found. *How could someone who sees and hears so much not see his own death?*

And maybe that was it.

Perhaps one could not see their own death coming even when they could see the death of an entire people.

Mikhail wandered the Infinite Glade.

4

SADINA

She hadn't slept through a single night since they'd left the shore, and it made her miss Old Man Frypan even more. On the *Maze Cutter*, there wasn't a fire to sit by or anyone to offer her advice. It was just her now, wide awake on her cot, listening to the boat creak and moan.

She sat up and moved over to the small window, lit by moonlight, and opened up *The Book of Newt*. If reading helped Frypan sleep, maybe it would help her, too. She didn't have the courage to read it front to back and witness her great uncle Newt losing his mind, but she hoped that flipping to a random page would reveal comforting words. She closed her eyes and her finger ran through the pages until it stopped on page 74 of Newt's journal:

You can't bloody prepare for what's next when what comes next has never happened before.

His words, in Frypan's handwriting, sent a chill from her feet all the way to the hairs on top of her head. He was *bloody* right. And it's exactly how she felt preparing to meet the Godhead. How could she prepare when she—or anyone on their ship for that matter—had never met a member of the Godhead before? Much less all *three*.

Dominic's snores echoed louder and louder. Sadina took in a slow breath through her nose and put all her fears into it, closed her eyes, and exhaled like Minho had taught her. The snores stopped. The Orphan was a miracle worker, indeed.

"Hey," Trish whispered.

Sadina jumped a little. "Sorry. Did I wake you?" She made room for Trish by the window, and they snuggled in the soft, bluish glow of moonlight.

"No, Dom woke me up. But then I woke *him* up and told him to lie on his side. When that kid's on his back his tongue clogs up his airway and makes him sound like a beached whale."

"Yeah, he gets pretty loud, huh?"

"Like those air horns we had back on the island. For the hurricanes. Actually, Dom is worse." Trish smirked but then her smile faded. "Sadina?"

"Yeah?"

"Do you think we'll ever get back home?"

Sadina was afraid to get Trish's hopes up. Every single day since they'd left the island felt like it took them further and further away—

not just literally, not just from their old life, but from ever being able to return to *life as they knew it*. Lacey and Carson were dead, as were two members of the Congress who'd helped plan their escape. Kletter was super dead, and with her mom not well, Sadina didn't know if she even *wanted* to go home when all of this was over.

"I don't know . . ." She finally said. "I honestly don't know."

"Can I tell you something without you getting mad?" Trish nervously played with the driftwood pendant around her neck that Sadina had made for her.

"Of course."

Trish paused and rubbed her forehead. "Don't be mad."

"I won't, I promise. What is it?"

"I left a note on the island . . ."

"Trish!" Sadina almost forgot everyone was sleeping. "Why? What did you say?" They'd all agreed when they left the amphitheater that no one on the island would know the truth. "We were supposed to pretend that Kletter did all that. The poisoning, the kidnapping, so that when we came back everything could be blamed on *her*!"

"I know, I know!" Trish held the piece of driftwood tighter. "But you had your mom with you and I was leaving my whole family behind. I couldn't *not* tell them. I didn't want them to worry. You know it would have killed my mom."

Sadina tried to find patience, to keep her promise. She understood why Trish did it, but she didn't want Trish's mom and dad telling the rest of the island. "What did the note say?" Sadina pressed. "I'm not mad. I get it. But I need to know what you told them."

Trish was on the edge of tears. "I don't even remember. I wrote it right before we left." She rubbed her head again. "I mostly just wanted to tell them that I was okay, I loved them, and that I'd be back soon. That we were going on an adventure."

Sadina sighed.

"You're mad."

"I'm not mad. It's actually perfectly understandable." She opened *The Book of Newt*. If Congress hadn't been split in the first place, then they could've just told the truth instead of leaving the island in a big cloud of mystery. "If you trust that they won't say anything then I trust them, too."

They sat in silence for a while, holding each other. Dominic started snoring again.

Trish motioned to the book and spoke softly, "Did you circle these pages because they're your favorites?"

Sadina didn't know what she meant. She hadn't circled anything so it must've been Frypan. She flipped through the book and to her surprise there were quite a few page numbers circled. She went through and said the circled numbers out loud, "1, 2, 3, 5, 8, 13, 21, 34, 55, 89, 144, 233. Page 1 is circled twice, I wonder what that means?"

"Maybe Old Man Frypan is a doodler."

"Maybe." But this didn't feel random. They felt connected. Like a code. She flipped through the pages with her thumb, again and again, repeating the circled numbers in her head until something literally started to add up.

"Trish. Look, these numbers, I don't think they're just page numbers . . . these . . . every single one of them, when added to the one that came before it, equals the number that comes *after* it. Simple math. Like, look, 5 plus 3 is 8. 8 plus 5 is 13. 21 plus 13 is—"

"34." Trish finished in wonderment. "But what does it mean?"

"I think . . ." Sadina's thoughts conflicted with the reality in front of her, they were just numbers but numbers that grew and evolved in a perfectly measured sequence. "I think it has something to do with the Evolution . . ."

CHAPTER TWENTY-ONE

Captive Audience

I

ISAAC

I t had been a long night

One bathroom break, a glass of water, and a couple small loaves of bread that tasted like uncooked flour and sand. They reminded Isaac of when he and Sadina were younger and made sand-pies on the beach. Back then, they'd only *pretended* to eat them. The young assistant that brought the food and gave Old Man Frypan and Isaac bathroom permissions didn't say a word to either of them and it only furthered the feeling that they were being held as prisoners.

In the morning, as soon as he saw the blonde-haired woman who'd helped take Jackie, Isaac jumped up and frantically pounded on the wall. He didn't care if the glass broke right then and there; in fact, he'd welcome it. "Hey! Hey! What's going on with Jackie?!" The glass in front of his mouth fogged up. The scientist walked over to him, clipboard in hand.

"We're still testing her blood."

"But she's alive?" Relief rushed through Isaac's veins. "You said hours ago that in thirty minutes you'd know if she'd made it—so she did? She made it? She'll be okay?"

"She's in bad shape but is on an aggressive decontamination drip." The woman barely looked at Isaac as she spoke.

He turned back to Frypan to make sure he'd heard Jackie was recovering. He nodded. And Isaac knew what that meant—they had to get out of the pot. "So what happened to her?" Isaac asked the scientist.

"Your friend suffered from a deadly neurotoxin that blocked her sodium channels. This caused her nervous system to shut down." She paused. "You're lucky neither of you had the same thing happen."

The word sodium had really jumped out at him. *Was Frypan right about the salt in the stew?* "What does all that mean?"

The scientist appeared very bothered with all the questions. "Tetrodotoxin is a common biotoxin in certain species of octopus, puffer fish, worms, toads—"

"The newt." Frypan stood up.

"Really?" Isaac asked him. "The little guy?"

The woman gave them her full attention now. Isaac could see *Pr. Morgan* stitched above the right pocket of her lab coat and another long set of letters that didn't mean anything to him. "I'm surprised Kletter didn't warn you about all this. . . . Bringing you all the way to California from your safe haven? There are things you need to know, here. It's very common to find birds and other animals dead from newt poisoning. It's part of the evolution that has become an epidemic . . ."

"Epidemic of evolution?" Isaac repeated.

"Yes. When one species becomes more present than others, the entire ecosystem tilts out of balance. Birds, rabbits, even snakes have lost large populations in recent years . . ." Morgan looked over her shoulder to the lab assistants and held up her finger for them to wait a moment.

Isaac tried to make sense of it all, how fragile life could be. "Jackie had touched Newt a hundred times at least and then that bug flew in her mouth and she scraped at her tongue. She put all that toxic crap right into her mouth!" Jackie drank from Isaac's canteen, too. It was a wonder he hadn't gotten sick.

"But she'll be okay?" Frypan asked. "You can get the poison out?"

Morgan nodded, "You're lucky."

But Isaac didn't feel lucky. He felt trapped.

"You got here just in time. Had it been a few more hours, she'd be dead."

Isaac felt a chill, then a rush of heat. He needed to see Jackie. "Take us to her." He hit his palm against the glass. "And Cowan." Morgan just stared back at him. He pounded louder on the glass.

Something wasn't right.

"Cowan is a different case." Morgan slowly unlocked the glass door. Isaac felt a wave of relief. "We'll move you to a lower floor. You'll be able to see them once they're both stable."

Isaac moved to go, anxious to get out of that room. To get the hell out of there for good.

"But first," Morgan said, blocking the exit from the pod. "You need to tell me exactly what you know about Kletter and where she is." She raised her eyebrows and folded her arms. *She knows.*

Frypan stepped froward. "What did you mean when you said Cowan was a different case?" The professor could cross her arms and raise her eyebrows all she wanted, but she couldn't deny a Glader of old some answers. "Something else from nature's evolution?"

Morgan shook her head. "Not from nature." She let her arms fall to the side. "Look. What Cowan has, we've only seen once before." She looked over her shoulder as she motioned for Isaac and Frypan to step out of the glass pod. Isaac gladly exited that prison but Frypan moved slower; his eyes didn't leave the corner of the lab where the curtained pod had revealed the flash of metal the day before. *Could the Griever have been a figment of their imagination?* Maybe they did have some slight poisoning from touching Jackie or drinking from the same canteen.

"But that other person recovered, they're alright?" Isaac asked, hopeful. If Jackie was okay, Cowan had to be okay too. He needed Ms. Cowan to be okay for Sadina.

Morgan frowned. "Where I saw it before wasn't in a *person*." She looked over her shoulder again and pointed, "It was on that shelf over there."

Isaac traced her gaze to a lab shelf filled with glass instruments and surgical equipment.

Huh?

What kind of infection did Cowan have?

2

MINHO

War tactics.

Funneling the enemy.

That's exactly how these islands, jutting from the ocean like the shoulders of giants, made the Orphan soldier feel. They left him little choice of direction. Like the ship was being led in by an enemy. A heavy wind blew along the choppy waters and made it all the more difficult to steer.

"We're going to get stuck," he said to Orange, but the truth was they already were. If he could turn the *Maze Cutter* around and try again, go back out farther west, outside of those little islands—he would have. "It's too shallow." The ship creaked from below. "That's not from water pressure, it's the rocks." He lowered the ship's speed to five knots. The wind howled at the windows.

Orange looked through her binoculars at the maze of islands ahead. "I don't know what happened. Two little landmasses turned into twenty big ones." The rest of the crew were on the deck, braving the gales and gawking at the beauty. The greenest of trees pointed up from the bluest of waters, shapes and colors that probably resembled the Earth before the sun flares and disease. It was breathtaking, but they'd have plenty of time to enjoy the niceness of it all when the boat became grounded. "Oh ship . . ." Orange pointed ahead. A shipwreck. One that looked like it had been there a hundred years.

Minho steered quickly to the right, away from whatever rocks and ship-destroying things were over there, trying to hug the other side of the waters, but Orange was quick to correct him. "There's another wreck over there. A newer one. You've got to stay right in the middle."

His hands shook on the wheel as he steered the boat between a changing center of water through long skinny islands. Dozens of islands. A hundred different paths. The wind pushed the ship back and forth, rougher than the tide at night, reminding them how small and insignificant they were. He'd been prepared for Cranks, and war, but not quite the wrath of nature, herself.

"Get everybody inside!" he shouted. The last thing he needed was someone falling overboard. Orange scrambled to get the islanders and Roxy away from the railings and below deck. Despite Minho's best efforts to steer to the center of the channel, the *Maze Cutter* hit something beneath. An ominous sound rumbled and groaned and scraped.

Minho looked desperately at Orange and she nodded.

She ran downstairs to check on things and came back within thirty seconds. "Yeah. We're taking on water."

"What do we do?" Dominic trailed right behind her.

Minho took the ship back up to ten knots, no longer caring about damage. Only speed. "Grab your stuff; we're docking farther south than we planned."

3
ISAAC

"My assistant will take you to the lower level," Morgan said. Old Man Frypan still couldn't take his eyes off the black curtain covering the corner pod, but Isaac was more concerned with the look on the young assistant's face. The fire in her eyes hadn't calmed down a bit from the day before.

"And that's where Cowan is?" The assistant only stared at him as if he were responsible for killing her dog or something. And then she walked away.

Morgan motioned for Isaac to follow the angry girl. "Cowan is in a separate safety pod on the lower level. You'll be able to talk with her through the glass." Isaac pulled Frypan's sleeve to break his stare from what haunted the old man behind the curtain. He snapped out of his trance and they caught up to the assistant. Isaac didn't care what they called the glass rooms, they weren't for safety. They were cells. He and Frypan didn't have a plan beyond telling Cowan what they'd learned about her illness and the folded-up Griever they'd seen—or hadn't.

"We'll see you for the dispensing this afternoon," Morgan shouted after them.

"Dispensing? What's that mean?" The assistant did not respond. She didn't even turn around. He and Frypan could barely keep up with her. For a second Isaac thought he saw a braided grass bracelet sticking out of her back pocket, along with a knife, but it couldn't have been. Couldn't. He rubbed his empty wrist.

The young woman led the two of them down a hallway, down a stairway, then another hallway before reaching a room with several glass pods like the one they had been in. Isaac exchanged glances with Frypan. There were at least a dozen of them, all empty except the one that held a very pale Ms. Cowan. She looked even worse than before. The layout of the bottom floor was almost identical to the lab upstairs; Isaac scanned the corners but there were no pods with black cloths hiding Grievers behind them. Grievers. He had to tell Cowan.

"Why's it gotta be in the basement? Nothing good happens underground," Old Man Frypan muttered as he glared at all the pods within the room. The assistant went to the next pod over to set up cots.

"Isaac, Frypan! Where's Jackie?!" Cowan shouted through the glass as soon as she saw them. Isaac couldn't tell if it was the lighting in the Villa or the stress on Cowan's body, but the skin around her eyes looked almost purple.

Isaac spoke loudly to ensure she could hear him. "Jackie's going to be okay. They've got her detoxing from a deadly bacteria the newt had on its skin." He examined Cowan's setup. They'd given her a bed and several buckets. She was hooked up to an IV.

"Oh. That's all it was . . . the newt?" Cowan rubbed her face. "I'm glad she'll be okay."

"Us, too." Isaac nodded, but he had bigger things he needed to discuss with Sadina's mom before the grumpy assistant made him and Frypan move to their separate safety pods. "Ms. Cowan," he said through the glass, "we need you to come clean with us. With Old Man Frypan, here." Isaac didn't want to have to tell Frypan about Kletter using the other kids as tests too. But with Cowan's illness and possible exposure to something so rare, they all needed to be on the same page. "It's not just about Sadina's blood . . ."

Cowan's chin dipped and she seemed ready to pass out. "I'm so sorry, Frypan. I never intended for you to get wrapped up in this," she coughed, "but Kletter's request went beyond just our family's bloodline, it was for as many bloodlines as we could escape the island with." The way Cowan said it, *escaping the island*, confused Isaac. The island was their home, they didn't need to run from anything there. This, now, here is what they needed to escape. He could only dismiss it as the sickness moving through her, confusing her, but she sounded like she'd been brainwashed or something.

"I know," Frypan said nonchalantly. This shocked not just Ms. Cowan but Isaac, too.

"You knew?" Isaac asked.

"What?" he chuckled, "I might be older than mung beans but I knew this wasn't just an off-island adventure for the Cure. As soon as we arrived at the Safe Haven all those decades ago, I knew that one day, someone would come looking for us. It was never going to be over, till it was over."

Cowan piped in, weakly. "It's still about the Cure. There was never anything nefarious other than lying to Congress and omitting some of the intentions. Having the potential use of control subjects within the same family bloodline if we needed them back on the island." Cowan coughed for what seemed like the hundredth time in the last few minutes. "But the Cure is the goal. Hear me? We owe it to the rest of the world to—" She coughed herself right into a fit until she hacked up liquid into a bucket.

Isaac couldn't tell if it had come from her lungs or her stomach, but either way, it wasn't good.

Isaac watched the sullen assistant open up the second pod and prepare it. "Ms. Cowan, did Kletter give you anything? Did she test something on you that you might have had a reaction to?" He looked back at Frypan to gauge how much he should tell her. The way Cowan blinked slower and slower, Isaac wasn't sure they should bother her with the threat of a machine upstairs that may or may not be a Griever.

Cowan seemed to be searching her memory. "I tested the sleeping substance before using it on the crowd at the amphitheater. Do you think . . . I had a reaction to that, it was so long ago though?"

Isaac questioned Frypan but he shook his head. "No. It wouldn't have been that. But, is it possible that she gave you something else while you were asleep?"

Cowan coughed again. "No."

"Maybe testing to see how it would react with a part of Sadina's blood?" Frypan asked as Isaac watched the assistant walk back over to them, dragging heavy feet.

"Kletter?" Cowan's purple-hued eyelids blinked. "You think she gave me something else when I was asleep?" She grabbed her head.

"Annie Kletter was a thief and a liar," the assistant finally spoke. Her eyes widened as if she dared anyone to correct her. "Is that why you killed her?"

"Annie?" Isaac had never known Kletter's first name, but for some reason *Annie* didn't fit. It was too nice of a name for that woman.

"We didn't kill her," Frypan said.

"No. We didn't kill her." Isaac was more than alarmed that the Villa even knew Kletter was dead. He'd hoped to use it as leverage to get out of there, but instead the walls were closing in on him. He had nothing left but the truth to use as a weapon. "A guy named Timon and a woman named Letti did. . . . I don't know which one actually slit her throat because I had a bag over my head before they kidnapped me, but *they* killed her." He was rambling, hating the memory.

"Where's the rest of the crew?" The assistant moved her left hand to her back pocket, where her knife was.

"The rest of our group is on their way to Alaska. I swear. We didn't kill her."

"Where's the rest of *Kletter's* crew?" Her voice had gone from demanding to desperate. "I need to know where they are."

"Kletter's crew from her ship?" Isaac asked, trying to think of something, anything to say about the eight people that arrived on the deck of the *Maze Cutter*, dead and beginning to rot. "Why?"

"Because my mom was with them."

CHAPTER TWENTY-TWO

Flaring Justice

I
ALEXANDRA

What a day. She wore her mustard-yellow cloak to match the endless crowd of Pilgrims before her, reminding them once again that they would all be Gods someday if they chose the Evolution alongside her. *What other choice did they have?* By furthering society, she would be placing Alaska back online. Not on the internet of old, but a new human-wired system that allowed humankind to accomplish things never dreamed before. Alaska, the site of the Maze, would be the leader of the future.

Flint worked to calm the crowd in front of her.

The Evolutionary Guards flanked her tighter than ever.

Alexandra searched the crowd for Pilgrims she might recognize from the six devout who, like Mannus and like the crazed woman in the streets, knew her secrets. She should have better committed their names and faces to memory, but she had other ways of flushing them out.

Her vision flashed red again with fire. Red and orange flames as if her mind itself was the very thing ablaze and she couldn't escape her own madness. The stress of the Evolution was getting to her, that was all. The stress of Nicholas *still* having control over her from beyond. His death had become a smothering blanket of wool, scratchier than the cheapest Pilgrim's cloak, and she was ready to be free of it already. Her ears buzzed a tone so high-pitched that she almost let out a scream. The Flaring Discipline be damned, she needed to control her mind. She recited the digits, a thing she was doing more frequently with every passing day.

"Goddess Romanov, they're ready for you." Flint directed her to the front of the stage, but she wasn't yet ready to address this Sunday crowd of Pilgrims, not without Mannus. He was her social experiment, her proof against any stigma or whispers that Evolution was anything but good. *Where was that horned human?*

"Goddess!" A man with long, matted hair screamed from the front of the crowd. "What of the murder? Who'll be charged for the death of our God?!" Others grumbled in agreement with his outburst.

"We need justice!"

"Send them to the Guardroom!"

Alexandra would calm them today, but in due time she needed a scapegoat or the Pilgrims would never settle. She looked over at Flint who voraciously tried to hush the Sunday chants, *Flare above, Maze below.*

The crowd finally settled.

She'd keep silly Flint around. He was good for some things.

There was commotion behind her as her Evolutionary Guard barricade let someone onto the stage, but it wasn't Mannus. It was a man in a dark robe, similar to what Nicholas wore. For just a moment Alexandra felt the scream of betrayal from her guards, as though Nicholas' ghost had whispered to them of her guilt. Her neck muscles seized with tension.

"How do I look?" The figure asked as it came closer.

Relief flooded through her. "You look . . ." She searched for the words but the only one that came to mind was "hornless."

Mannus, missing his ratty beard along with the horns, looked softer, more human than ever. He winked and gave a chuckle that made Alexandra feel violated. *Did he just read her thoughts?*

"Indeed. Impressive, isn't it?" he said. "That Cure gave me some fun gifts."

Her jaw tightened. His lips hadn't moved.

Just as she had gotten rid of Nicholas' telepathy she had now apparently inherited Mannus', but she had to embrace the fact that some gifts of evolving would be like those of the Maze Trials. It was inevitable. Neural networks were a part of the Evolution.

But unlike Nicholas, she had *control* over Mannus.

You look like Nicholas in that cloak, but don't be an idiot. Follow suit and you can keep your head. She made sure to think the words loud and clear before stepping forward and addressing the people.

"Good afternoon, dear Pilgrims. We want to assure you that there is nothing more important to the Godhead than your safety and that is why we are moving quickly with our plans for the Culmination of the Evolution." She paused, considering how delicately she must balance her motives with the fears, desires, and survival needs of her followers. She pushed the fire and buzzing out of her mind, into the embrace of the Flaring. "Not only is the serum for the Evolution a preventative to the Flare, but it will also unlock your highest potential in every way."

"Serum? We have to drink it?" an older man griped, as if they didn't drink every night at the pub, anyway. Alexandra hated getting hung up on semantics, but she wasn't exactly sure how the vials would be distributed. *Serum* sounded better than *dispensing*, the term the Villa had used.

"How do we know it's safe?" another shouted.

"The details will be available soon enough, but we've begun with our first set of human trials." Alexandra waved at Mannus to join her at the front of the stage, conveniently leaving out the fact that their Godhead had been the *real* commencement of human trials. "Mannus, please step forward."

Her eyes wandered the crowd before her, waiting for each unique reaction of those Pilgrims who knew Mannus as a lower-rung member of society. A rung just above the dead moss above the site of the Maze, trampled on daily. A horned being, more beast than man, barely more man than Crank.

Mannus pulled back his cloak to reveal his face, and more importantly, his hornless head. A gasp drifted over the gathered, from front to back. Alexandra smiled as the Pilgrims turned to each other, sharing their wonder. "You may know Mannus as one of you, but he is now raised to a God-like status through the help of the Evolution."

A bit of a stretch, even she was ready to admit. But no matter. Means to an end, all that.

The heckling began soon after the initial shock.

"He's no God. He just got rid of his horns!"

"We don't care about this—we want justice for Nicholas. Justice!"

"Flaring justice!"

Flint attempted to silence the growing dissent, but his waving arms and shouts were little help, drowned out by the noise. The buzz in Alexandra's ear started again, coupled with fierce head pain.

"Flaring justice, flaring justice, flaring justice . . . ," they chanted and Alexandra pressed her tongue to the roof of her mouth in anger. She simply would not be able to roll out anything to do with the Evolution today. Instead, she'd have to pacify their wants for justice. The Flare be damned, she'd give them justice. She stepped forward with her hands in front of her in prayer position. "Please, settle yourselves. We know who's responsible for the murder of our dear Nicholas." A hush fell over the audience just as she knew it would.

She turned to Mannus.

Name them, the four others who accompanied you, Alexandra *thought* at him.

He shook his head, stood firm. Challenging her.

It's you or them, she thought, along with all the *feel* of warning she could muster. Mannus stood there in his robe, unmoving and unspeaking. Fine. She'd show him that she wasn't bluffing. "Dearest people of Alaska. Look to—"

"Pilgrim Gilbert!" Mannus shouted aloud in a deep, booming voice.

The crowd turned as one toward a round-headed man, no horns, but with the names of every single Glader of old tattooed on his face. Alexandra remembered him now. *How could she ever have forgotten those fanatical tattoos?* As soon as Mannus spoke the name, it was as if the robe of Nicholas' transformed his word into law; the surrounding people mobbed the tattoo-faced man, throwing punches and kicking him to the ground. From beneath their grapples, the man tried to defend himself, tried to speak, but the violence only worsened. Alexandra didn't like it, but she let the people have their moment, restraining the Evolutionary Guards with a glance, allowing the Pilgrims the reprieve of vigilante justice.

The tattoo-faced man suddenly broke free from the mob, every last inch of him bruised or bloodied. "It was the Godhead turning on their own! It was—" A man in the crowd slugged the tattooed Pilgrim so hard he collapsed to the ground, completely lifeless. The Evolutionary Guard dragged him away.

She kept her face still. Sometimes, violence was the only option. Sometimes, an example had to be made. For the greater good.

"Yes, the rumors are true." She spoke loud and clear. "The Godhead has turned its back on its own kind, as well as the people of Alaska." The crowd quieted. "Mikhail has murdered our dear Nicholas and used the weakest of the Pilgrims to do his bidding." She barely got the words out before the people before her erupted in screams of disbelief. Horror. They clawed at their own skin and eyes.

Flint tried to calm them down by yelling one of the chants. "Flare above, Maze below! Flare above, Maze below!" But nothing of the sort would fix this. The people needed to heal, and in order to heal they first needed the wound ripped wide open.

Keep going. She sent her thoughts to Mannus, finding the task easier and easier. *You wanted power, well this is how you take it.* Her ears rang with the piercing buzz as she observed Mannus announce the names of another man and two women. The mob went after the Pilgrims before the Evolutionary Guard ever had a chance.

"Godkillers! Traitors!" The people shouted, their voices rising in waves of strength. They nearly murdered the four Pilgrims before the Guards could take them captive. The prisoners were lucky to be alive.

Meanwhile, Alexandra was trying to shake the madness from within. The buzzing, the visions of fire. *It was over now*, she told herself. There would be no more outbursts. No more demands from the crowd. Mannus looked particularly annoyed, probably realizing the price of betrayal. Alexandra could hardly feel sympathy. If he wanted to wear the cloak of a Godhead, then he had to carry the burdens that came with it.

She wasn't done with the crowd. "The people of Alaska want justice and we must deliver that today!" She allowed a long, dramatic pause. "We will send them to the Maze—for Nicholas!"

The Pilgrims cheered.

Too easy.

2

XIMENA

La verdad siempre saldrá a la luz.

She grilled the boy standing in front of her, needing the total truth about Annie. "Was she with a group of people when you met her or not?" Deep down in the middle of her bones she knew that her mom was dead, but within the center of her heart remained the smallest bit of hope.

"I . . . I don't . . . know . . ." The young man's eyes darted to the two others in the room, the old geezer and the sick lady, but Ximena had heard disappointing news from adults her entire life. She wanted to hear this from the boy.

"You *do* know." It couldn't be more obvious that he was lying. Weakness. The immune's blood might have been strong, but the rest of his body was weak. His eyes were tired, wounded, like whatever he'd seen wasn't something he ever wanted to say out loud. There was no way he'd killed Annie. Ximena put the knife back in her pocket. She softened. "What's your name?"

"About time someone asked. I'm Isaac. And that's Frypan, and this is Ms. Cowan."

"Isaac." Ximena slowed down her words, "I need to know where they are. The people who were with Annie Kletter. Can you tell me that?"

He nodded, almost looking relieved.

"They're on our island back home," he said softly, and Ximena allowed herself the slightest sense of relief. Of course her mom and Mariana wouldn't want to come home from the island, with so much to study and learn from the immunes. Absent-minded Annie didn't leave them behind—they *chose* to stay.

Ximena looked back to the old man, named Frypan of all things. He had a strange look in his eyes. "What? What is it?" she asked. The Cowan woman coughed. They all avoided Ximena's stare as if they knew how *different* she was. A uniqueness that her mother called *special*, but Ximena felt differently. Every time she met someone outside her village and they learned the truth about her, they ignored her, stayed away from her. "Did my mom tell you about me?"

"What is your name, dear?" The sick lady asked, and Ximena realized she hadn't told them yet. Not that it mattered; they'd never see each other again after today.

"Ximena."

"What a beautiful name." Ms. Cowan coughed. "I'm so sorry to have to tell you this, but . . ."

"The boat, when it came in . . ." Isaac continued, and Ximena froze. Anything that started with an apology and needed two people to explain wasn't good. She gazed into each of their weak, tired eyes. The old man returned a look of sincere sympathy, as if he'd seen all the worst things the world had to offer during his long life, and that he was sorry for it all.

She shook her head, wanting to deny it.

The omen of the dead, blackened jackrabbits.

Her premonitions.

Despite already knowing the truth, she couldn't stop shaking her head.

Frypan stepped forward and put his hand gently on her elbow. "They didn't suffer." He said it in a way only someone who'd lost a loved one could. Or many loved ones.

Ximena started to cry before she heard the how and the why of it all. *Her mom was gone.* She wiped at her eyes, promising her Abuela that she would find the truth. She owed it to her whole village, and it all started with these islanders. "Get in the pods. One each." She motioned with the keys in her hand.

"We're really sorry," Isaac said.

But could he possibly know what it felt like to lose a parent? To not get to say goodbye? She doubted it. "Get in the pod," she ordered, refusing to look him in the eye.

3
SADINA

Trees. Mountains. Rocky cliffs.

Air almost as chilled as the water crashing ashore.

Alaska.

The *Maze Cutter* anchored inside a small bay with a rough bump that jolted Sadina. Trish helped her gather their stuff; Miyoko and Dominic got the rest. "Should we bring the other palm mats too?" Miyoko asked.

Minho snapped his answer. "Nope. Only what you need to survive. Bags, food, weapons."

Sadina tucked *The Book of Newt* into her satchel. "We don't need weapons."

As if her very words triggered the entire changing of the world, the skies darkened. Above them, approaching from the wooded horizon inland, were six Bergs. Bergs! *Six* of them. Then the sound caught up, shaking the air and the land, rocking the boat. It had all happened so fast.

"What's happening?!" Miyoko shouted, directed at Minho, dropping the palm mats she'd been defying orders to bring.

"Shit!" was the Orphan's reply. He grabbed his armory bag. "Orange!" He motioned something to his longtime companion, a sign language that Sadina didn't understand.

"Do you know who that is, son?" Roxy asked. "Last time we saw those things, it wasn't good."

"Not sure." But Sadina saw a watery look in his eyes that worried her. Something like fear, so unusual for him. "It's *not* good, you're right. Reminds me way too much of the Remnant Nation's war formation. Everyone grab a weapon."

Of all the things running through Sadina's head lately, *war* was not one of them. The island where they'd grown up was so peaceful and dedicated to generational growth that war wasn't even in their sphere of thinking. What would Old Man Frypan say if he were here? Probably something like, *nothing good ever happens in Alaska.*

"Here." Minho handed Dominic a small knife no bigger than the ones he'd been scaling fish with. "Don't be scared. Maybe they'll fly right over us. Or even better, seems like they're heading north, not right at us."

The boy shrugged, trying to hide the tremble in his shoulders. "How'd you know I'm scared . . ."

"Just a wild guess," Minho responded, and then he handed a small gun to Sadina. She knew absolutely nothing about how to use it.

"I don't want it." She tried to give it back to him, but he pushed it against her.

"Armory is an extension of your *arms*," he insisted, placing the gun in her right hand and showing her how to hold it correctly. "Respect. Control. You can handle it." She looked over at Dominic with his knife and wished she had that, instead. But Dom never had control, likely would shoot his foot off.

Sadina met eyes with Trish, and Trish nodded as if she could hear what Sadina was thinking. "Wait." Sadina tried one more time to give the gun back to Minho. "You'll be with us, you can protect us. I don't wanna kill anybody!"

"I can only use one weapon at a time," Minho said. "Everyone listen up. We're going to make a pack-run for the woods and go as far in as we can and then slightly north once we're under cover. Keep quiet and keep alert. I don't think the Bergs will spot us or care about us. Not yet, anyway."

Sadina didn't know what that meant, exactly. She put the gun in her back pocket but it felt like it was weighing her down in more ways than one. She wished Minho could've said something a little more encouraging like, *don't worry everything will be okay.* Her mom would have if she were there. But Sadina was never more aware of the danger all around. "Trish," she reached for her hand as they left the ship. "You okay?"

Six more Bergs whipped past them overhead, a little closer this time. Miyoko covered her ears and asked, "How many of those things are there?"

"That makes twelve," Roxy said as she strapped a long gun across her chest and a knife around her waist.

"Are you okay?" Sadina whispered to Trish again.

"I don't know what to think . . ." Trish watched in fascination as the Bergs flew farther north. "But wherever you go, I'll go." She clasped her fingers around Sadina's and held them tight. Sadina was thankful to feel something other than fear in that moment, and she squeezed back just as hard. She whispered her response into Trish's ear.

"Wherever you are, I'll be."

4
ALEXANDRA

Bergs. Lots of Bergs.

Six of them. They appeared as suddenly as a stroke.

Dizzy from the spectacular, horrifying sight, she almost had to grab on to Flint for balance. The sound of the flying machines was like anger from the ancient gods, displayed with thunder and lightning.

Her ears ached from it, the noise much worse than the maddening tone that had inflicted her of late. Perhaps it had been a warning all along. *But what good was a premonition if she could do nothing to stop it?*

Six *more* Bergs appeared. Twelve!

Her vision flashed red.

Just as the monsters of metal, exhaling blue fire like dragons of ancient lore, spread out in the sky above, the people of New Petersburg dispersed through the streets in a mad panic. As if her body had taken charge, taken over her troubled mind, Alexandra abruptly realized that she, too, was already running for cover, her Evolutionary Guard and Flint right beside her.

Her feet pounded the ground like never before.

A wild, foreign feeling of fear rushed through her.

She turned to her Evolutionary Guard and shouted over the Bergs above, "We have to get back to the—"

One of the Guards dropped to his knees.

"Get up!" *They had to get away from the city.* A mild grunt escaped the Guard's lungs as he collapsed fully onto his stomach. An arrow stuck out from his back.

"Goddess!" Another one of the Guards pulled at her, but she looked up, tracing the arc of the arrow. A Berg, as loud and bright as the sun, hovered above them; Alexandra swore she could see a child holding a bow. *A child? Is that all it took to kill her strongest Guard?* Panic filled her like an aurora in the night sky.

The remainder of the Guard yanked her into a building to escape the crossfire, then pushed her through the empty bakery, all of them running to nowhere. But the Berg was targeting the Goddess with more than just arrows.

Explosives. Bombs.

Walls crumbled around them, the world becoming dust and noise, cracks of cement and the warping of metal. And death. Several Guards crushed.

She knew nothing of wars. For years she'd played nice with Nicholas and Mikhail so that tensions never escalated. As she scrambled to avoid the falling debris, choking on the dust, it hit her like its own explosion.

Mikhail.

Somehow, in his Crank-riddled mind, he'd been able to orchestrate this.

Two Guards pushed Alexandra out the back exit. She coughed and gasped for air as they emerged into a city full of flames and destruction. She pulled her cloak tight around her as if it had magical powers of protection.

"Get me to—" But when she turned around it was only Flint behind her.

"They—they . . . ," Flint stuttered.

"Nevermind! Come on!" She ran, and Flint followed. She tore through the south streets, farther from the child army and farther from the Bergs. She zigzagged and dodged things falling from the sky, cinched her hood around her face so that no one could see it was her— their Goddess—running away from her people. Gunfire rang in every direction. She considered fleeing to the ruins of the Maze, but if she fled below ground it would surely be her burial site.

And so, she ran.

She ran, Flint beside her, weaving between the Pilgrims who chose to stand their ground like maniacs and fight for their land, and between the bodies on the ground that lay already dead. She jumped over a woman on the street, eyes glazed over, who she'd seen earlier shouting for justice. *Flaring justice, flaring justice.*

The Flare be damned.

The Evolution be damned.

Mikhail be damned.

She saw a black cloak that just for a moment made her think Nicholas had returned from the grave with the armies of the dead, seeking revenge.

Mannus.

He turned to her with the dead stare of a man crippled by terror. He was alive, but his mind seemed on the edge of flight, the escape of madness. And then she remembered.

The boat.

Docked along a southern port from when they'd returned from the Villa.

"Flint, there's a—" Alexandra stopped at the sight of her faithful servant's expression, crooked with pain. They locked eyes for just a moment before he gave her an apologetic look and fell. His knees hit the ground, a single red arrow jutting from his neck.

Flint.

All these years, she could never even be bothered to use his real name. His dying eyes searched her face and the greatest shame she'd ever known washed through her every cell.

"I'm sorry . . . ," she mouthed to him. And then he was gone.

The only thing remaining in all the world was for her to run.

Goddess Alexandra Romanov ran.

CHAPTER TWENTY-THREE

Dispensing Disbelief

I

MINHO

E ndless training.

Constant threats.

Everything the Orphan experienced in his life had led to this moment, a war that he'd doubted at times would actually happen. But the bullets firing off in the distance convinced him it was real. *Would the Godhead even survive an attack like this?* No ragtag Alaskan army of Pilgrims could ever be a match for the Orphan Army. Minho continued to lead the group inland, through forest, over hill and rockslide. Far enough to be safe, far enough from the attack until things calmed down.

"How long does something like this last, anyway?" Miyoko asked while looking through the binoculars. Minho knew she wouldn't be able to see anything. The tree cover was too thick.

"From the history books, wars can last months . . . years . . . decades," Roxy said. Minho would have to to ask for one of her grandpa's war stories later, but for now he wanted silence. He needed to hear what was happening in the distance.

Orange took her binoculars back from Miyoko. "It won't last longer than a day. This skirmish will be over by sunset or tomorrow's sunrise."

Minho had to agree with her, especially from what he'd heard about the people in this city of Gods. Lacking weaponry and its people unskilled in the ones they had.

Dominic held up his knife like a candle. "I just want to point out that I was the only one who voted to go home."

"What's going to happen . . . ," Sadina asked in a whisper, walking slower than the rest of them.

Minho certainly didn't love the answer to that question. He could only think of two possible outcomes, and figured he'd better be honest with her. "Either the Remnant Nation will take over the city of New Petersburg and kidnap the Godhead or the Remnant Nation will take over and the Godhead will be dead."

The group got quiet.

War raged on in the distance.

2

XIMENA

Their building had as many bedrooms on the upper floors as it did safety pods on the floors below, and it didn't take Ximena long to find the small room that had belonged to her mom. She sat down on the bed and looked out the window at the dusty sunset, wishing she could go back home and tell her Abuela about everything: Kletter dead, her mom and Mariana buried on the island of the immunes, how she couldn't bring herself to tell Carlos until she knew more.

Until she had a plan.

Estar entre la espada y la pared, her Abuela would say. She was in between the devil and the deep blue sea. A rock and a hard place.

Ximena wanted to run back to her village, through the desert and the littering of dead jackrabbits to her home and curl up in her favorite blanket and just mourn everything. Drink tea with her Abuela and spend time with those in the village who she had left. But that wasn't a solution, it was what her mom would call escapism, and she knew that. The world wouldn't get any better by people hiding under blankets.

That was one of the few pieces of advice from her mom that still stuck in her brain. As soon as Isaac said the words out loud confirming her mom's death, it was as if all of the precious memories had evaporated in an instant and Ximena couldn't grab on to anything.

Carlos appeared in the doorway. "You disappeared right quick?"

"Yeah. I'm just tired."

"You're disappointed." He wasn't wrong, but he didn't know the full extent of that disappointment, and she wasn't going to share it all just yet. She knew that once Carlos found out the truth that his grief would overwhelm him to a point of no return. It wouldn't just be sorrow for Mariana's death but also for the life they'd planned to have. The baby. Everything. He'd be inconsolable.

Ximena spotted a water container on the dresser and handed it to Carlos. "For the red clover flowers you picked." Although she knew Mariana would never see the sweet sentiment that Carlos brought for her, hope was important to Carlos.

"Thanks. Hey," he said excitedly, tipping the water at her like a toast. "Got the dispenser fixed."

She didn't know what the dispenser was, and she didn't care. "Good job."

"You coming down for dinner?" The words reminded her of her mom, finally, and she was glad for it.

"You're calling lunch dinner now?" she asked. "You're working for the Villa one day and they got you changing already." She suddenly remembered Kletter's skeletal body and thought she'd probably never eat again.

"Yes, at the Villa it's called dinner and at the Villa we respect tradition."

Ximena gave him her best sarcastic smile. "I don't care if it's lunch, dinner, breakfast, supper. I'm not hungry."

"Okay, but don't miss the dispensing," he said. "I know it sounds lame, but this is history, they started working on this before you were even born."

Ximena nodded. She tried a more genuine smile for Carlos and his work, but she knew all too well the things that had started before she was born. Not a single one of them good.

3

Ximena tried to portray excitement to Carlos when he showed her all the hard work he'd put into the hydraulic thingy, even if she didn't have much belief in the Villa anymore. As far as she was concerned, working for the Villa was like working for the devil. *La hierba mala nunca muere*, Abuela would say in defense of the villagers who did just that: **the devil looks after his own**. But Annie Kletter was something worse. She'd failed to protect the people under her wing.

But Carlos beamed with pride. "You'll see. The whole Villa will see today. It'll work, I know it will." She'd never seen him so taken by one of his own achievements.

She responded half-heartedly. "I'm glad you could fix it, if it means there's hope for the future."

"This isn't just hope for the future, Ximena, if this works—it'll fix some of the errors of the past."

She had no idea what he meant. As they left and walked into the main lab, she saw another young girl her own age, with Professor Morgan. It shocked her so much she almost stumbled. Ximena felt an instant connection to this human standing in front of her, merely because they were the same age. How silly, yet how remarkable a feeling.

"Ximena, good morning," Morgan said. "Before you do rounds in the basement, I want you to take Jackie here and put her in a safety pod down with the others. She's healed enough that she can reunite with the group."

Dios mío. She was one of the immunes. "Sure," Ximena said, and her eyes landed on Jackie's grass-braided bracelet. Exactly like the one she'd found near the scene of Kletter's murder. "Where'd you get that?" She checked her back pocket, half-expecting it to be gone, stolen. Still there.

Jackie touched the bracelet on her wrist, "I made it. With my friends."

"Oh." Ximena didn't know what to think of that response. "I found one just like it. Near Annie's body."

"Who?" Jackie frowned.

Morgan didn't seem to care about bracelets right then. "Put her in the back pod, the furthest corner. The front pod will be for the rest of us when we come down later to test." The professor smiled. Morgan never smiled.

"Come down later to test?" Ximena asked. She had never once in all her time at the Villa seen any of the lab techs go *into* a safety pod. They had people like her go in and out with cots and amenities, cleaning, whatever was needed. It was as if the scientists themselves were afraid of the pods. "What do you mean? The lab techs, too?"

"All of us." Carlos was practically skipping. "To watch the hydraulics in action."

He was way too excited about whatever was about to happen. It made Ximena nervous. She looked behind her shoulder at the others in the lab, all of them shuffling around, busy busy. They had a buzz about them. *¿Qué estaba pasando?*

"Just come with me," Ximena said to Jackie, then led her down the hallway and then the stairwell. With every step Ximena took, her stomach tightened. Something bad was going to happen. Maybe it was because she had never before seen a kid her age, here, or because the lab techs and Carlos were losing their monkey minds about this test they were going to do. Even as they reached the last step to the basement, she couldn't let the feeling go. She pulled Jackie into a corner.

"What are you doing?" Jackie asked.

"Shh. There aren't any cameras in this spot." Ximena pointed to the rounded safety viewers in other places. Safety pods, safety viewers, everything was meant to make guests feel safe—but Ximena knew it was the exact opposite. Everything inside the Villa was a risk. The scientists simply tried to minimize the casualties involved. "I need you to be honest with me."

"Okay," Jackie whispered, then shrugged. The immunes were too trusting. Too weak. Too kind.

"Annie—" Ximena corrected herself, "Kletter. Who killed her?"

"Oh, um . . ." Jackie smacked her head in a funny way, as if they hadn't just met. "I can't think of their names. The gentle giant and the weird lady with him. They kidnapped Isaac and Sadina and cut Kletter's throat. It was horrible."

Her story matched the others, and she certainly didn't seem the murdering type. But there was something else Ximena wanted to know. "And what about the crew on the ship with Kletter?" She'd only gotten so much out of the other immunes: *That her mom didn't suffer, that they buried her on a plot of land with honor,* but she needed to know more—like why Annie killed eight people, and how.

"Oh, that Kletter friend of yours was something else. Gave that whole crew a sleeping drug and then shot them in the head. Right in the center." Jackie tapped her forehead.

Ximena tried to slow her breathing, tried to wrap her mind around the horrific details. She could hear Morgan at the top of the steps. "We've got to go," she whispered.

She led Jackie into the lower level with the others.

"This place is really weird," Jackie said as she followed. "I mean, I know you guys saved my life and all, but this doesn't feel . . ." She stopped talking once she saw her friends locked inside safety pods. "What's going on?"

"Don't worry, they're okay. Just don't make a scene." She walked Jackie back to the designated safety pod in the corner and talked as quickly as she could before shutting the glass door. "Listen, the lab techs are coming down here to initiate a test." She said it just loud enough for the others to hear, as well.

"To test our blood?" Isaac asked through his glass speaker.

"No. It's more than that. It's something they've never done before." *Mantengase Calma.* She didn't know if the message to stay calm was for her inner self, her hands shaking, or if it was for the others. "Just remain calm. Whatever happens, stay calm." She fought the urge to not lock Jackie's pod, to just release Isaac, Frypan, and Cowan right there and tell them to run for it. But even if she wanted to help them, Cowan was growing sicker by the day. And *the devil took care of its own.* She needed time to think.

The Villa workers began to arrive. Professor Morgan came into the room first with a walkie-talkie in hand. *Why did she need that?* Carlos headed into the glass pod closest to the doorway and waved Ximena over, but she was frozen in front of Jackie's pod. Thinking of Annie, shooting her mom, Mariana, the others, right in their heads. *Why would she kill every single one of them like Cranks?* They couldn't have had the Flare. There was no way anyone from their village could have gotten any variant of the Flare. They must've finally been turning on her. To see her lies for what they were. There was a chance that the crew of eight finally realized, out there on the vastness of the ocean, what Ximena had seen in Annie all along. That she was a poison. A germ. A disease.

An overhead light flickered and Ximena blinked.

"What's going to happen?" Jackie asked.

Ximena shook her head; she really had no idea. The other lab techs filed in and crowded inside the largest of the glass pods. Ximena locked eyes with Isaac, and he looked as if the air had just been sucked out of his own pod. She knew the feeling from when she'd been a child, but unlike back then, the Villa wouldn't be testing on her today.

Ximena stepped away from Jackie's pod but turned back to her. "*Sorry,*" she mouthed.

"We didn't want to come here," Jackie said listlessly. "We voted. We didn't want to come."

"You shouldn't have," Ximena said to herself as she walked away.

4
ISAAC

With every lab tech and assistant that came on to their floor, Isaac felt like he was drowning in another foot of water. Frypan sat on the floor of his pod, arms relaxed on his knees, but Isaac knew better—the old man wasn't relaxed. Not with this many people looking at them like test subjects.

"Jackie!" Isaac shouted to get her attention but beyond that he didn't know what to say. He wanted to tell her that everything would be okay like some kind of hero, but he didn't know that for sure. He didn't know anything for sure anymore. And Cowan barely looked alive. *How had she faded so quickly overnight? Why weren't the lab workers able to help her like they had done with Jackie?*

Isaac turned to watch Morgan in the larger pod next to him. She held a black box in her hand, surrounded by workers, what seemed like every single person who was a part of the Villa. *What was happening?* He looked at Ximena, questioning with his eyes, but she just dropped her chin. Morgan nodded to those in the pod and then walked out, into the center of the room.

Morgan, square box in hand—with what appeared to be a little antenna jutting from the top—walked over to Cowan's pod and unlocked it. "With Kletter gone, and your infection spreading," the blonde-haired scientist spoke to Cowan as she entered her glass pod, "we have very few options for your treatment." She gently unhooked Cowan from her IV, helped her stand up, then led her outside the pod.

What nonsense was this?

"You see, Kletter's work was quite advanced and may have seemed unorthodox, but she was ahead of her time, like many of the scientists of old." Morgan tapped Cowan's shoulder three times, gently, as if to say *you'll be okay* before walking back to the large safety pod with the others, then sealing the door. She'd just left the sickly woman standing, weakly, all by herself. "Please stand by and await the test."

"What test?" Isaac yelled, but no one responded. Half of the scientists and lab workers watched Ms. Cowan and the other half watched the main entrance as if expecting a special visitor.

What test?

5

XIMENA

"Release the dispenser!" Morgan shouted into the walkie-talkie, and every muscle in Ximena's body tensed. The lab techs whispered to each other in anticipation.

"What *is* this?" Ximena asked Carlos.

"Just watch." His eyes didn't leave the doorway, as if he might miss something if he looked away for a single second. Ximena turned her gaze back to the middle of the room to see Cowan sway on her feet. Barely standing. Metallic, staccato noises from the stairway clanked loudly but it didn't sound like footsteps. Ximena had been up and down those stairs a thousand times, but she didn't have a reference for what that clanking sounded like.

A hush came over the techs.

Silence.

Clanks had turned to clicks and whirring. Loud, mechanical clicking. But there was no preparing Ximena for what she saw next. As soon as the long, spikey, silvery legs came into view, she felt a fear that Cowan must've felt a thousand times stronger, pumping through her weakened veins.

There was a collective gasp in the pod from all the scientists, except Carlos, who just smiled. A Griever made its way on to the main floor. Different from the ones of old—those fleshy, sluglike monsters in stories of the Maze Trials. This new version was almost completely machine. Mostly gone were the biological elements that had once slowed them down, though enough remained to give the impression of a live, breathing nightmare.

"It's working . . . ," Carlos whispered in awe.

Ximena had never seen anything so terrifying in all her life. So ugly. So big and frightening. The Griever paused at their pod and hissed at everyone inside with its wet, slimy beast-like face, then sniffed the air in front of Isaac's pod. Ximena instinctively grabbed the knife from her back pocket, knowing it would accomplish nothing if things went awry.

Isaac banged both fists on the glass.

I wouldn't do that, Ximena thought.

"How can you do this to her?" Isaac screamed at Morgan and Ximena could see how betrayed he felt. Ximena understood, feeling the exact same amount of distrust toward Carlos, who continued watching the Griever with a fanatic, childlike glee.

She slapped him on the arm. "*This* is what you were working on? How could you!?" She screamed the words, everything she'd thought she'd known about him vanished, like vapor in wind. The Griever rolled forward, using all of its appendages, whirring and clicking with each movement, a sound that sent Ximena's mind to a dark place.

Cowan was at first frozen in terror, but she now stumbled backwards, crab-walking past Frypan's pod toward the one in the back that held Jackie. The burst of adrenaline that made her move was a sight to behold. All the while, the Griever sniffed and snarled and clicked its legs forward. "Stay calm!" Morgan instructed, as if the horror story in front of them wasn't happening. Of the islanders, only the old man named Frypan came even close to following her order—he looked *unusually* calm.

Ximena couldn't hear Jackie over the terrifying noise of the Griever and people yelling and shouting, but she was trying desperately to open the pod from the inside for Cowan. But they didn't have the keys, Ximena did.

Isaac gave her a pleading look.

The keys.

She could do something.

Ximena reached in her pocket and fingered the pod keys as she walked forward. This felt like the first time in her life she could really and truly help someone in need. If she could just get past—

"Stop." Carlos grabbed her arm like he'd done a hundred times before. Always in charge, always telling her what to do or what not to do. She shook off his grip, done listening to him.

"No! Not this time!" Her hands shook as she reached for the door handle, as she pulled the keys from her pocket. But then Morgan stopped Ximena with nothing but her voice.

With just a gentle whisper she held Ximena in place. "It's going to work. I know it will." Ximena could not move. "*Fear* is an important tool in the healing process."

Cowan had reached the wall, her back against it, trembling in terror. The Griever slowly moved closer, as if it had been programmed to stretch out the agony. As if it had been programmed . . .

Ximena turned to Carlos, who was still smiling. She didn't know if she could ever trust him again. His naive hope for the future had turned into darkness, had spilled over into blind trust in the Villa. Blind trust could get you killed.

Morgan spoke as if she were giving a lecture to students, even as the Griever inched closer to Cowan. "When the body feels true fear, it pumps the blood faster and releases special chemicals and endorphins to its each and every part. Amazing, really. *Terror* boosts white blood cells, and Cowan needs that most right now. She'll need as many white blood cells as possible to help with the incoming dosage."

Mechanical growls vibrated the glass of the pod. Cowan had gone rigid, obviously in shock as the Griever crawled ever closer to her. The Villa scientists, doctors, and lab techs watched it all with an almost sickening display of anticipation, bordering on pleasure. A reckless power watching their experiment unfold.

"You're just going to let it sting her?!" Ximena shouted. She should have followed her intuition when she first brought Jackie down to the basement. A pit of deep regret formed in her stomach.

Morgan answered with the utmost serenity. "The Griever takes the patient's blood, runs it through the algorithm, and then dispenses the Cure dose accordingly. A quantum algorithm that no human could match. From the terror to the dispensing, it's all part of a beautiful solution. It will save your friend's life." She smiled like a proud parent.

"This is the only way."

6
ISAAC

Isaac's heart raced itself to a clatter; his palms slid down the glass of the pod from sweat. Every moment since Ms. Cowan first showed him her rash flipped through his mind in a blur. If only he'd known what the Villa was capable of, he never would have brought her here.

The Griever clicked; the Griever whirred; the Griever crawled forward, prolonging the agony of every person watching. Isaac had no words to describe such a thing. It was half creature, half machine, full-on nightmare.

"Ms. Cowan!" Isaac pounded the glass to get her attention, remembering what Ximena had said earlier. "Just stay calm! Stay still!" She'd gone from shocked stillness to flailing her arms, an impossible effort to ward off the Griever, now right in front of her. Its glistening, shapeless face leaned in, came within an inch of her own. Isaac held his breath. Cowan screamed. One of the Griever's arms pulled back with a series of clicks louder than all the others, revealing a large needle as if it had one horrible finger. In a snap, it slashed forward and stabbed Cowan right at the shoulder.

Ms. Cowan unleashed a sound from her throat that sounded like all the demons of hell coming back to life. But she didn't move to resist, and a metallic section of the Griever's midsection started spinning in place, noisy and clanking.

Morgan's voice seemed artificially amplified. "It's calculating your needs for the serum. It processes your DNA at near quantum speed."

Quantum speed?

The Griever let out what sounded like a series of short, breathless cries of pain. Cowan winced, closed her eyes. Isaac looked around him, helpless. Tears poured down Jackie's face. Old Man Frypan held his head in his hands. Ximena stared at nothing.

The monster hovered over Cowan, churning out sounds but otherwise staying in place.

What was it waiting for? Isaac wondered. He just wanted the whole thing to end.

Morgan issued more commands. "Open your eyes, Ms. Cowan. It needs to read your face." But Cowan squeezed them shut even tighter.

Isaac pounded on the glass again. The only choice now was to do exactly as they were told. "Ms. Cowan! Just do what she says! Open your eyes!"

The Griever cycled through several motions with its arms, legs, whatever the hell those spiky things were and raised one at a time until Cowan finally acquiesced and looked, wide-eyed and terrified, at the creature. As if pleased with her obedience, it placed two of its appendages on Cowan's shoulders, almost lovingly. With a final *CLICK, CLICK, CLAAACK,* needles flashed out, sinking their points into her skin. Her eyes closed and she slumped to the side. Lying there, limp.

What had they done?

The Griever rolled and whirred its way over to Frypan's pod and pressed its face against the glass. The old man no longer held his head, but instead stared right back at the monster. Isaac could only imagine the haunting memories of the Glade that must've filled his head. Of all the lives that had been lost. Time stretched out. It was as if he and the creature were reminiscing, a silent exchange. Until one of its spiky machine arms pulled back then punched the glass of the safety pod.

It hissed a noise then slammed another of its arms in the same spot, splintering the glass into cracks.

"Frypan!" Isaac shouted. He looked over at the main pod, filled with a dozen Villa workers, "Stop that thing! You've got to stop it!" They ignored him, as if no one was really in charge of the Griever machine at all.

Old Man Frypan moved to the back of his pod, as far from the creature as possible, watching in silent terror as it punched the wall again, then again. The next one stabbed its way through, spraying pellets of glass on to Frypan.

Isaac, beside himself, pleaded for them to stop the Griever. But the lab workers weren't even watching. All of their attention, each and every one of them, was on a lifeless Ms. Cowan. *What the hell were they waiting for?* Then Cowan suddenly came to life, gasping for air.

Morgan spoke loudly into her black box.

"We're done. Insert the code."

CHAPTER TWENTY-FOUR

Bogged Down

I

SADINA

The sounds of war swirled around them and they were some of the worst that she had ever heard. Explosions. Gunfire. Screams. Minho led them through the thickly wooded forest and kept reassuring them that they were still far from the battle, but it seemed right on top of them. He held up his hand to signal something to Orange, and the group came to a stop.

For the barest of seconds she thought she heard Old Man Frypan, rinsing his iron pan with tiny pebbles and stream water, cleaning up after a fresh stew. But the fantasy vanished immediately, and there was only the harsh clanking of metal somewhere beyond the white-barked trees ahead.

"Shhh . . . ," Minho whispered.

The noise grew louder, as if a dozen Frypans had gone from cleaning pans to banging them together. "What *is* that?" Trish asked quietly.

Sadina's heart thumped hard enough to feel it in her ears, and she pulled the gun from Minho out of her back pocket.

The crack and warp of metal grinding on metal stopped, oddly replaced by a gurgling noise. Garbling. Mumbling.

"Something's there," Dominic said, pointing his knife somewhere straight ahead, but a lot of good that was going to do.

"Minho?" Sadina asked, wanting him to take control like her mom would have, to tell everyone it would be okay, but he remained silent. The wind blew through the bog trees beside them, creepy pine trees that looked like they weren't willing to leave the ground no matter what came after it, be it an ax, storm, or avalanche. They were full on the bottom but skinny all the way to the top, like the sky had grabbed hold and stretched them as far as they would go. Trees that looked like tall weapons themselves. Spears.

Minho shushed them again. He and Orange stood still, listening intently. The rest of the group did the same. Roxy obviously wanted to say something, but she didn't. She just held her long gun tightly in both hands.

"Guys . . ." Dominic broke the silence when the source of the metal clanking came into view.

Cranks.

Six . . . no, *eight* Cranks chained together in a row came through the white-barked trees up ahead. Like the kind of weird Crank-contraption they had seen on the Berg with those Grief Bearers. They stumbled over roots and smacked their heads into low-hanging branches, but stayed upright, walking closer to Sadina and her friends. They were normal humans, all sexes and ages, but with eyes full of deep emptiness. Soulless.

"Oh shit." Without hesitating, Minho pulled up his gun and started shooting them, one by one. Trish grabbed Sadina's arm as the Cranks fell alone but also together because of the chains fastened around their wrists and ankles, binding them into one fighting force. Before the last Crank in the group of eight fell from Minho's death shots, another fence row of Cranks came trampling through the woods. And then another one. And another one.

"What in the Iblis is going on!" Roxy straightened out her gun and started firing like an Orphan veteran, obviously taught well by her adopted son, but Sadina remained frozen. Gun or no gun, she could only hold Trish and walk backwards from the wall of Cranks coming at them, pushing them deeper into the creepy pine trees. Dominic and Miyoko walked backwards, too. The islanders weren't meant for war and they weren't meant for whatever this Crank-stuff was.

"I told you!" Orange shouted over to Minho as she put down one after another in a line. Two, three, four bodies fell. Sadina watched as Orange, Minho, and Roxy all fired away, the cracks and smoke of gunfire filling the already misty air. Despite the relative ease of picking them off, more and more waves of them were coming, weaving through the trees, stumbling but then dragged upright again by the chains.

The war had come to them, after all. *Dammit.*

"I told you!" Orange said again. Her gun fired three times in succession, each shot hitting a target. More came.

"What?" Minho asked, clearly annoyed as he reloaded his own weapon.

"How many Cranks need to be tied together and marching toward us before you'll admit there's an underground Crank Army in the Remnant Nation?" She huffed as she shot yet another Crank in the head and skipped a rock into the temple of another one.

Minho refused to take the bait or even look at her, keeping his eyes on the heads of the Cranks he was blasting. "Not much of an army without weapons!"

Orange allowed herself one moment to glare at Minho. "They *are* the weapons, idiot."

Roxy shot at them with relentless consistency, like it was a hidden talent no one knew about. "She's quicker than both of them . . . ," Dominic said.

He was right, but he was also wrong. Miyoko pointed out the obvious. "No. It's because there's only four or five Cranks on some of her group's chains." Miyoko freaked a little. "Where's the rest of them?" It was as if she'd spoken it into existence, the fact that there were now

Cranks on the loose. They appeared out of the nearby bog, crawling on arms that ended in bloody, raggedy stumps, their hands sawed or chewed off at some point. They came anyway, dragging themselves between the pine trees.

"Minho!" Sadina shouted. There were two freed Cranks coming at the islanders but Minho, Orange, and Roxy still had their hands full.

"I'm out of ammo!" Roxy pronounced and moved to the next chain-link fence of Cranks with her knife. Sadina stared in awe at such bravery.

"Minho!" Sadina cried again, squeezing Trish tighter and moving away from the trees.

"Dominic, get it!" Miyoko screamed, pointing at the Crank closest to them. Sadina couldn't process what she was looking at, all this insanity and terror. For the first time since getting separated, she was glad that Old Man Frypan wasn't there with them to suffer such pain and anguish. "Dominic!" Miyoko yelled.

"Stab it in the neck. You can do it." Minho quickly showed Dominic where exactly to stab and slash his blade.

Dom stomped in place like he was going to pee his pants. He gripped his knife then looked directly at Miyoko, then Trish and Sadina and said, "I voted to go home!" And then he charged the Crank crawling at them from the pine trees. He stabbed it in the neck with a war cry like Sadina had never heard. He'd been so loud that it made Minho and Orange stop shooting for a second and turn around. "I got him!" Dom raised his knife in the air.

"Good job," Minho said and went back to holding the line of chained Cranks coming out of the woods. Dom had a renewed strength and went after the next Crank crawling from the pine trees. This time it took two stabbing thrusts to kill it. Sadina let Trish's hand go with a sigh of relief.

Dominic wasn't quite smiling, but a sense of pride had glistened his eyes with tears. In that moment of terror and violence, Sadina realized two things at once: First, Dom didn't have something he was particularly good at like the other islanders, he didn't have a trade to learn and train for on the island and grow into, and even though he wanted to go back home, he really had the least to go back to.

Second, Sadina realized there'd been three Cranks missing from Roxy's chain and Dominic had only stabbed two of them.

And like a tall, creepy, pine tree in the bog, a Crank rose up from the ground and stood behind a proud Dominic. Hovering with horror.

"Dom!" Sadina cried, but her voice shook and it was too late. She watched Dominic's expression change as he realized what was grabbing him. Fear paled his features and a struggle ensued. Miyoko cried out. Trish stepped forward as if to help Dom, then hesitated, then stepped back with a wash of shame swept across her features. And just as panic impaled itself within Sadina, she remembered the gun. She knew next to nothing about shooting the damned things, except the sniper breathing routine Orange and Minho had taught her. "Dom, don't move!" She sucked a long breath into her nose, deep into her lungs, and then she put every fear and all the terror into the exhale, blowing it out through her mouth.

Fear of Cranks.

Fear of Dominic dying. Trish dying. All of them dying.

Fear of every last thing in the world.

She steadied the gun in both hands then blew a bullet through the Crank's head.

2

ALEXANDRA

Far to the south, where she finally couldn't smell the smoke any longer, she stopped to catch her breath. The Goddess' feet and lungs had never been so spent, so exhausted. She had never run so far, so fast. Alexandra could still hear the explosions and gunshots and the cries of war in her mind, haunting replays of the sounds that had shattered her heart. A ratchety *BOOM* in the distance shook her, reminded her it was all too real. Flint, her Evolutionary Guard, gone. The Pilgrims. The shops. All overtaken.

Her feet sank into the soft swampy ground, and she tried to remember where Mannus had beached the little boat. It was near a string of birch trees, she peeled the bark while he'd gathered their things. She should have forced Mannus to flee the city with her, *why didn't she?*

Nicholas. He'd looked too much like Nicholas.

She'd figure it out, recover what she could, perhaps even live on the remote island with the three scientists for a while. Once she told them of the surprise attack, they'd surely understand the raised importance of Culminating the Evolution.

Her shoes and feet were soaking wet, her hands trembled. She shoved them in her cloak pockets. *Some Goddess.* In her right pocket she felt the spikey bog rosemary that she'd used to poison the rogue Pilgrim. Alexandra pulled out the stems and threw them to the ground. The last thing she needed was to accidentally poison herself. She slapped her hands clean of the spiked leaves and returned them to the warmth of her cloak, only to feel something else. The letter from Nicholas she'd stashed away in stubbornness and spite. Avoidance, not wanting to hear his *I told you so's* from beyond or whatever the letter held. But she pulled it out now.

She needed to know what *he* saw that she could not.

What were his last words to her? Had he predicted the war? Had this been a part of his emergency shutdown plan? She took a breath and slowly reached into the envelope that had her name scribbled in Nicholas' handwriting. His penmanship was sloppy as hell—he'd always explained it as his mind moving far more quickly than his hands were able. She thought it showed his lack of control. Her heart raced as she unfolded the letter. She had to remind herself that she didn't need to control her own thoughts anymore—even so, it felt like Nicholas was right there, lording over her. Something rustled in the woods and caused her heart to quicken even more. Her palms squeezed the letter.

A squirrel. Just a squirrel.

Alexandra sighed.

The attack from the skies had heightened her fight or flight senses and there wasn't enough tea in Alaska to calm her nervous system, now. Of course, she'd try with the Flaring Discipline all the same. She returned to the letter, and upon unfolding it saw how short it was. Not even a full page. *Did she want a dead man to say more?* She was embarrassed by her misplaced disappointment.

The squirrel, the culprit, ran toward her and disappeared up an oak tree.

But behind the squirrel was a man.

He walked with a dreadful, pained scowl worse than any of the faces of death Alexandra had just witnessed in the streets of New Petersburg. Some faces were indeed worse than death. Cranks.

The man emerged from the line of trees and held its arm up, missing a chunk of wrist and two fingers. Alexandra crinkled the letter and shoved it deep into her pocket again. She backed up, looking for a stick on the ground, something, anything, to defend herself with, but it was mostly marsh. Not even a rock to throw. Nicholas was surely taunting her from the beyond.

She walked as quickly as she could between the maze of trees and brush, no choice now but to put her back to the Crank and get out of there. Her foot twisted on a jutting root, but she dodged a swinging punch from the oncoming Crank. She pushed him away and ran, toward a thicker part of the forest, despite the pain lancing up her leg.

She yelled the digits out loud as if to amplify their power.

"1, 2, 3, 5, 8!"

The Flaring Discipline was her only weapon.

"13, 21, 34, 55, 89, 144 . . ."

3
MINHO

Someone in the distance shouted, kept shouting, almost melodic against the distant sounds of battle. It took him a few moments to place in his mind that the voice coming from the trees ahead was reciting numbers. *Counting down cannon fire?*

He motioned Orange to walk farther west. They didn't have enough ammo for another ambush and needed to conserve energy.

"Trish!" Sadina was next to him and pointed toward the strange voice, almost a chant, now.

Trish stopped walking and listened for a moment. "The numbers." She had a weird look on her face. Something like relief.

Minho glared at them both. They certainly didn't have time for island games. "No. we're going that way." He pointed to the right, west of the noise, but Sadina ignored him and walked in the other direction.

"*The Book of Newt* had these numbers circled," she said. "Whoever that is, she's chanting the exact same numbers! You're telling me that's a coincidence?"

"13, 21, 34, 55 . . ." Trish counted along with the woman's voice in the background.

"They're the same, I swear!" Sadina turned to Miyoko and Roxy for support.

"Then we should go check it out," Miyoko said.

Roxy shrugged. "Lady sounds innocent enough."

Minho waited to hear a cannon blast, but he didn't. "Fine. But stay behind me and be on guard." He went into stealth-mode, watching each footstep to prevent noise as they approached the crazed voice reciting numbers aloud. She appeared, running frantically at them, a woman with long black hair, wrapped in a wooly yellow cloak. She was being chased by a Crank, probably the last one who'd escaped the chained collectives.

Minho positioned and aimed his gun. "Drop to the ground!"

She slipped instead, sliding right between two trees. Whatever worked. He took the shot.

The bullet landed home, middle of the forehead. The Crank dropped, landing only a few feet from his prey, dead. Minho scanned the tree line for any more loose Cranks. "Did we get them all now?" he asked Orange.

"Hope so." She helped the woman get back to her feet, the odd robe muddied and torn.

Sadina walked right up to her. "Those numbers. What are they?"

The woman just shook her head and straightened her heavy cloak.

Minho pointed his weapon at her. "Tell us everything you know about the Godhead and what's going on up north." The stranger looked at each and every person in their group as if they were apparitions. She stared at Minho the longest, then glanced down at his uniform.

"You're never going to kill the Godhead." She spoke with an unreal confidence.

"Lady, we don't care about killing the Godhead." Orange tossed a piece of tree bark to the side; it was the first time Minho heard her admit she didn't want to kill their lifelong enemy.

"The numbers," Sadina insisted. "What does 1-2-3-4-8—mean?"

"Four *isn't* a sacred number!" the woman snapped, and Sadina took a step back.

Trish motioned to Sadina's pocket. "Show her the pages that Old Man Frypan circled in *The Book of Newt*."

"Newt?" The woman perked up as if she'd been shocked with electricity. She limped over to Sadina to see the ratty book that Frypan had given her. Minho exchanged glances with Roxy and Orange. The three of them were more worried about Kletter's captain's log than deciphering some island bible.

"Newt was one of the subjects of the Maze," Dominic said proudly, but there wasn't any way in Flare's hell this woman from Alaska didn't know who Newt was.

"Yes, dear Newt." The woman ran her fingers over the cover of the book. She then eyed Sadina, Trish, and Miyoko with a bit of awe, as if she wanted to touch their faces. "You're . . . you're from the island of immunes." She seemed dreamy, as if a giant battle wasn't taking place in the background. Like she'd gone to an island in her own mind.

"Yeah, we four are," Miyoko said. "They're from—"

Minho cut her a look that said *never mind where we're from*. He still held his gun in a readied position but had lowered it a little. "We're trying to get to the Godhead," he said. "Any idea how or where they're holing up—"

"I *am* the Godhead. Goddess Alexandra Romanov." She folded her arms in a way that might have looked powerful if she weren't wearing a bulky, dirty old cloak.

Minho lowered his weapon all the way to his side and motioned for Orange to do the same. She hesitated as if to ask *are you sure* before following his lead.

He didn't believe this woman was a God. She was wearing a common cloak and she sounded just about as crazy as a Crank. Looked it, too. But she seemed harmless enough.

Trish had a one-track mind. "And those numbers, 5, 8, 13, 21 . . . what do they mean?"

"They're a part of nature, of all evolution. The sequence of life, itself. The Culmination of the Evolution can't be stopped no matter how many wars your people wage on us." She raised her eyebrows at Minho.

"Goddess . . ." Minho started but he forgot her supposed name.

"Romanov." She waited.

"Goddess *Romanov* . . ." He didn't bother hiding the disbelief in his voice, but he didn't know if he could outright mock the poor woman, either.

Dominic stepped forward, his Crank-killing knife still in hand. "If you're a member of the Godhead, why are you hiding out here in the woods like some loon?" Miyoko elbowed Dominic. "What?"

But Minho had been thinking the same thing. "What good is a God in the middle of a swamp?"

Alexandra cleared her throat. "I was led into the woods and the southern bog for a reason." She moved closer to Dominic and glared at him until he looked away. "We don't always know the reasons for our intuition, but I trusted it enough to find myself here and *you* found me. The blood of immunes." She straightened out her cloak. "Evolution is brilliant like that." She turned and smiled at Sadina.

Something about her reminded Minho of the Grief Bearers. "Then where are the other two members of the Godhead?"

"They no longer exist."

"Oh?" Roxy questioned.

"I'm the only one left, now. The only God." Alexandra spoke loudly and confidently, but Minho didn't believe the Godhead could just . . . *dissolve* so easily. Something about this person wasn't settling right with him. Only a devil would destroy the other Gods, at least according to Roxy's Grandpa's story.

"What's your plan, then?" he asked. He couldn't get the sounds of explosions out of his head. Knowing the Remnant Nation, the destruction would be vast. "Your city is being destroyed."

"You're *all* a part of my plan now." The Goddess smiled at each and every one of them, unfazed by the decidedly mixed reactions. At least Trish and Sadina returned the smile. "We'll continue with the Culmination and we'll Cure the world of the Flare once and for all. It's really that simple."

Minho wanted the Flare gone, of course he did.

The Flare was still his devil.

But something about this woman didn't feel much different.

CHAPTER TWENTY-FIVE

The Last

I
XIMENA

It should not have surprised her that the woman who killed her mom also resurrected the Grievers of old, but impossibly, she was even more disgusted with Annie after the terrifying scene with Cowan. When the moment was right, Ximena sneaked down the basement stairs without Morgan or Carlos seeing her.

Ximena was done with the Villa and everything to do with it. She pulled out Annie's knife and sheath, onto which her mom had sewn an eagle, and traced the threads. Ximena had promised to sew the truth through the land and she would still do that in her own way. She walked to a small room in the basement, far in the back that held the electrical components. Wires. Cables. Cords. The room smelled of heat and dust and disease. She stood inside for a long time, her knife in hand.

There was no going back.

She cut each and every cord in front of her. Solar wires to pods.

Cable cords to safety viewers. Fluid funnels to hydraulic machines. She cut them all, figuring she'd have about eight minutes before Morgan realized what was going on. A minute for each of the dead crew members Annie had slaughtered—and Ximena would make each of them count. She stepped out of the utility room and moved quickly to the islanders' pods.

"Where's Ms. Cowan, is she going to be okay?" Isaac asked frantically as Ximena unlocked his pod. Cowan *would* be okay as far as the power and machinery she'd been hooked into—she had her own breaker unit on the west side of the property. But Ximena didn't know that she'd ever be *okay again.*

"She's in a medically induced coma," Ximena told Isaac before she moved over to Frypan's pod. She paused momentarily and shivered at the splintered glass along the front where the Griever had attacked. It had been a close run, Morgan finally shutting the creature down at the last minute. Ximena opened his pod and set him free.

"Thank you," the old man whispered.

"We don't have much time, they'll be down here in about five minutes." She rushed to Jackie's pod.

She wondered if Morgan and the team would miss the islanders more than they missed her. Carlos might not, but that was all. The others would miss having her blood to study and having her on standby if they needed anything—but they'd never truly cared about her.

As soon as Jackie was freed, she ran to hug Isaac. "What's going on? I feel like I'm hallucinating again."

Isaac was teary by the time he let go of Jackie. Then he addressed Ximena. "Thanks for letting us out, but we can't leave without Ms. Cowan."

"Look, I don't care what you do or where you go. Just get out of here before they run some other *test*, okay?" Ximena threw the pod keys into the corner, remembering how it felt when the Villa once studied her. She was setting herself free. She turned toward the black metal door that led to the outside.

Isaac reached for her. "We can't leave without Cowan. Her daughter, Sadina, supposedly has—"

"Cowan's not going to get better," she snapped at him, forgetting how weak the islanders could be. Even after seeing what they had seen —they *still* had hope?

"I think we're overdue for getting out of this, Isaac," Frypan said.

Jackie fiddled with her grass bracelet, avoiding the terrible choice.

Isaac didn't stop, as if staying at the Villa were really an option. "I know, I know, but Sadina . . . they were going to come and . . . what about the Cure?"

Ximena opened the door and welcome sunlight poured inside. She debated for a second and a half telling the islanders the truth about things. She held the heavy door open and looked the three of them up and down. Her Abuela would've asked what good was freedom without the truth?

"The Cure is just another lie of Annie Kletter's." Ximena couldn't help but think of the silver ring on her dead skeletal hand. The snake eating its own tail. A perfect symbol for the world when humankind continued to destroy itself. She'd said enough; they could figure the rest out. She stepped outside and let go of the door.

"Wait!" Isaac and the other two followed her, after all. Of course they did. "I get not trusting Kletter, but what if there really is a Cure?"

She looked back at them. If she was going to sew truth in the land to honor her mom, she might as well start here. But they needed to get the hell out of there. "Come on, let's get to the woods, we'll talk and walk. Annie Kletter came to our Village twenty-nine years ago to give us the Cure."

The three immunes were right on her heels.

"So you *do* have the Cure? But . . ." Isaac took a moment, probably to gather his thoughts. "Why would Kletter tell us that we had to leave the island to help *find* a Cure if she already had one and took it to your village?"

"Is it a real Cure for the Flare?" Jackie asked. "I mean, it really works?"

Ximena nodded as she quickened the pace. "No one in the village has gotten the Flare in twenty-nine years."

"Then what's the problem? That's almost three decades, two generations, without disease and Cranks and—"

"No generations," Ximena said. "There *are* no more generations." She let that settle in as they reached the cover of the wooded hills. Ximena pictured her mom and Mariana. They would have wanted to tell the islanders the truth from the beginning. Maybe that was their ultimate downfall and the reason Annie killed them. The truth was a weapon that Annie took away from every single one of those eight crew members, but it would be the weapon that Ximena carried with her for the rest of her life. "Kletter went to your island for a cure *from the Cure.*"

"Oh, man," Jackie said under her breath, obviously understanding.

"The Cure needs a cure?" Isaac asked.

"It created its own type of disease." Ximena looked behind her again to make sure no one on staff was nearby. She was surprised at how well the old man could keep up. "In my village, I'm the only child born in the last twenty-nine years."

"I'll be . . ." Frypan rubbed his eyes. "And you guys wonder why I never trusted any of this."

Ximena continued, ducking under a low-hanging branch. "They studied me here from the time I was born until I was six years old. Then my mom agreed to work for the Villa, trying to help them decode the Cure."

Isaac and Jackie looked at each other. "That's . . . ," but neither of them could finish their thought. Just as the Cure had wiped Ximena's village of children, it wiped the words right out of their brains.

Ximena could only imagine the shock of learning such a thing all at once. "The Cure might rid the population of the Flare, but it also *rids the population.* They obviously didn't mean to do it, but something about the sequencing that blocks the Flare also blocks reproduction." A part of her wished she hadn't burst their hopes and dreams. "Carlos and his wife volunteered to help Annie's studies because they wanted children. My mom volunteered because she somehow was able to have *me*. They studied us in those same pods."

"The Cure," Frypan scoffed. "More like the Curse. The truth ain't always the truth." He couldn't stop shaking his head back and forth, as if chastising himself for some reason.

Ximena wanted to hug the old man.

"It's a curse, alright," she said. "The Evolution will cause our extinction."

2

ISAAC

As they trampled their way through the hilly, dry forest, he tried to process what Ximena had told them about the Cure. How it can save the population while ensuring it ceases to exist. *How could both realities be true?* It had to be one of the worst things he'd ever heard.

And of course he couldn't let it go. "Okay, so maybe if Sadina's blood really is the cure for the Cure then everything will be okay? Kletter had to have some basis for coming all the way to our island." Ximena wasn't having it, her face saying that nothing would ever be okay again and Old Man Frypan hadn't looked the same since the Griever of old practically stabbed him through the glass.

Ximena walked even faster, as if she wanted to leave the topic behind forever. "Or maybe it'll just create a new disease. Maybe everything we thought was wrong was right, and everything we thought was right was actually wrong."

Isaac was already sick of Ximena's riddles. He was thankful to be free of the glass cell, but he had no idea what came next and he hated, absolutely hated that they'd left Ms. Cowan behind. "So what's your plan? What did you do back there?" She had something in her eyes that reminded him of Sadina when she got a big idea in her head that wouldn't go away. A plan was brewing, here.

"I destroyed the electrical room in the basement of the Villa and I'll do the same thing at the next one."

"Next one?" He didn't know where they'd end up. Mostly he wanted to run up the coast as quickly as possible and wait at the spot that Minho had designated for their return. What killed Isaac more than anything was that Sadina had been right. Letti and Timon had been right. The Villa was a bad, bad place.

"So yeah, what do you mean by *next one*?" Jackie asked.

Ximena had something move across her lips that half-resembled a smile. She then delivered a cutting jab, "You all really did live on a desolate island, didn't you?" She was breathing hard from the ups and downs of the hike. "This isn't the only Villa, and we aren't the only people Kletter worked with. There's quite a few of them, all the way from the southern desert to the site of the Maze in Alaska."

Old Man Frypan bristled at that but didn't say anything.

"Alaska?" Jackie repeated. "That's where the Godhead is."

Isaac felt like he was practically running to keep up with Ximena and the others. He liked her. She knew a lot and they'd still be trapped in a glass prison if not for her. He had a feeling they needed her and maybe she needed them.

He had an idea. "Ximena, come to Alaska with us to find our friends. And to see the Godhead." He didn't know what he expected her to say, but her sharp laugh surprised him.

"The *Godhead*." She eviscerated the word as she spoke it. "The Godhead is just another disease."

EPILOGUE
A Final Letter

Dear Alexandra,

You're reading this note in the event of my death and in the event that the Culmination of the Evolution will be shut down for good. Patience was never your strong suit, but you must understand that the bulk of the experiments were not a success. The Cure can work on Cranks because you cannot kill a man who is already dead inside, but providing healthy humans with the Cure is a risk that's not always successful. I have always told you and Mikhail that you both were the first of the test subjects: X1 and X2, but that was a gentle lie. I didn't want you to look at me as a monster or to look at yourself as anything but a miracle. But dear Alexandra . . .

There were thousands.

You were the first successful study of a non-Crank at Villa X.

I have sent my work across the world in the last 30 years, and the reason I stood firm on the Culmination of the Evolution being restricted to certain members of society is that I've watched what happens within those who have held too much power through their evolutionary gifts. I had hope for you until the very end. You were my greatest trial. But one person's deity is another person's demon.

You once thought of me as a God.
Now you think of me as a devil.

But dearest Alex, you have not seen the world like I have. There are many more Villas than you know. On the surface, as far as anyone could see— the trials of the Maze ended long ago.

But they had only ever just evolved.

yours in life, and now in death,
Nicholas

End of Book Two

The #1 New York Times Bestselling Maze Runner Series From

JAMES DASHNER

Published by Delacorte Press, an imprint of Random House Children's Books, and by Riverdale Avenue Books.

 @JamesDashner

 @DashnerJames

JamesDashner.com

Check Out the Mortality Doctrine Series by

JAMES DASHNER

Welcome to the VirtNet.

A world beyond your wildest dreams . . .
. . . and your worst nightmares.

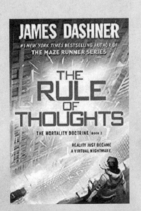
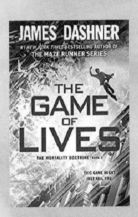

Published by Delacorte Press, an imprint of Random House Children's Books.

 @JamesDashner

 @DashnerJames

JamesDashner.com

ABOUT THE AUTHOR

James Dashner is the author of the #1 *New York Times* Bestselling *Maze Runner* series (movies by Fox/Disney) including *The Maze Runner*, *The Scorch Trials*, *The Death Cure*, *The Kill Order*, and *The Fever Code*, and the bestselling *Mortality Doctrine* series (*The Eye of Minds*, *The Rule of Thoughts*, and *The Game of Lives*). Dashner was born and raised in Georgia, but now lives and writes in the Rocky Mountains with his wife and their four children.

Join the #DashnerArmy for exclusive content and giveaways at <u>JamesDashner.com</u>